──────────── ★ ────────────

The dead girl was sprawled on the floor not two feet from the door. Her arms were outstretched, palms up, and her legs akimbo so that she looked like an obscene Raggedy Ann doll. There was a thin virulent red line around her neck.

"Do we know who she is?" Gerald asked as Ransom silently crouched beside the body for a closer look.

"Her name is Laura Shay."

"What?" Ransom turned his eyes to Becker and rose slowly. He looked as if he hoped he hadn't heard correctly.

Becker shot a blank glance at Gerald, who was looking at his partner quizzically.

"Laura Shay," Becker repeated. "You know her?"

Ransom looked down at the girl, then closed his eyes and slowly shook his head. "Why did this have to happen in our area?"

──────────── ★ ────────────

FRED HUNTER

RANSOM FOR A KILLING

WORLDWIDE.

TORONTO • NEW YORK • LONDON
AMSTERDAM • PARIS • SYDNEY • HAMBURG
STOCKHOLM • ATHENS • TOKYO • MILAN
MADRID • WARSAW • BUDAPEST • AUCKLAND

RANSOM FOR A KILLING

A Worldwide Mystery/December 1999

First published by St. Martin's Press, Incorporated.

ISBN 0-373-26329-5

Visit us at www.worldwidemystery.com

Printed in U.S.A.

For Eleanor Taylor Bland

PROLOGUE

May 1989

THE STEADY, hollow thrum of the basketball could be heard, echoing off the surrounding close-knit houses, late into the evening. It was Friday night and Ben Harvey didn't have to be in early, so he was filling his time by shooting hoops on the cement court behind John Quincy Adams High School. Ben was a gangling youth with long awkward legs and arms, and a torso with such prominent ribs he looked like a human marimba. He was six feet tall and his head was an elongated oval, which made him appear to be even taller. He wore green shorts of fake silk and a matching T-shirt, both of which his mother had bought for him at Woolworth's.

Most of his friends were out on dates, or out with each other, or running in groups or gangs that night—"up to no good," as Ben's mother would say. But she didn't have to worry about Ben: he focused all of his free time and spare energy on perfecting his athletic abilities. Some of his classmates had remarked on how he would be a "natural" in basketball. If he gave any thought to it at all, he was apt to recognize the none-too-subtle racism of what they were saying, but he excused it. His mother had brought him up to believe that people who talked like that just didn't know any better, and that he had to forgive them. It still rankled him. It tainted his enjoyment of the sport, making him feel as if he shouldn't play for fear of perpetuating a stereotype. But Ben had enough self-assurance to put these petty thoughts aside and allow himself some innocent fun.

He didn't have any dreams of an athletic scholarship or a place with the pros. His mother had seen that his head was on straight. He was going to become a lawyer. He'd kept his grades up, though not enough to win a scholarship, but Mrs. Harvey believed in her heart that, if Ben made a good showing in his first years at Harold Washington Junior College, he wouldn't have any trouble getting the financial assistance he needed to go on from there.

Ben kept the ball in motion with his left hand while he checked the Timex watch his mother had given him as a graduation present. He knew the watch wasn't expensive, but coming from his mother, it was literally the widow's mite, and he cherished it as if it were gold. It was just after eleven o'clock, and time to head home, or at least to stop bouncing the ball. Pretty soon the neighbors would be complaining.

He made one more run at the hoop, shooting from just beneath it. The ball skimmed its way around the rim twice before dropping through.

"All right!" he exclaimed, cheering his own prowess as he caught the ball. He continued bouncing it as he left the court.

He stopped when he reached the sidewalk and tucked the ball under his left arm. He was about to set off for home when he noticed a young woman hurrying down the opposite side of the street. Ben wasn't surprised by the speed at which she was walking—to his mind, it was normal for girls to hurry along, especially if they happened to be out at night alone. But he noticed that she wasn't very steady on her feet, and he thought he could hear her making some kind of noise that didn't sound quite right.

Ben crossed the street, passing unnoticed under a burned-out streetlamp, and got to the other side just as the young woman was about to pass. Lost in her private distress, she didn't see Ben until she almost ran into him. She let out an abbreviated scream and started to run the other way. Ben caught hold of her arm.

"Laura?" he said. "Laura? It's me, Ben."

She stopped struggling and turned her face toward him. Ben was shocked at the state she was in: she'd been crying so much her eyes were puffy, and there were trails down her face through her makeup. Her hair was in disarray and her dress was torn, both on the right sleeve and the hem. There was a noticeable bruise just under her right eye and scratches on her arms. The sounds she was emitting were the last, choking sobs of someone who's almost cried herself out, but is still upset enough to cry some more. Her eyes were almost wild with fear.

"Let go of me!" she yelled.

"Laura, it's me, Ben Harvey."

"Ben?" She repeated his name in one short burst.

"From school," he said, although he figured she had to know him. They were in homeroom together. He didn't sit that far away from her. "Laura, what's wrong? What happened to you?"

There was a split second of recognition in her eyes, as if for one moment she knew him. Then the terror returned and she resumed struggling.

"Let go of me!"

In the house in front of which they were standing, one of the window shades moved and someone cautiously peeked out.

"No," he said, trying to sound older and more in control than he felt. "No. You're in a state! If you don't want to tell me what happened, then I should just walk you home. You shouldn't be out like this.''

There was another flicker of recognition. Then she suddenly screamed ''No!'' and took a swipe at his face with her free hand. Her fingernails tore across his cheek and, as the pain cut into him, he involuntarily released her and stepped back. Laura fled away down the street.

Ben stood for a moment holding his hand against the deep scratches. He could feel the warm blood wetting his palm. He flexed his other hand against the basketball, holding it tighter to his side as if it were a teddy bear from which he could wring some comfort. He shook his head and started off down the street.

The window shade fluttered back into place.

THE EMERGENCY ROOM doors slid open with an asthmatic whoosh. George Shay kept a protective arm heavily draped over his daughter's shoulder as he propelled her into the hospital, but the unsteadiness of his gait made it difficult to tell which of the pair was most in need of support.

Being Friday night, the emergency room was filled to overflowing with the usual assortment of cases: victims of driving mishaps, participants in brawls, and an assortment of people who, through an overindulgence in alcohol, had come to harm in one way or another. The staff was busily attending to the patients' needs and took no immediate notice of the father and daughter who had just entered.

George Shay cast a confused look around the bustling room with his small, glaring eyes, which he seemed to be having trouble focusing. When he was able to comprehend that his daughter was not receiving prompt attention, he announced loudly, "My daughter...my daughter's been...attacked!"

There was a sudden pause in the activity as if patients and staff alike were paying homage to the girl with a moment of silence. Laura buried her face deep into her father's shoulder as if she thought she could escape everyone's notice, like a child who believes it can hide from its parents by covering its own eyes. Then the pandemonium resumed as if nothing had happened.

Shay was about to raise his voice a notch higher when a young man in a bright blue shirt and white pants hurried to his side and said, "Your daughter's been attacked? Come this way."

He laid a comforting hand on the girl's shoulder, but removed it quickly when she flinched. He led them along a row of curtains that reached only partway to the floor, behind which various degrees of moaning and conciliatory murmurs could be heard. He ushered them into a small open area at the end of the row, in which there was an unoccupied gurney and several other pieces of hospital equipment. Shay eyed them suspiciously as he took a seat on a small plastic chair in the corner.

Laura shrank from the young man's touch as he gingerly helped her onto the gurney and asked her to lie back and try to relax.

"She's your daughter?" the young man said over his shoulder to Shay.

"I said so, didn't I?" His tone carried the belligerence of a man who is anxious to take action but doesn't know at whom it should be directed.

Satisfied that Laura was as comfortable as she was likely to be, the young man crossed to Shay and said quietly, "What was the nature of this attack?"

Shay looked up at him with eyes that seemed to be coated with thick fluid. He said, "What do you mean?"

"Was the attack of a sexual nature?"

Shay's frown deepened. "What do you think?"

"Okay. Don't worry. We'll take good care of her."

The young man drew the curtain across the area, shutting it off from the rest of the emergency room. "The nurse will be in in a minute."

"We don't need a nurse, we need a doctor! Can't you see that?" Shay's voice boomed.

"Yes," the young man replied patiently, "and the doctor will be along directly."

He disappeared through the slit in the curtains, and although he spoke very low as he walked away, Shay heard him say to an unseen comrade, "We'll need a rape kit in here."

Shay raised his bleary eyes to his daughter, who was lying on the gurney staring at the ceiling as if in a trance.

"Don't you worry, sweetheart," he slurred. "We'll get you fixed up and then we'll get that bastard! We'll make him pay!"

A nurse walked briskly into the curtained cubicle, placed a box and a clipboard on the bedside table, and stopped by the side of the gurney. The nurse was a short, slight Filipino woman who spared a tender smile for the girl before launching into the business at hand. She took Laura's vital signs in a crisp, professional manner that would have pleased George Shay had he been fully cognizant. When she was finished, she grabbed the clipboard from the table and jotted down a few notes, then crossed to Shay on the other side of the gurney. Though she was very small, she seemed to loom over him as she asked him a series of personal questions about his daughter, each of which he responded to slowly as if he was having trouble remembering such information as her name, address, and birth date. The nurse noted each answer on a sheet on the clipboard, and when she ran out of questions, she snapped the clip once as if the exercise needed some sort of punctuation to mark its completion. Then she disappeared through the curtains.

The nurse had barely been gone for a minute when another woman came through the curtains. She was tall and wearing a muted floral dress covered almost entirely by a long white coat. She had short, graying brown hair and wire-rimmed glasses that were perched on the bridge of her nose. The glasses slipped down slightly as she read something on the clipboard in her hand, apparently the same board the nurse had held.

She retrieved a stool from behind the gurney and sat down next to the young girl. She said, "Hello, Laura. My name is Dr. Hutchins. Laura, I understand that you've had a very unpleasant experience, and I'm going to try as much as I can to help you. We'll dress those cuts on your arms and legs in just a minute, but first I'm going to have to perform an examination. I know you probably don't want that, but it really is necessary, and I promise I'll make it as gentle as possible. Do you understand?"

Laura continued to stare at the ceiling as if she were oblivious to everything that was going on around her. Dr. Hutchins waited a while for a response, then repeated the girl's name. There was no sign of recognition in her eyes, nor did she answer audibly. But after a long pause, she inclined her head just slightly, which Hutchins took as a nod of assent.

She rose from the stool and said, "Mr. Shay, I'll need you to wait out there for a few minutes. There're some chairs by the door where you came in and a coffee machine if you should want any."

Shay stared at the doctor for a moment as if he would have liked to protest. Then his eyes turned to his daughter. The understanding of what the examination would entail seemed to sink in at last, and he struggled up from his seat and started out of the cubicle. He paused for a moment when he reached the doctor's side and said, "Thank you."

Hutchins recoiled at the noticeable smell of gin on his breath. She said, "It won't take very long," and was relieved when Shay nodded and stepped out through the curtains.

Shay sat uncomfortably wedged between two other men who waited anxiously for the verdict on loved ones receiving aid in the other cubicles. Periodically, he leaned forward and peered down the aisle at the curtains behind which his daughter was being examined. The nurse came in and out as he watched. He sat back and sighed heavily as he raised his eyes heavenward, but the top of the chair cut sharply into the area just above the small of his back, so he soon had to lean forward again.

It was about twenty minutes before Dr. Hutchins emerged from the cubicle, just as a pair of uniformed officers entered through the sliding doors. She signaled to them and they crossed the room to her and held a short, hushed conference during which she pointed to Laura's cubicle. The three of them headed for the curtains, and Shay climbed out of his seat and wavered his way across the room. Despite his level of intoxication, he managed to intercept them before they passed through.

"What are you doing?" he said.

"Mr. Shay?" said the taller of the officers. Shay nodded. "We'd like to talk to your daughter about what happened."

Shay looked from one officer to the other, then at

Hutchins, who looked back at him as if she were wary of how he would react. Shay appeared to be trying to decipher what was best. After a few moments he said with a measure of decision, "Yeah. Yeah. Okay."

Dr. Hutchins silently breathed a sigh of relief, but she was not completely satisfied with the tone of the father's acquiescence. He sounded almost reluctant, but Hutchins was always one to try to give the benefit of the doubt. She chose to believe that he was just worried about his daughter's welfare and feared that it might upset her further to be questioned. Hutchins held back the curtains. Shay and the officers passed through, and Hutchins followed, closing the curtains behind her.

Laura had been bandaged and was lying on the gurney, still staring at the ceiling but no longer quite as oblivious as she had been. Hutchins indicated the box beside the gurney to one of the officers, who nodded his understanding.

"Miss Shay?" said the shorter officer. "I'm Officer Canton, this is Officer MacDonald. Can you tell us about what happened to you?"

The girl made no movement, but her eyes began to brim with tears.

"Miss Shay," said MacDonald with gentle firmness, "we'd like to catch whoever did this. Do you know who did this to you?"

Laura's lips began to tremble and the tears escaped the corners of her eyes and ran down to her ears. She reached out with her left arm and flexed her hand as if she were clutching at air.

"Daddy?" she sobbed. "Daddy!"

George Shay went to her side but didn't take her hand. She dug her fingers into his cloth coat. "What, honey? What is it?"

"I want to go home. Please take me home!"

MacDonald persisted with his questions as gently as possible for a couple of minutes, but the only result was that Laura pressed her face into her father's coat and clung to it so tightly that she almost pulled him over. Shay looked down at his daughter with a bewilderment born of intoxication, but eventually it broke in upon him that Laura was nearly hysterical. He drew himself up as best he could and with a sudden burst of fortitude said, "That's all! She can't talk now! Can't you see that?"

Officer Canton nodded with practiced sympathy and said, "It might be best to wait until morning. Miss Shay, you think it'd be all right if we send somebody around tomorrow to talk to you?"

The only response he received was a muffled sob.

"Good, then," Canton continued. "Why don't we do that?"

Canton nodded to MacDonald, and Dr. Hutchins drew back the curtains to allow the officers to pass through, then followed them out.

"Should she go home in that condition?" MacDonald asked.

"Maybe not," Hutchins replied. "But this isn't a jail. She can go home if she wants to."

MacDonald heaved a weary sigh that seemed to express the opinion that victims were their own worst enemies. Then he and Canton headed for the desk to get the Shays' address.

Inside the curtained enclosure, Laura's panic subsided once the police were out of sight, though she continued to cling to her father's coat, resting the side of her face against his stomach.

George Shay laid an unsteady hand on his daughter's head and slowly stroked her hair.

"Don't worry, baby," he said quietly, "we'll make him pay."

DETECTIVE BERGER towered over Detective Collins, a diminutive woman who had only recently made detective. Collins was of two minds as they climbed the steps to the front door of the Shays' modest bungalow: without having set eyes on the girl yet, Collins felt inclined to be sympathetic toward her, as she would anyone who'd suffered the trauma and humiliation of rape. At the same time, she resented that sympathy was expected of her by her superiors and that it was the main reason she had been sent to question the victim.

Berger was also torn by conflicting emotions. Since he was the senior partner in this team, he would have expected to take the lead in any investigation, and he considered himself equal to handling the victim with the kid gloves that MacDonald and Canton's preliminary report indicated would be necessary. At the same time, if the victim was as skittish as he imagined, he would just as soon hold back and let Collins handle it.

Collins rang the doorbell and the two detectives stood and waited. It was a full two minutes before the door was opened by a large-boned woman in a faded cotton nightgown, the background of which had at one time been white. The woman's hair was the color of steel wool and looked as if an attempt had been made to brush it back and flatten it. However, several stray hairs floated straight up as if propelled by static electricity. The woman's eyes were brown and bloodshot, and her lips were small and tight.

"Are you Mrs. Shay?" Collins asked, since the woman offered no greeting.

The woman nodded.

"I'm Detective Collins and this is Detective Berger. We've come to talk to your daughter."

Mrs. Shay's eyes narrowed at the sound of their names. She said, "Yeah," and pulled back the door, allowing the detectives to enter.

They found themselves in a small living room, darkened by the heavy drapes drawn across the single window in the front. The scant light seeping in through the drapes was supplemented by the cold glow of a television set that sat in the far corner of the room on a low pressboard stand. Directly across from the television was a tattered love seat that listed to one side, apparently having lost one of its casters. Laura Shay was seated there, her legs drawn up beneath her and hidden from view by the afghan she had wrapped tightly around her. She stared dully at the screen and gave no indication that she was aware of the detectives' presence.

"Laura," Mrs. Shay said loudly, "these people are here to see you. They're detectives."

Laura didn't move. Mrs. Shay crossed the room and hit a button on the television set, which emitted an electric crackling noise as its picture disappeared.

"Miss Shay?" said Collins softly. "Laura? I'm Detective Collins and this is my partner, Detective Berger."

Berger fought the urge to glance at Collins. He felt an inward stab at his vanity at being introduced as Collins's partner as if he were an afterthought.

"I understand that you had a...bad experience last night."

Laura didn't respond. She continued to stare at the blank television screen as if she could will the picture to return.

"Can you tell us about it?"

Mrs. Shay stepped in front of the television set to be

in Laura's direct line of vision and folded her fleshly arms
across her chest. Although Laura didn't move, Collins
could sense a change in her. Laura's dull gaze seemed to
intensify, as if she were trying to bore holes through her
intrusive parent to get through to the television.

"Laura?" Collins said again, trying to draw the girl's
attention. "Laura, do you know who it was that attacked
you?"

The question was followed by a silence interrupted only
by the increased heaviness of Detective Berger's breathing
as he tried to stifle a frustrated sigh.

Collins tried again. "Laura, who did this to you?"

The girl's eyes did a fast trip to her mother's face, then
immediately returned to the midsection of the faded nightgown.

"Ben," she said after a long pause. "It was Ben Harvey."

Mrs. Shay let out a single "Hmmph." She sounded like
a stern parent who was only moderately satisfied with her
child's performance.

ONE

March 1997

THE FIRST SET of sturdy metal bars slid back with a loud crash that reverberated inside Ben Harvey's skull just as vividly as when they'd closed on him eight years earlier. His lawyer, John Livingston, shook his hand and led him down the stark hallway. There was a guard standing against the wall with his arms folded defiantly across his chest. He had greasy, gray-streaked hair and a matching mustache from which a few crumbs of food were dangling. He narrowed his eyes, his expression clearly showing that, evidence or no evidence, he believed Ben had gotten away with something. Ben returned the gaze coolly, then turned away and faced forward, determined not to make eye contact with anyone else.

Ben had grown into a man behind bars. There was no more of the gangliness of his youth. He carried himself slowly and carefully, like a man accustomed to the encumbrances of invisible fetters. All of the awkwardness of his teenage years was gone, replaced by a cold stoicism that made him look as if his skin had tightened around his already slight frame and was holding him hostage. He wore the dark brown suit that Livingston had brought for him, a white shirt, and a brown tie. The clothes hung on him as if he were a human coat hanger.

"There are some reporters outside," said Livingston as they continued down the hall. "It figures. They'll want to know how you feel."

Ben glanced at him out of the corner of his eye.

"But you don't have to talk to them if you don't want to," Livingston continued. He'd long since grown used to his client's silence. "I can talk for you if you want."

They passed through the last checkpoint, and the final set of steel bars slid open with the usual sickening clang. It occurred to Ben again that they sounded exactly the same when they opened as when they closed, and he'd learned enough to know that there was a reason for that: whether he was coming in or going out didn't matter. Now that he'd spent almost a third of his life here, he would never be free.

They passed through the last door and out into the blinding sunlight of the parking lot behind the prison. Just as Livingston had said, several reporters were there, some carrying microphones that they jabbed in his direction as they shouted questions to both the lawyer and his client. They were accompanied by several cameramen jockeying with each other for position, occasionally bumping into each other but by longtime tacit agreement not stopping for apologies for fear of missing something important. It was apparent that these people traveled in packs, familiar with each other from all the time they'd spent covering the same events. Most of the questions were variations on a theme: how did Ben feel?

Ben said nothing as he made his way through them. In his mind the same answers played over and over again: "I don't feel anything, any how, any way."

When a particularly aggressive reporter from an evening news team darted forward and loudly asked the same thing again, Livingston interposed himself between the reporter and Ben and said, "My client is naturally happy that his conviction has been overturned. The DNA test has proved conclusively that he was not guilty, and both my client and I could only wish that these tests had been more widely available back when he was falsely accused.''

Livingston propelled Ben forward toward his nearby car as the reporters shouted follow-up questions, most of which concerned what the future held for Ben, legally. As Ben was climbing into the passenger side of the front seat, the same reporter yelled out, ''How do you feel toward your accuser? How do you feel about Laura Shay?''

All of the reporters fell silent: it would be the big question on the minds of their audiences. Ben stared dispassionately over the roof of the car at the reporter who'd asked the question. After a lengthy pause he replied, ''Those people have taken up enough of my life. I'm not gonna give them any more.''

He dropped into his seat and closed the door softly. Livingston got behind the wheel and with one continuous motion slid the key in the ignition, started the motor, and shifted the car into reverse.

''Well, you're a free man now, Ben,'' he said as he hit the gas pedal.

Ben didn't respond.

LAURA SHAY hadn't slept since she heard the news. She could hardly leave her apartment because of the reporters that kept coming around. She hadn't been back to work for days. She learned of the release of her supposed attacker from a reporter who showed up unexpectedly at the drugstore where she was a cashier, shoved a small tape recorder in her face, and asked her what she thought of the fact that the man she swore had raped her eight years ago was about to go free. Laura was caught completely off guard by the question, not just because it was so unexpected but because the case hadn't even made the news when it originally happened. Like the majority of crimes, it had passed through court like a greasy hamburger, not stopping for general digestion. Laura was shocked that Ben Harvey's release should be news when his conviction had been so quiet.

"Why...why are you here? What do you want?" she stammered at the reporter.

The reporter realized at once that Laura didn't know what had happened, and was more than happy to break the news to her so that he could avail himself of the opportunity to get her first reaction.

"He was...they think he didn't do it?" Laura had said, her eyes wide.

"They *know* he didn't do it," the reporter replied.

"They know..." Laura's voice trailed off, and it seemed for a moment as if she had trailed off with it.

"So what do you think, Miss Shay?" the reporter pressed, trying to get some reaction from her. "You were *sure* he was the one that attacked you, weren't you?"

Laura suddenly had come back to the present and nodded vigorously. "He *did* do it! I don't care what anybody says!"

She burst into tears and fled into the back room of the store.

She gave a hurried, practically incoherent explanation to Mr. Gibson, her employer, for why she had to go home early, then slipped out the back door. She walked all the way home to her dingy studio apartment, keeping mostly to the alleys for fear of running into another reporter. Even though the alleys were considered dangerous, facing them was preferable to facing more questions about what had happened that night eight years ago and how she felt now. All the way home, she had had one thought in her mind: now the truth would come out.

She spent the next two days locked in her apartment, barely getting out of bed and never getting dressed. The third morning found her lying in bed staring at the tiny black and white TV that sat across the room on the dresser she had taken with her when she moved away from home. She absently picked at the threadbare elbow of the pink sateen housecoat she had bought three years earlier at Kmart. When she saw it on the rack, she felt there was something comfortably familiar about it, and after a long internal debate over the cost, she had bought it. When she got it home and put it on, she realized why it was familiar: it was exactly like something her mother would wear. In fact, when she looked at herself in the mirror, her expanding waistline accentuated by the wide sash of the robe, she realized how much she was starting to look like her mother. This realization brought on a flood of tears, during which she sat on the foot of the bed and gently stroked the hem of the robe, lamenting the fact that she wouldn't be able to enjoy it.

Though she was still young, that experience had left her strongly aware that up to that point, her life had been a complete and utter failure, and there was no reason to believe that would ever change. And now even the housecoat was falling apart.

She reached over to the nightstand and wrapped her fingers around the neck of a bottle of vodka. She tilted some of the liquid into a tumbler. She had long ago convinced herself that she would be all right as long as she didn't drink it straight from the bottle. When she righted the bottle, her hand brushed against an empty carton of orange juice, knocking it onto the floor. She thought for a moment that she would really like to have some more juice to mix with the vodka, but that meant a trip to the store and the possibility of being spotted by a reporter.

Besides, she thought she had reached the point where it was easier to drown her sorrows undiluted.

Laura managed to keep her senses dulled to the point that she was only dimly aware of the slow passage of time during the morning and afternoon. Her mind was clouded with thoughts that seemed to inflate inside her head until they were too large and too close for her to see them, but she sensed their general theme. It was that horrible night her senior year in high school that had ruined her life. It had all been so promising, but something had gone wrong. Through her mental haze she could remember the attack and how awful it had been. But then beyond it there had been a ray of hope that something that had been so horrible could be the turning point for her, would end up being the spark that would change her life for the better. It was like that Bible verse they used to read to her when she was in Sunday school: all things work together for good. Laura had seen the good that could come out of that terrible night. Her father had made her see that. But the rug had been pulled out from under her, and the good she had tried to make for herself was coming back to haunt her.

And now things were worse. She could barely afford the rent for her tiny Uptown apartment as it was, and she hadn't been able to go to work for fear the press would show up again and spread her shame across the front pages of the news and on television. Not that they weren't doing that anyway. And maybe things would get even worse. She hadn't heard from the police yet, but if the newspeople kept harping on the story, might the police want to reopen the case?

She drained the glass, then reached for the bottle again and found it was empty. She let the bottle slide from her fingers onto the floor, then lay there on the bed looking

down at it glistening on the filthy rug. She realized with
disgust just how much she hated the place. All of the
furniture except the dresser was other people's throw-
aways; the rug was never cleaned and the walls never
painted because the building owner couldn't get high
enough rent in this neighborhood to make keeping the
place up worth his while. Half the time when she came
home from work there was someone lying drunk or passed
out on the stairs, and the hallways smelled of urine. What
made it all worse was knowing that there'd been one
chance for her to improve her lot in life all those years
ago, and she'd blown it. She'd made a fatal mistake.

She lay back on the bed and let her tears flow. In a
way she felt like that same young teenager she'd been
when the attack occurred. The shame and humiliation, and
mostly the anger, all washed over her again.

But in the midst of the swell of emotions a single
thought fought its way through the fog in her mind: maybe
it wasn't too late. As she considered once again the possibility of renewed interest in the case and all the media
attention it was getting now, what her father had tried to
do for her back then came back to her. Maybe her father
had been right, and only his timing was wrong. Maybe
Ben Harvey's release and the attention it had drawn was
a blessing in disguise. Maybe it was all God's way of
giving her one last shot at improving herself. For the first
time in days, she felt like getting out of bed.

Laura hurriedly threw on an old gray sweatshirt and a
pair of jeans, then pulled open the top drawer of her
dresser. The little cup which she kept full of quarters and
dimes for the laundry was empty, but occasionally some
coins would fall out when she opened and closed the
drawer, so she ran her hands under the disarray in the
drawer searching for loose change. She found two quarters

and three dimes, which she stuck in the pocket of her jeans. There was a pay phone down by the 7-Eleven and she could use it to make the call and even pick up some more liquor while she was at it.

She stopped for a minute and frowned down at herself in the hand mirror that was lying on top of the dresser. Did she have enough money for booze? She knew there was seven dollars in her purse, but she was going to use that for food, since her minuscule paycheck wouldn't be coming for another four days. A smile slowly broke out on the image in the mirror as she realized that after tonight, that wouldn't be a problem anymore. She grabbed her keys and headed out the door.

Laura paused in the poorly lit vestibule and looked out through the cracked glass panel in the door. Nobody was there. Whatever reporters had been there on the day of Ben's release had gone away. For a moment, she was stopped short in her newly formed plan. Maybe the media wasn't interested anymore. But her smile reappeared. She knew they would be interested if she decided to talk.

Laura wove her way unsteadily down the sidewalk to the store on the corner, at first praying that one of the two public phones on the outside of the building would be working, then praying that the person she needed to call would have a number that the phone company would give out. If the number was unlisted, then her plans would be over before they were begun. At least for the time being.

Her first call was to Directory Assistance, and they gave her the number she wanted, which Laura took as a sign from God that she was on the right track. She carefully repeated the number over and over to herself as she replaced the receiver, then picked it up again and dialed.

The phone rang five times before it was answered.

"Hullo?" It was the voice of a small child, drawing the word out tentatively.

"Hello there," said Laura, trying as best she could not to sound drunk. "Who is this?"

There was a beat before the child said slowly, "Uh... I'm not supposed to say."

"That's all right," Laura replied. She was starting to enjoy herself. "Listen, is your daddy home? Can I talk to him?"

"Okay," said the child. There was a loud double knock through the receiver as the child clumsily put the receiver down. It was picked up almost immediately.

"Very good, honey," said a male voice to the child. Then he said into the receiver, "Hello?"

Laura took a deep breath and said, "Hello. Remember me?"

"Who is this?"

Laura laughed inwardly. "It's Laura. Laura Shay."

The mention of her name was met by a stunned silence.

"I know you remember me," she added.

"Why are you calling?"

"Why am I calling? Don't you read the papers?"

There was a pause before the man said, "What about it?"

So you do know about it, Laura thought. Then she said, "There've been some reporters want to ask me questions about that night. Seems a lot of people are interested now that Ben's been cleared. Funny, nobody was interested back then."

The man gave a smug laugh. "You know you can't prove anything."

"I don't have to," said Laura, measuring her words carefully to give them more weight. "All I have to do is *talk.*"

TWO

LAURA SHAY was right about one thing: people were interested in the story. Several miles from Laura's squalid apartment, while she made her call, Emily Charters sat in the kitchen of her small gray house reading about the case in the newspaper. Emily had seen the rise and fall of many things in her seventy-odd years, and as she read the article she emitted a gentle "tsk" at what she perceived to be the general decline of journalism in her lifetime.

"This says that Mr. Harvey was 'curiously subdued' as he left the prison. Now, I wonder what exactly that's supposed to mean."

"They probably mean they expected him to be dancing with joy at the thought of being released," said Lynn Francis.

"Really." Emily pursed her lips with mild disdain. "Well, I would think he'd be experiencing a lot of conflicting emotions. He certainly wouldn't be dancing at the thought of the injustice he's suffered."

"You're much more practical than reporters."

"Oh, dear, dear, dear," Emily said softly as she continued to read. "And what exactly is aggravated rape?"

"Emily!" Lynn exclaimed. Her face reddened at the thought of explaining it to the old woman.

Emily looked at her with a glint in her eye and said, "Well, I know what rape is, of course, but wouldn't you think that it was, by nature, aggravated?"

"You have me there."

Emily watched Lynn as she finished arranging the lettuce she'd been tearing into bowls. Always a shrewd judge of her fellow human beings, Emily had recognized Lynn as a woman of strong character the moment they had met, and that recognition had grown into fondness over the ensuing months.

"You really don't need to wait on me," Emily said. "You're a guest. You're not on the clock." She bestowed a kind smile on Lynn, who stood at the kitchen counter carefully quartering cherry tomatoes to put in the salads.

"I enjoy doing for you, mum," Lynn replied with a comic curtsy and a flip of her long, tawny hair.

Emily laughed and said, "That's very kind of you to say, but it's you we have to think of now."

Lynn's smile faded as she concentrated her attention on the tomatoes. "It's best if I keep busy."

Lynn Francis had been hired to come in and clean for Emily two days a week after the elderly woman had undergone a bypass operation several months earlier. She had proven efficient enough at her work to meet with Emily's high standards, which was saying a lot, and was kept on even though Emily's health had improved to the point where she no longer felt the need of assistance—not that Emily had ever acknowledged that need. Lynn had been hired for her by her friend, Detective Jeremy Ransom. But it wasn't in her capacity as a cleaning woman that found Lynn staying with Emily at that time.

Lynn had once been the personal assistant to a high-powered businessman, but had given up that position and offered her services as a much less highly paid cleaning woman, a change that allowed her a more flexible schedule. That flexibility was the most important thing to Lynn, who needed it in order to take care of her lover, Maggie Walker. The past two years had been an emotional roller-coaster ride for Lynn as she constantly faced the prospect of losing the companion with whom she had shared her life for over a decade. Maggie had gone through several bouts of pneumonia; a very serious infection with a long Latin name that Lynn could never remember, but which had fortunately responded to antibiotics; and a tuberculosis scare, at which point Lynn had truly felt that it was all over. But the tuberculosis had turned out to be a false positive, and Lynn felt a reprieve that had her fostering the hope that just possibly Maggie might survive a while longer. The scare was no sooner over than Maggie suddenly developed lymphoma, and the virulence with which it attacked her, coupled with the ravages of everything that had gone before, left her unwilling or unable to fight anymore. She had succumbed quickly.

When Emily heard the news, she had insisted that Lynn come and stay with her for a while so that the young woman wouldn't be alone. Lynn hesitated to accept the offer at first. Her initial reaction to Maggie's loss had been to retreat within the walls of her apartment as the overwhelming sense of grief washed over her. But after a couple of days, the walls of the home the two women had shared began to close in on her. The place was so thick with memories that at times it was difficult for her to breathe.

In the end Lynn had accepted Emily's offer, and found the old woman's kindly attention to be a balm that she couldn't have hoped to receive from anyone else. And Lynn's temporary residence in Emily's home also served to keep Emily from slipping back into the lethargy she'd experienced after her operation.

As Emily watched Lynn continue the meal preparations, she couldn't help but marvel at the turn her own life had taken over the past couple of years. She'd lost the last of her old friends, a woman she had known all her life. There was no longer anyone who could remember with her the days of her youth, or her late husband, or any of the milestones that mark the normal passage of time in one's life. Emily had found herself at a turning point where she could either fade away from this life, which she thought with a smile would be expected or maybe even desired of someone of her age, or she could begin again. The turning point had instead become a new beginning for her. Far from fading into obscurity or oblivion, Emily had undergone a renewal that found her almost happier than she'd ever been. *If I were a fanciful woman, she thought, I might go so far as to say that my heart operation was part of that renewal. She smiled to herself. But I'm not a fanciful woman.*

"What are you thinking about?" Lynn asked, breaking in upon Emily's thoughts.

She sighed. "I was thinking about the inevitability of change."

Lynn stopped with her hands resting on the counter and looked at the old woman. She was tempted to ask why, but she thought she already knew the answer to that. Instead, she simply said, "Really."

Emily shifted in her seat. "Yes, well, what I mean is that when you reach my age you would think that things would stop changing, but they never do, you know. When I look back at it now, it seems as if life is a series of turning points with a lot of living in between. But it's always the turning points one remembers."

"I see," Lynn said softly.

Emily sighed. "I suppose change, though, is a sign that we're still living."

There was a long pause before Lynn decided that Emily wasn't going to continue, so she went back to preparing dinner. Both of them were lost in their own thoughts.

Their silent musings went uninterrupted until the arrival of Jeremy Ransom. He was clad in a dark blue suit and carrying two large sacks of groceries, one in each arm. Ransom's visits to his adopted grandmother had become more frequent since her operation. It was unusual now for a day to go by in which he didn't at least stop in to check on her.

"Oh! Jeremy!" Emily exclaimed with a start. "I didn't hear you come in."

"No matter how often I visit, you always sound surprised to see me," he said as he placed the bags on the opposite side of the counter from where Lynn was working. "I think I managed to find everything you needed."

"Lynn," said Emily, "would you bring me my purse, please? It's on the stand by my bed."

"Sure thing." Lynn quickly wiped her hands on the yellow checked kitchen towel and left the room.

"You know, Emily," said Ransom as he took a seat at the kitchen table across from her, "if you pay me I'll feel just like a delivery boy."

"Nonsense!" Emily replied with a smile. "I may be a woman of limited means, but there's really no need for you to be paying for my groceries."

Ransom cocked his head and eyed her slyly. "Emily, I don't think anyone would ever accuse you of having limited means."

Lynn returned with Emily's purse and then busied herself with unloading the groceries and putting them away. Emily carefully counted out the money and pushed it across the table to Ransom, who pocketed it without looking at it. Much as he disliked the idea of accepting the money, he thought in this case, it might be the better part of valor. Despite her advanced years, Emily was a deeply independent person, and to have refused her would have done nothing but cause unpleasantness all the way around.

"So what have the two of you been doing all day?"

"Keeping busy, as always," Emily replied. "I've just been reading the paper."

"So late in the day?"

"I'm afraid I didn't get to it this morning. Since Lynn is here, I thought perhaps it might be time to go through the things in the attic, clean out the things I didn't need anymore, and get it all straightened out."

There was a twinkle in Emily's eyes that told Ransom that the project was designed more to keep Lynn occupied than from any real need. Ransom gave a slight nod of understanding.

"We were just reading about that young man who was released from prison. The one they just found innocent of rape," said Lynn as she arranged some bags of vegetables in the freezer.

"Ah," said Ransom, "Ben Harvey."

"You know of the case?" said Emily, her eyebrows arching with interest.

Ransom gave a short laugh. "Not firsthand. Only what I read in the papers."

"It seems terribly sad," said Emily, "that the D-N-A testing is such a recent development." She pronounced the letters of the test slowly, as if she were spelling out a foreign word.

"Only if you think in terms of the past," Ransom replied thoughtfully. "It's a shame it wasn't there for people who were wrongly convicted before, but in future terms, it can hopefully keep the same thing from happening again."

Emily tilted her head slightly to one side and looked off in the distance as she considered her own thoughts.

"You know," she said at last, "this Mr. Harvey seems an extraordinary young man."

"How so?"

"Well, according to the paper—understanding, of course, that you can never take what you read in the paper as absolute fact—Mr. Harvey has no feelings whatsoever about the woman who accused him of rape. He says he just wants to get on with his life. Now, that seems unnatural, doesn't it?"

Lynn chuckled to herself as she folded up the brown paper bag she'd just emptied. Ransom shot her a glance and said to Emily, "Why do you say that? I would think he'd want to make her the farthest thing from his thoughts."

"Perhaps," said Emily, "but I believe there's a bit of Shylock in all of us. I think everyone wants their pound of flesh to some degree."

"So it's *The Merchant of Venice* this time, is it?"

Emily's cheeks turned slightly pink. "I do happen to be reading it at the moment."

"And what about you, Emily? Is there a bit of Shylock in you?"

"Oh, no," Emily replied with a gentle laugh. "I'm much too old for vengeance."

"Would anyone like some tea?" said Lynn as she folded up the second bag.

"Thank you," said Ransom.

Emily closed the newspaper, laid it aside, and folded her hands on the table. It was a position that Ransom always thought made her look like a schoolmarm.

"And what are you reading at the moment, Jeremy?" she said in a tone the reinforced the image.

"I'm rereading *Oliver Twist*, which I'm happy to say

has absolutely nothing to do with Ben Harvey.'' He added to himself, *And thankfully, neither do I.*

IT WAS PAST MIDNIGHT, and Laura had made so large a dent in the new bottle of vodka that she could barely hold her eyes open. But if she'd been drinking out of sorrow or frustration before, since making her call she was more inclined to drink to celebrate. She'd even bought another carton of orange juice. She knew she wouldn't have to worry about money anymore. The man she called had told her to go to hell. He said he wasn't afraid, and she wasn't going to get a penny out of him. But Laura knew better. She knew that once he had time to think about it, he would realize she meant business and what it would mean to him if she told her story. Then he would come around...and come across. She wouldn't have long to wait.

She was just dozing off when she thought she heard a knock at the door. It was so light that she wasn't sure, but after a pause it was repeated. By that point she'd had so much to drink that the knock came as a surprise, even though she was expecting it. She struggled out of bed and started for the door, dragging the top sheet from the bed almost halfway across the floor with her before she realized it was tangled around her foot. She did an awkward one-footed dance back to the bed, looking as if the sheet were reeling her in. She fell backward into a sitting position on the bed, knocking the nearly full carton of orange juice off the nightstand as she fell. She then lurched forward to disentangle her foot.

There was another knock at the door. Laura stood, careful to go slowly enough to not lose her balance, and headed for the door again. She opened it and found a man standing there, backlit by the dim hall light. The energy

she had expended in getting to the door seemed to revive
her enough that she remembered who she thought would
come to her, but she was so bleary-eyed and the hall was
so dark that she wasn't sure that the man standing in front
of her was the one she expected. She squinted at him and
was struggling to focus her eyes when the man's hands
flew up, and Laura felt something slip tightly around her
neck. Instinctively her hands clutched at whatever it was
that was cutting off her oxygen, but before she was even
cognizant of what was happening, it was all over. Her
body went limp and she slumped to the floor.

THREE

"DID YOU KNOW that this area used to be one of *the* places to live?" said Ransom.

His partner, Gerald White, grunted in reply as he steered the car onto a side street just south of Wilson and just west of the lake. Gerald was born and raised in Chicago, and felt as deeply as anyone that it was his home. But he was no more interested in its history than he would have been in having a list of the previous owners of the house he shared with his wife, Sherry, and their two daughters.

"It's hard to imagine that any area by the lake could be allowed to slip so far."

They pulled up behind the squad car in front of a red-brick apartment building that had definitely seen better days. What had once been a fine example of urban elegance now looked like an imploding monster with dried mortar popping out from between the crumbling bricks, as if the building were being crushed under its own weight. The building had a small paved court fronted by huge rectangular pillars on each side. There were two sets of large, rusted hinges on each pillar, evidence that at one time there'd been a tall gate, most likely for ornament rather than for security. The court was barely wide enough to allow for the three doors that offered admittance to different sets of apartments. A uniformed officer was waiting for them just inside the door to the left.

"You the detectives?" said the officer as he opened the door.

"I'm Ransom. This is my partner, Detective White."

"I'm Becker," said the officer as he led the detectives up the stairs to the first landing. The stairs were covered with a red carpet so dirty that it looked as if it had rusted.

A man was sitting on the stairs at the top of the landing. He was about fifty years old and was wearing a pair of black Levis and a blue jacket over a white shirt and tie. He was staring forward, giving no indication of seeing the approaching men, and absently rubbing his knees with his hands. Just to his right was another officer standing in front of the door to the scene of the crime.

"This is Jones," said Becker as they walked past him into the apartment.

"And the man on the landing?" Ransom asked.

"Bill Gibson. He's the one who found the body." As Becker said this he pointed to the floor.

The dead girl was sprawled on the floor not two feet from the door. Her arms were outstretched, palms up, and her legs akimbo so that she looked like an obscene Raggedy Ann doll. There was a thin, virulent red line around her neck.

"Do we know who she is?" Gerald asked as Ransom silently crouched beside the body for a closer look.

"Her name is Laura Shay."

"What?" Ransom turned his eyes to Becker and rose slowly. He looked as if he hoped he hadn't heard correctly.

Becker shot a blank glance at Gerald, who was looking at his partner quizzically.

"Laura Shay," Becker repeated. "You know her?"

Ransom looked down at the girl, then closed his eyes and slowly shook his head. "Why did this have to happen in our area?" he said quietly. "What a mess this is going to be."

"Jer? Who is she?" Gerald asked.

Ransom rolled his eyes toward his partner and said, "Have you heard of Ben Harvey?"

Gerald stared back at Ransom, his brow furrowing as he tried to recall where he'd heard the name before. Finally his face lit up and the creases on his pale forehead disappeared. "Oh!" He looked at the body and added, "Oh, God!"

"Indeed," said Ransom.

"Well, who is she?" said Becker with irritation. He knew he was outranked, but he still didn't like being treated as if he weren't there.

Ransom gave the officer a coy smile and said, "I think you should read the newspapers."

Becker frowned but thought the better of pressing the matter. With a grunt, he joined his partner on the landing.

"You realize," said Ransom, "this isn't going to be pretty."

"Uh-huh," said Gerald, who was scrutinizing the empty vodka bottle that lay by the bed.

Ransom slowly surveyed the room, making mental note of the condition and quality of the contents. In addition to the empty bottle on the floor, there was another bottle, three-quarters full, sitting on the small table by the bed. There was an empty carton of orange juice on the floor and another by it that had been knocked over, spilling its contents into the carpet. The doorframe and the lock appeared to be intact.

Gerald said, "There's cuts on her fingers. Looks like she tried to stop it. Struggled with the wire. It would've been very quick."

Ransom nodded.

There was a pause. Then Gerald asked with a noticeable

lack of confidence, "I don't suppose this could be a really bad coincidence?"

"Bad for who?" said Ransom as he continued to look around the room. "And we can rule out robbery. Not even a blithering idiot could have hoped to find anything of value in this building." He sighed heavily. "The minute the press hears about this they'll jump to the conclusion that Ben Harvey had something to do with it."

"Uh-huh."

Ransom paused for a moment, tapping his index finger against his lips. "There's something definitely not right here."

"Aside from the dead body," said Gerald with a smile.

Ransom ignored him and continued, "No sign of forced entry."

"If she didn't have the dead bolt on, he—whoever it was—could've opened the door easily enough."

"Yes, but look at the place. Outside of the bottle on the floor and the orange juice, it certainly doesn't look like anything's happened here…" He shot a glance at his partner and added wryly, "Aside from the dead body. It doesn't look like there's been a struggle. If she was here when someone broke in, I would've expected some kind of struggle."

Gerald pointed to the empty bottle and the other one on the table in turn. "There's an awful lot of booze missing. Maybe she was in no condition to fight."

"Hmm," said Ransom as if he were giving the suggestion at least cursory consideration. "Perhaps. But I would expect a drunken struggle to be even messier."

"Yeah, but if she was drunk enough he could've broken in and killed her before she even knew he was here."

"I suppose…" said Ransom slowly, "but look where she is. She's right by the door."

Gerald shrugged. "She could've ended up there in the struggle."

Ransom thought about it for a moment, then sighed. "Well, if we're ruling out robbery we're left with two options. The first is that somebody broke in here and killed her."

"You mean Ben Harvey."

Ransom narrowed his eyes. "I mean somebody. And the second possibility is that she let the killer in."

"Only if she was drunk, that could've been anyone, whether she knew them or not."

Ransom pursed his lips. "Perhaps. But if Laura Shay let the killer in, there's no way it could have been Ben Harvey. Even drunk, I can't believe she'd do that."

Gerald glanced at the dead girl as if he thought she might offer some explanation for her actions.

"And if it was someone she didn't know," Ransom continued, "that still leaves us with the question, what would a stranger hope to gain here?"

Gerald looked back at his partner. "Maybe sexual assault?"

"The autopsy will tell," said Ransom with a very heavy sigh, "but I certainly hope not. Things will be bad enough as they are."

The detectives paused for a moment, looking down at Laura Shay's lifeless form. To the casual onlooker it would have appeared as if they were pronouncing a silent benediction over the girl. At last Ransom sighed and said, "Let's talk to Mr. Gibson."

They went out onto the tiny landing, interrupting a whispered conference between the two officers. The officers stepped back just inside the door to allow the detectives more room. Gibson was still seated on the top stair and rubbing his knees like a mute, misdirected Lady Macbeth. The detectives towered over him.

"Mr. Gibson?" said Ransom. When there was no response, he repeated the name.

"Yes?" Gibson's voice sounded hollow, as if he was answering them from within a dream.

"Mr. Gibson, I'm Detective Ransom. This is my partner, Detective White. We'd like to have a word with you."

The rubbing stopped and without a word Gibson rose and turned to face them. He made no move to take the last step up onto the landing, so his staring eyes were about level with Ransom's throat.

"How did you come to find the body?"

There was a pause so long that Ransom wasn't quite sure that Gibson was going to respond. Then Gibson swallowed hard and said, "No phone."

"I beg your pardon?"

"No...she doesn't have a phone." He swallowed again and added, "I've never seen a dead person before."

"I understand," said Ransom somewhat curtly. He didn't really understand. He couldn't see how anyone of Gibson's age could've avoided seeing a dead body, at least at a funeral. Then again, he reminded himself that at funerals they try to make the body look as if it were alive. Laura Shay looked unmistakably dead. "Now, Miss Shay had no phone, and you needed to talk to her for some reason?"

"Yes." Gibson cleared his throat in an attempt to pull himself together. "Yes, Laura works for me. I own Gibson's, the drugstore over on Broadway. She hasn't been to work for a few days. We haven't heard from her, and I came over to see if she was ever coming back to work."

"And what did you find?"

"What?" said Gibson, allowing his eyes to meet the detective's directly for the first time.

"What did you find when you got here?"

"You saw her," Gibson replied, his eyes widening.

"Yes, I know, but when you got here did you just walk in?"

"No, I knocked on the door. There was no answer."

"So you just went in?"

"Uh-huh."

"Hmm," said Ransom, once again touching his index finger to his lips. "How did you get in?"

"What?" Gibson's eyes had widened even further. He looked as if each question was a new, unpleasant surprise.

Ransom smiled. "How did you get in? Was the door open? Unlocked?"

Gibson shook his head slowly. He looked like a man who has just discovered he's walked into quicksand. "No. I have keys."

"Do you, now?" said Ransom, raising one eyebrow.

"Well, yes..." Gibson replied slowly, as if any sudden movement would sink him further.

"So you have more than an employer/employee relationship with Miss Shay?"

"No! No, it's not that. I'm a married man. I have a wife. No, Laura just gave me a set of keys in case she got locked out. She wanted to make sure there were keys someplace safe if she lost hers."

"Hmm," said Ransom again, giving Gibson a half-smile. "How does your wife feel about that?"

"She doesn't—" Gibson broke off, shook his head, and amended what he'd been about to say. "I never saw any reason to tell her about it. Why should I?"

Ransom paused, more for effect than anything else, then said, "Why did you bring the keys with you?"

"What?"

Ransom sighed. "If she gave you the keys just in case she was locked out, why did you bring them with you? Were you anticipating trouble?"

"No, I..." He stopped and his face took on a deadly pallor. For a moment, Ransom was afraid that the man might faint. Gibson looked at Gerald, then back at Ransom, then to the floor. "No, I carry them with me. You were right. I'm sorry. Laura and I *were* more than employer and employee. Sometimes. I just...didn't want anyone to know. So we tried to be discreet."

"Have you quarreled with her lately?" Ransom asked.

Gibson turned his large, pleading eyes up to him and said, "No...no. We were the same as always. I mean, we were close, but there's only so close you could be with Laura. She didn't...trust, really."

"She trusted you with her keys."

They stared at each other until Gibson turned away. He said softly, "She liked me as much as she could like anyone, I guess."

"And how did you feel about her?"

"I liked her," Gibson replied weakly.

Ransom turned to Gerald and said, "I think we should have the keys, don't you, Gerald?"

"Oh, I think so," Gerald replied with a solemn nod.

Gibson's hand was shaking when he handed a small ring with two keys on it to Ransom, who pocketed it and said, "This will be returned to you as soon as we're done with our investigation."

Gibson lowered his eyes to floor and said, "That's okay. I won't need them now. What would I want with them?"

Ransom sighed serenely. "So you got here and you found the door locked?"

"Yes."

"Both locks?"

"What?" Gibson looked up, again seeming startled.

"Were both locks on?"

"Oh…" He thought for a minute then said, "Yes… well, no, I don't think so."

Ransom gazed at him as if through sheer force of will he could clear away Gibson's mental debris. "You don't *think* so?"

Gibson shook his head. "I turned the top lock first— that's what you usually do, right? And then I did the key in the doorknob, but the door didn't open like it should. So I did the top one again, and the second time it worked. So I think maybe the top lock was off, and the first time I tried it, I was locking it instead of opening it."

"Has that ever happened before?"

"No, I—" Gibson caught himself and blushed deeply. "I don't know. I haven't used the keys before."

Ransom smiled. "Of course. Can you tell me why Miss Shay has stayed away from work?"

"Oh, she hasn't been to work since… Did you know about…?" He looked from Ransom to Gerald and back again.

"We know about the rape case."

Gibson shook his head sadly. "I didn't. Not until the day that guy was released. A reporter showed up that day. Laura was…it was the first she'd heard that that guy was getting out. She was beside herself when she heard. She ran to the back room. Goddamn reporter didn't care. He stayed out there waiting for her to come back out. All he wanted to do was ask her questions. He didn't care that he was making her crazy."

"Crazy?" said Ransom, once again raising a single eyebrow.

"Wouldn't you be?" said Gibson. "Finding out that the guy that raped you was getting out?"

Ransom paused before saying, "But he didn't rape her."

Gibson eyed him doubtfully. "That's what they say. But you should've seen Laura. She was scared to death when she heard about it. And it looks like she should've been, too. Look what's happened!"

"But did she tell you that she was afraid of Ben Harvey?"

Gibson seemed momentarily taken aback by this question, as if he thought Ransom might be trying to trick him. "No. She just kept saying 'What am I going to do?' Just like she was afraid something would happen to her."

"I wonder..." said Ransom, letting his voice trail off as he narrowed his eyes at Gibson.

Gibson glanced at Gerald as if he thought he might be able to explain his partner's actions, but Gerald had taken out his small spiral notebook at the beginning of the conversation and was now staring down at it like a disinterested third party, heedless of Gibson's silent entreaty.

Gibson turned back to Ransom and said, "You wonder?"

Ransom breathed deeply and said, "Mr. Gibson, do you know who we should notify of Miss Shay's death?"

"Um...yeah. Her mother. If I remember right, her name's Miranda. So far's I know, she's the only one of Laura's family that's still..." His voice faltered and he glanced toward the open door to the apartment. The murdered girl's left leg was the only thing visible through the space left by the two officers. He cleared his throat again. "Her mother is the only living relation I know of."

"What about friends? Did she have any friends?"

Gibson shook his head. "We never talked about them.

Maybe the other girls at the store, but I don't know. There's three other girls that work there." He gave them the names, which Gerald jotted down in his notebook.

"I have one other thing to ask you, Mr. Gibson," said Ransom, "which I would need to ask anyone in your position." He paused and noted that Gibson didn't look pleased at the mention of his being in a position. "Where were you last night?"

"Last night?" His eyes widened. "Where was *I*?"

"From the looks of the body she's been dead a matter of hours, not days. I'll need to know where everyone close to her was last night."

There was a lengthy silence before Gibson replied hesitantly, "Well...I was home. All night. With my wife."

"She'll be able to verify that?"

"Yes," Gibson replied without enthusiasm. Then his eyes quietly shifted back to Ransom. "Will she have to?"

"We'll try to be discreet," Ransom replied with a wry smile.

THE DETECTIVES waited at the scene for the men from the crime lab, which gave them time to ring the bells on the other apartments to see if anyone was home. There were no answers, which was to be expected since everyone was most likely at work. But the detectives knew that this was the type of neighborhood where people were reluctant to answer an unexpected doorbell, and even more reluctant if they knew the police were the ones ringing.

Ransom called in to Sergeant Newman to let him know what they'd found. Although not issued by the department, cellular phones were becoming a standard piece of equipment for detectives. While Ransom was not necessarily averse to new technology, he greatly disliked the idea that carrying a cell phone would make him so readily accessible. But he chose to look at it from the plus side: it made his work easier, and it allowed Emily to be able to reach him whenever she needed or wanted to, which gave him some comfort given the state of her health over the past few months.

Newman was understandably displeased when told the identity of the victim, knowing that he'd have to brace himself for an onslaught from the press. While Ransom was reporting in, Gerald used his own cell phone to make some necessary calls and jotted down information in his notebook. One of these entries was Miranda Shay's address. Once Ransom was finished talking to Newman, they set off for Shay's home.

"Gibson's wife verifies that he was home all night," said Gerald as they walked back to the car.

"Hmm," Ransom replied. "What reason did you give for asking?"

"The truth. I told her one of his employees has been murdered, and we were making a routine check of everyone that knew her."

The corners of Ransom's mouth slid upward. "One can only hope that she'll raise questions of her own."

"He's a bit old for her, isn't he?"

"Hmm."

"He did solve one thing, though."

"What's that?"

"The locks. If what he said was true, then the girl's top lock wasn't on. Anybody could've slipped something in the other lock and walked right in."

"The lock being open this morning doesn't necessarily mean that," said Ransom with a half-smile. "The lock on the doorknob was set to lock automatically. The killer wouldn't have had the means to lock the dead bolt."

Gerald looked at him for a moment. Then his normally white cheeks turned a bit pink. "Oh, yeah."

"We're going to have to question her coworkers and see if anybody knows what she's been doing lately. And we'll have to see if they know anything about this relationship between her and Gibson. If I know my coworkers, this 'well-kept secret' will be common knowledge." He stopped for a moment, looked back at the apartment building, and sighed. "Oh, dear," he said as they climbed back into the car, "I suppose Mr. Gibson has given us an indication of what this case is going to be like."

"How do you mean?" Gerald asked as he turned the ignition.

"He assumes that Ben Harvey is the murderer. It's my guess that everyone else will, too. Harvey will prove to be a very convenient scapegoat."

Gerald paused in the act of putting the car in gear and turned to his partner. "Unless, of course, he really murdered her."

"Yes, there is that possibility."

Gerald didn't immediately turn away. In the years he'd spent with his partner, he thought he had grown to know him pretty well, and although they disagreed on occasion, they had never had a serious argument. Gerald was almost as confident of Ransom's detective prowess as Ransom was himself, and he knew that Ransom was usually right. But that didn't mean that Gerald ruled out the possibility that Ransom could be wrong.

"What?" said Ransom, chafing under the scrutiny.

Gerald sighed. "Look, I know we haven't even started yet, but I wouldn't want…" He faltered for a moment. He'd been about to make his statement more specific than would have been wise, but he caught himself in time. When he continued, he chose his words carefully. "I realize we don't know anything about the girl and who else might have wanted to kill her—"

"Who *else?*" Ransom interrupted, cocking his head slightly to one side.

"Who else in addition to Harvey. But I don't think we should rule him out, either."

"Rule him out?" Ransom repeated, staring at his partner in a way he usually reserved for difficult suspects. "Do you actually think I would do that?"

Gerald paused long enough to make his doubt evident. "No," he said as he turned away from Ransom and put the car in gear. He really didn't think Ransom would ever consciously ignore a suspect, but he also knew how Ransom could be if he felt he was being pushed in one direction.

Ransom pressed the lighter into the dashboard and extracted a plastic-tipped cigar from the inner pocket of his jacket. "I know that Harvey is a suspect, if for no other reason than circumstances, but I'm not going to focus on him before we have any evidence just because he had the misfortune to be released from prison just before the murder. Anyone could've seized the opportunity to kill Laura Shay now, knowing that suspicion would automatically fall on Harvey."

"I know," said Gerald with a weary sigh.

The lighter popped out of the dash and Ransom lit the cigar with several short puffs. Then he stuck the cylinder back into its slot, sat back, and took a long, satisfying drag, exhaling the smoke with a sigh. Emily had been after him for a long time to quit smoking, and he'd tried on occasion, only to find himself lapsing back into it with a vengeance at the first sign of stress. Since his failure to quit had been a source of irritation to him—and a reminder that he was still subject to human frailty—he'd ceased his efforts to give up the habit for the time being, if for no other reason than to stop accentuating his failure. Besides, he enjoyed it.

"We know very little about this yet, Gerald," he said in a more conciliatory tone. "But we know one thing that I find very interesting: Laura Shay was *afraid* when she heard that Harvey was released from prison."

"Why's that so interesting?" said Gerald as he executed a three-point turn before heading south.

"Why would she be afraid?"

Gerald shrugged. "I think most women would be when the guy that raped them is released." He stopped and his brow furrowed. "Except...except he didn't rape her."

Ransom smiled broadly. "Exactly."

"I suppose she could've been afraid that he'd be mad. I know I would've been if that'd happened to me."

"I suppose," said Ransom, pausing to take another puff of the cigar. "Or she could've been afraid of something else."

It was a long drive down Sheridan Road to Lake Shore, and then to the Dan Ryan Expressway. They had driven almost the entire length of the city when they exited the expressway at 111th Street.

The far southwest side of Chicago was unusual in that it had managed to accept integration without the "white flight" that had occurred in many other parts of the city in the sixties. That left the area with a very broad mix of ethnic diversity and socioeconomic classes.

The detectives came to a stop when they reached Lynnwood Avenue, the street on which Mrs. Shay lived. On the corner of 111th and Lynnwood, taking up the entire block north of 111th, stood John Quincy Adams High School. At one time, it had been the neighborhood's dividing line between black and white, with whites living to the west in the statelier homes that spread up a hill into expensive, upper-middle-class residences, and the blacks living to the east in more humble working-class homes. Over the years the nonviolent integration to the west of the school had muddied the division, so that the school no longer drew the line between the races.

"That's where it happened," said Ransom, rapping the window with the knuckle of his third finger.

Gerald leaned forward slightly and looked past him. "What?"

"That's where the rape was supposed to have taken place. Behind the school. At least that's what it said in the paper." He mentally repeated Emily's disclaimer about believing what you read in the press. He sighed heavily and said, "Well, let's go talk to the mother."

Miranda Shay's house was a couple of blocks south of the school in an area that had run down from working class. Most of the houses were serviceable if undistinguished, though it was evident that most of the residents, presumably through pride of ownership, made some effort to keep up their property. Shay's house was one of the exceptions. It was a small wood-frame, later in date than its neighbors and apparently built at a time when memories of the Chicago Fire had dwindled. The paint was warped and peeling, and the four steps leading to the front door sagged as the detectives mounted them. Gerald rang the bell and they waited.

After a lengthy interval, the door was opened by Miranda Shay. Her once-steel-gray hair had gone completely white, and although she still brushed it straight back it had thinned enough that her blotchy scalp was plainly visible. The blotches continued down onto her forehead and joined together on her cheeks, giving her the red flush that Ransom associated with heavy drinking. She was wearing a flannel nightgown, dirty white with small sprigs of flowers all over it, and there were smudges across the stomach that seemed to indicate that she used the midriff as an apron. She had a pair of old vinyl mules on her feet.

"Yeah?" she said.

"Mrs. Shay?"

"Yeah?"

"I'm Detective Ransom. This is Detective White. We'd like to talk to you." He showed her his badge.

She didn't look down at it. Instead her eyes widened at the introduction, revealing angry red lightning bolts that cut across the whites. "*Detectives.* What do you want with me?"

"We'd like to speak with you. Do you think we might come in?"

"*Detectives.*" She stared at him a moment; then the memory of the last time detectives had visited her home seemed to come to her. Her eyes widened further and her mouth dropped open. "Detectives! What's happened? What's going on?"

"If we could just come inside and have a word with you?"

She pushed back the door with her left hand, on which a large blue vein pulsated. The detectives passed through into the living room.

The room hadn't changed for the better since the time of Laura's rape, although since neither Ransom nor Gerald had been involved in the original case, they couldn't have been expected to know this. Everything was in the same place but in worse condition. The carpet was so threadbare in spots that the cheap foam pad was visible through it. A mustard-yellow bedspread was thrown over the love seat, covering it but not hiding the fact that it still sloped to one side. Clouds of dust spun up through the stream of light pouring in through a break in the closed curtains. It looked as if the room were in the process of decomposing.

Mrs. Shay dropped onto the love seat, which emitted a puff of dust in response to her weight. A bottle was heard rolling away under the seat, apparently from an inadvertent kick. Ransom pulled a wooden chair up to face Mrs. Shay. It was all he could do to stop himself from dusting it off before sitting down. Gerald sat in the corner in a chair whose seat had sprung. He opened his notebook, adjusted himself around the exposed spring, and waited.

"Mrs. Shay," said Ransom carefully, "I'm afraid we have some very bad news."

She glared back at him as if defying him to find some news bad enough to touch her. "It's Laura, right?"

"Yes."

"She in jail?"

There was a beat before Ransom said, "No. I'm afraid she's dead."

Mrs. Shay curled her lips and continued to stare at him. Ransom found her reaction both interesting and puzzling. Instead of tears or expressions of disbelief, which would have been perfectly natural, she looked as if she were angry.

"You're telling me Laura's dead?" she said.

"That's right."

She sat back and folded her arms under her breasts, her expression coming close to a sneer.

"Hmmph," she said with a heave of her chest. "Well, at least she's out of it."

Ransom raised an eyebrow. "I beg your pardon?"

"Out of it. It's all over for her. She's better off where she is. It's not like life treated her too good."

Ransom waited for a few moments, allowing Shay room to relent if she saw fit. Although he'd seen many peculiar reactions to news of the death of a loved one, he'd rarely seen the news accepted so clinically. When it was apparent that Shay had nothing more to say, Ransom said, "Mrs. Shay, your daughter was murdered."

"Murdered," she shot back with distaste. The scowl that accompanied her exclamation made her look as if she thought the murder was the last in a long line of affronts perpetrated by her child. The tone of her voice caused Gerald to shoot her a curious glance from his corner.

"Yes. She was strangled. Do you have any idea who might want to kill your daughter?"

Shay shook her head brusquely. "Haven't seen her in a long time. We were never what you call close, and after her daddy died we were nothing. I think it's been two years since I even set eyes on her."

"So you wouldn't know anything about her friends or acquaintances."

"No."

"You never heard from her at all?"

She wrinkled her nose. "No."

Ransom glanced at Gerald, then asked, "Was she close to her father?"

"Yeah…" Shay replied, drawing the word out as if the memory still made her angry. "They were close." She stopped and continued to glare.

Ransom allowed a few seconds to pass before he said, "Is there something wrong with that?"

"Ha! No. I 'spose not. Just I never did know why she liked *him*. He wasn't worth nothing. He was just a night watchman at that canning company over on Western. Never made much money, but he was always going to. Always had some scheme to make money. And he never did nothing. Died and left me nothing. And Laura's the same way."

For a moment Ransom thought perhaps Mrs. Shay was referring to the possibility of an inheritance from her daughter.

"She'll never amount to anything," said Shay, apparently switching to the future tense through force of habit when speaking of her daughter's prospects. "She'll never amount to anything. Never did. Just like her father. Couldn't even make it work when he had the chance."

"I'm sorry," Ransom interrupted. "He couldn't make *what* work?"

Shay eyed him suspiciously, then said, "Nothing. He couldn't make nothing work. And Laura didn't even finish college."

Ransom glanced at Gerald again, who appeared as struck by the sudden shift in topics as Ransom was.

"We had hopes for her there," Shay continued, "but George—that was his name, George—his hopes for her were just like his hopes for everything else. All came to nothing."

Ransom studied the woman in silence. To say that he felt a dislike for her would have been putting it mildly. She sounded as if everything that had happened to her husband and daughter were personal offenses aimed at her. Ransom knew he had to keep a level head and remain objective, but he could feel himself hardening against the woman. And although he knew virtually nothing about Laura Shay, he felt almost compelled to defend her. Or at least to shoot some holes in Miranda Shay's rough exterior.

"Mrs. Shay, I understand that your daughter was raped just before graduating high school."

"Yeah?" she replied warily. Once again her tone caused Gerald to pause in his note-taking and look at her from across the room. "What does that have to do with it?"

The expression on Shay's face made it evident to him that there was something about the subject of the rape that made Mrs. Shay uneasy. Ransom tilted his head to one side, which made him look like a malevolent elf.

"Yeah?" she said again, this time more forcefully.

"Well, I was just thinking that sometimes an experience like that can severely alter the course of someone's life."

"Huh?" Shay said dully.

Ransom closed his eyes to collect himself, then opened them and said, "What I mean is that an attack like that can have very bad effects. Those effects might have held your daughter back."

Shay's face went blank for a moment. Then she blinked and said, "Oh." Her relief was noticeable, which Ransom found even more curious. She rubbed the blue vein on her left hand with the index finger of her right for a few seconds, mulling this over. Suddenly her features tightened again and she let out a derisive "Huh."

"Yes?" said Ransom calmly.

"You didn't know Laura," she said, taking a swipe at the air as if she were slapping a vision of her daughter. "Before she got herself raped, things weren't that great, neither."

Ransom crossed his legs and folded his hands on his knee. "You don't think very highly of your daughter, do you?"

Shay took another swipe at the air, this time backhanded. "She was just like her father."

Ransom adjusted himself on the hard seat, which was becoming distinctly uncomfortable. He refolded his hands and said, "Mrs. Shay, do you watch the news?"

"What?" she said, drawing back slightly as if the question was another affront.

"Do you watch the news? Or read the paper?"

"Course not. Ain't life bad enough without adding to it? I got problems of my own."

You certainly do, thought Ransom. Aloud he said, "So you don't know."

"What?" Shay said. The redness of her cheeks deepened. Ransom smiled inwardly. To him this was the typical reaction of someone who was undereducated: she eschewed gaining knowledge, and yet was angered at the idea of not being in the know.

"Do you remember Ben Harvey?"

Shay's face went blank. She looked as if she thought she ought to remember the name. She said, "No," then clamped her lips together and shook her head as if to demonstrate that anybody she couldn't remember was unimportant.

Ransom tried not to sound patronizing as he said, "He was the young man that your daughter accused of raping her."

"Oh, him!" She glared at Ransom as if he'd been trying to trick her by using the young man's real name. Then her thick, curved eyebrows slid inward. "Hey, what do you mean, 'accused'? He's in jail."

"Not anymore. He was released a few days ago."

"It figures. They always let 'em out sooner or later."

"Oh, he wasn't just let out, Mrs. Shay. He was proven innocent."

"What?" Shay exclaimed, for the first time looking completely off guard.

"He was proven innocent," Ransom repeated.

"But...how could they do that?"

"DNA testing. Surely you must've heard of it. DNA

testing has come into play since your daughter's rape. It's a scientific test that can be used to positively identify a criminal in some cases...or clear someone. That test has proven Ben Harvey's innocence.''

Shay looked almost wild-eyed, though she didn't move or speak for a minute. She simply stared at Ransom as if she thought he might be there to tear down the foundation of her house. When at last she spoke, she'd regained some of her hardness, although it was tempered with a lack of certainty. ''I bet people can buy those test results. Just like everything else. I bet people can give payoffs.''

''Not *poor* people,'' said Ransom with a quick glance around the room to make it clear that he included Mrs. Shay in that category. ''If what I've read is correct, the Harveys are not wealthy people.''

''Well, then, there's gotta be a mistake! That was the kid that raped my daughter!'' It was the first time that Shay demonstrated any sort of defensiveness on behalf of the dead girl, and Ransom would have found it more convincing if she hadn't sounded so defiant.

''Did your daughter actually *tell* you that he was the one?''

''Course she did,'' said Shay, looking more unsure of herself by the minute. ''She told the police! She told the court! You think she would've done all that if he wasn't the one?''

''But he wasn't the one, Mrs. Shay.''

''I don't care what some damn test says, he was the one that did it!''

Gerald had looked up from his notebook and was casting a concerned glance at his partner. Gerald had never interrupted him in the middle of questioning someone, but he was tempted to do it now. Mrs. Shay was holding tightly to the cushions of the love seat as if she needed to physically hold herself down.

"I'm sorry," said Ransom in a tone devoid of expression. "I didn't mean to upset you."

She didn't look mollified. "What's that got to do with anything, anyway? You come here and tell me Laura's been murdered, then you gotta bring up that time—" She stopped suddenly and her mouth dropped open. Her eyes widened, but all the anger was gone. "You think he might've done it? You think he might've killed Laura because..." She let go of the cushions and sat back against the seat. She looked as if the cause-and-effect possibility had just gotten through to her, though much more sharply than Ransom would have expected. To Ransom, Mrs. Shay looked like someone who'd just realized she'd accidentally set off a bomb.

"Because of what, Mrs. Shay?"

"Because..." She turned her eyes to his and attempted to harden them again. After a few moments, she seemed to win the battle, at least somewhat. She said as calmly as she could, "Because she sent him to jail, of course!"

"WHAT IN THE HELL was that all about?" said Gerald as they walked back to the car.

"What do you mean?" Ransom replied, choosing to ignore his partner's tone.

"For Christ's sake, Jer, you just told her her daughter was dead. Then you acted like she didn't care."

"Correction," Ransom said as he opened the passenger door. "*She* acted as if she didn't care. I acted on that."

Gerald dropped into the driver's seat and started the car. "You know as well as I do that when somebody hears about a death they can act strangely. I know how that woman was behaving, but you don't know whether or not she *really* cared about her daughter.''

Ransom's right eyebrow slid upward as he turned to face his partner. ''Do you think for a minute that that woman gave a fig about the dead girl?''

Gerald paused and took a deep breath, releasing it slowly. He stared straight ahead. ''I like to think so.''

Ransom looked at him for a moment, then said, ''That's because you're a parent, and a decent human being. But you don't believe she cared, either.''

''She might, for all I know—for all *you* know, for that matter. She might just hide it well.''

Ransom propped his elbow against the window and rested his temple against his hand. ''She didn't react to the news of her daughter's death. Well, I should say she *did* react, but not as I would've expected any mother to. So I pressed her to see if there was anything she *would* react to. Maybe in a moral sense it wasn't the best time to do it. But when would be? After she's had time to let all the ramifications of the death sink in, and after she's had time to think of how it would be best to answer?'' He paused for a second, then said, ''Besides, we needed the answers.''

''You don't think she had anything to do with it?''

''She didn't like her daughter,'' said Ransom with a noncommittal shrug. ''But I can't imagine her thinking enough about anyone else to kill them.''

Gerald turned toward Ransom with his pale lips slightly parted and his pasty forehead furrowed. After a brief pause, he sighed. ''I suppose you're right.''

''You know, Gerald,'' Ransom said slowly, still staring out through the windshield, ''there is something very strange about that rape.''

''What do you mean?''

"The only thing that Mrs. Shay *did* react to was when I brought up Harvey and the rape case."

"Well, that's only natural. It brought back painful memories."

Ransom turned to his partner and curled his lips. "More painful than hearing that her daughter was dead? I think there's something very wrong about that rape."

"Of course there is," said Gerald with a laugh. "Laura Shay identified the wrong man. It happens."

"Yes, but the item I read in the newspaper said that she still insisted that he was guilty."

"I think that's natural, too. She's spent eight years thinking he was guilty. That sort of thing gets burned in your mind."

"Without a doubt? I would think after hearing the news that he was *proven* innocent, she would've at least *entertained* some doubts. But she was adamant about it being Harvey. So was her mother just now...but..."

"What?"

Ransom sighed. "But didn't it seem to you that she was protesting a bit too much? Harvey served a sentence and her daughter's dead. What possible reason could she have for insisting that Harvey was the rapist against positive proof?"

Gerald sat for a while, mulling this over. Finally, he said, "You know, I've never really understood how someone could finger the wrong guy for rape. You'd think they'd have to know who raped them. But I guess trauma will do funny things."

Ransom sat up and looked at his partner for a moment, then pulled out a cigar. "I think we'd better talk to Harvey."

"Before we get the report from the crime lab? There might not be a reason to."

"I thought he was your favorite suspect," said Ransom, feigning surprise.

"I didn't say that," Gerald protested, mentally kicking himself for falling for his partner's needling. "I just think he's a *likely* suspect."

Ransom pushed the lighter into the dashboard. "We'll probably have to talk to him sooner or later. I'd rather he heard about the murder from us instead of on the news." He unwrapped the cigar, crumpled up the cellophane, and stuffed it in his pocket. "And I'd like to see how he takes the news. Do we know where he lives?"

"Seventy-seventh and Jeffrey," said Gerald as he shifted into drive.

Ransom shot him an amused glance.

Gerald coughed, then said, "I got that when I called for the information on Mrs. Shay."

Ransom pulled the lighter out of the dash. As he lit the cigar, he said, "Good old Gerald. Always anticipating my every whim."

FOUR

IT TOOK a little over half an hour to reach Harvey's neighborhood. He was staying with his mother in a house on Luisa Street, a couple of blocks west of Jeffrey and just south of 77th. Unlike in the Shays' neighborhood, the white residents had fled this area when blacks started to move in in the late fifties. Now the area was predominantly African-American.

Luisa Street was lined with rows of nearly identical redbrick cracker boxes built shortly after World War II. Very little had been done to distinguish the outside of the houses other than the planting of borders and flower boxes, none of which were blooming at that time of year. Whatever attempts the inhabitants had made to individualize the interior of their houses were hidden from view of the street by the small front windows and the uniform venetian blinds. It was a street where the houses could be identified only by the midsized, fake brass numbers that clung precariously to the bricks just to the right of each front door.

The detectives located the Harveys' house, parked, and climbed out of the car. As they went up the narrow cement walk to the front door, Ransom noted that this house was probably less expensive than the Shays' home but was infinitely more presentable. The outside was quite clean, the low row of bushes along the front was neatly trimmed, and although it was still a little early in the year for lawn care, the grass showed that it had at least been cared for in the past.

Gerald pressed the doorbell, but they couldn't detect any corresponding ringing inside, so after a moment he opened the outer door, which still had its storm windows in, and rapped his knuckles against the inner door. The cheap, light wood sounded hollow.

After a brief wait, the door flew open and the detectives were faced with Ben Harvey. He was wearing dark blue pants that provided more than ample room for his legs, and a T-shirt that fit snugly at the shoulders, but his meager torso was unable to fill the rest. Ransom had never seen a face so completely devoid of emotion: no twitches, no unnecessary movement of the eyebrows or muscles around the mouth, not even the telltale pulsating of the veins at his temples. It was as if Ben had spent the years in prison learning to master every fiber of his body, including his circulatory system, so as never to let anybody know what he was thinking or feeling. The one thing he couldn't control was the adjustment of his eyes. At first sight of the detectives, there was a slight retraction of his pupils, completely involuntary, that made him look as if he were retreating into himself.

"Ben Harvey?" said Ransom. Ben inclined his head slightly, and Ransom completed the introductions. "May we have a word with you?"

"About?"

Ransom was going to answer when another voice was heard approaching the door.

"Who is it, Ben?" It was the voice of an older woman, slow and slightly hoarse so that it sounded like dry ground being pelted with light gravel. "Who's at the door?"

She stepped into view. She was about five feet tall and heavyset, with hair that was unnaturally black for her age and tied in a bun that spiraled up from her head like a funnel. She wore a green knit dress that showed signs of heavy washing. Ransom mentally noted that Mrs. Harvey must've given birth late in life.

"It's a pair of detectives, Momma."

"What?" said the woman, her eyes opening wide. She stared straight at the detectives as she said, "What do they want?"

"They want to come in and talk to me."

There was a brief pause, then Mrs. Harvey said, "Well, then, they should come in, I suppose." She sounded like someone who was accustomed to giving solace to her enemies.

Ransom introduced himself and Gerald to Mrs. Harvey as she led them down a short hall into a tiny living room. Ben glanced out the door, checking to see if anyone had noticed his visitors before closing it and following them in.

The furniture was what Ransom called "oppressively old," but all in very good condition and kept polished and clean as if the owner knew their value, and that value came not from age but from the difficulty in finding the money to replace them if anything should ever happen to them.

"This house belonged to my brother," Mrs. Harvey explained. "I moved in here with him after...a while back. It worked out good because he was ailing and needed somebody to take care of him. His wife passed almost ten years ago. My brother's name is Nathaniel, and he's in a nursing home now."

"I see," said Ransom.

"Mr. Ransom, you sit there," she said, gesturing to one end of the couch, "and Mr. White, you can sit on the other side. I'm sure you'll be comfortable. If you don't mind, I'll sit in my easy chair. It's not that nice to look at, but it's high enough off the floor that I can get in and out of it easy, you see?''

"Yes, Mrs. Harvey," said Ransom with an understanding smile. All three of them then turned their eyes toward Ben, who stood in the center of the room looking down at the detectives.

"What do you want?" he asked with no trace of emotion.

"Ben!" his mother exclaimed. "I was just about to ask these gentlemen if they'd like something to drink."

"No, thank you," said Ransom, answering for both of them.

"This ain't a social call, Momma. They got work to do." He turned to Ransom and added, "Don't you?"

"We're on duty, yes."

"Well, the least you could do is sit yourself down, son," Mrs. Harvey said lightly. "You make me nervous standing up there like that. You always were a tall boy, but when I'm sittin' down you're way up there! You sit down, now."

Ben didn't look at his mother, but after a beat he complied. He sat on a chair that had two removable cushions covered in a yellow fabric and wooden armrests that were considerably shorter than Ben's arms. The chair was low and slanted, which caused him to bend in the middle with the upper part of his legs slanting upward, jutting his knees out like arrows. It made him look as if the majority of his height were made up of legs.

"You gonna tell me what you want?"

Ransom glanced at Gerald, then said, "I'm here to deliver some news."

After a pause Ben said, "Yeah?"

"You remember Laura Shay?"

Out of the corner of Ransom's eye he noticed that Mrs.

Harvey's face was starting to sag, as if the weight of sorrow was dragging it down. There was no change in Ben's expression. He waited just a second before he said, "Yeah. I remember her."

"She's dead. She's been murdered."

"What?" Mrs. Harvey exclaimed. She suddenly began to breathe deeply and rapidly, as if she were working hard to draw enough air into her lungs without much success. Ben was out of his chair in a shot. He knelt beside her and took her right hand in his, rubbing her back with his left hand.

"Calm down, Momma," he said softly. "It's all right..."

"But that girl's dead! What happened to her? What will they think?"

"You already know what they'll think," he said, keeping his voice modulated so that no matter what he said he didn't betray any animosity. "That's why they're here."

"It's all gonna happen again, only this time it'll be worse! Murder!"

"No, Momma, it's gonna be all right."

Mrs. Harvey closed her eyes and took a couple of deep breaths that seemed to calm her down. Then she looked over at Ransom and said, "Is that why you're here? Are you going to take my son away again?"

"No, Mrs. Harvey, I'm not. It's my case—" He shot another glance at Gerald, who was smiling down into his notebook, then corrected himself. "It's our case, and you can rest assured that I will not assume that your son has done anything." He paused for a moment to give more import to what he was about to say. "But I think you are wise enough to know what's going to happen."

Mrs. Harvey's eyes slowly moved from Ransom to the

carpet. She seemed to be reading the consequences there so clearly that one might've been tempted to ask her about the future. Her shoulders began to droop as if what little energy she possessed was draining out of her. "Everybody's gonna think he did it."

"Quite possibly," said Ransom.

Ben dropped back onto his chair. "Including the police. That girl gets killed and of course you come straight to me."

Ransom smiled. "I thought it might be better if you heard if from me rather than hearing it on the news."

There was a brief silence during which something within Ben seemed to intensify. Ransom wished he was sitting close enough to see his pupils clearly.

"Sorry I disappointed you," Ben said at last.

"Disappointed me?"

Ben nodded once. "How did you expect me to react? You think I'd be scared? I don't have nothing to be scared of anymore. Maybe nervous? Maybe I'd play at being shocked?"

Ransom shrugged smoothly. "I never know what to expect."

Ben continued, missing Ransom's tone. "Or maybe you think I should play like I'm sorry she's dead."

"Ben!" his mother remonstrated. "You keep talking like that and they'll think you killed her!"

"Go on, Momma. They think I killed her anyway. Like I'd waste my time. You know what kinda girl she was."

"What kind of girl was that?" Ransom asked.

Ben replied after a pause, still with his ghostly calm voice. "The kind of girl that would accuse an innocent man of raping her, even when she knows he's innocent."

Ransom eyed him for a moment, then said, "*Did* she know you were innocent?"

Ben's hands flexed once on the ends of the armrests. "She knew I didn't do it. She knew who I was. I wasn't just another nigger."

"Ben…" his mother protested softly.

"She saw me every day. I sat near to her in homeroom. She talked to me face-to-face all the time. Night she was attacked, I tried to help her. She looked at me, right in the face. She knew who I was then, and she knew who I was when she lied to the police and told them I done it."

Ransom's smile had faded, not because he was displeased but because a more sober aspect was now appropriate.

"You sound as if you had every reason to hate her."

"Yes," he repeated solemnly, "I had every reason to hate her."

Ben stopped, and it didn't escape Ransom that he hadn't answered the implicit question.

"Did you hate her?"

His expression still didn't change. "She took away eight years of my life. Would've been more if they hadn't come up with that test."

He still hadn't answered the question, but Ransom decided that instead of pursuing it, he would try a different angle.

"That was an awfully stiff sentence, wasn't it?"

"She was beat up. And I'm black."

"Still," Ransom continued with calculated caginess, "for somebody with no record…"

Mrs. Harvey looked at her son, who continued to stare at Ransom without flinching. After a pause Ben said, "It was a stiff sentence any way you look at it."

"Very stiff. I would think eight years would be time enough to learn to hate someone, even if you weren't the type of person who would normally hate."

"I suppose some people would do that," Ben replied.

Although Ben remained dispassionate in his demeanor and his delivery, Ransom was sure that he was enjoying deflecting the questions: he'd probably been practicing for a long time.

Mrs. Harvey, however, was not enjoying herself. Tears had welled up in her eyes, and after Ben had finished speaking she said aloud to herself, "Oh, my Lord! They took my boy away once and they're going to do it again!"

"I'm not planning to take him away, Mrs. Harvey," Ransom said as gently as possible.

"Don't you worry, Momma. If they were gonna take me away, they'd'a done it already. That means they don't have any proof of nothing. It's not like it was before. This time they need proof."

Ransom leaned forward. "I always need proof, Mr. Harvey." He sat back again and added, "They must've had some proof when they arrested you before."

"See that?" Ben ran his index finger along three stripes on his cheek, slightly darker than his skin and not very wide, but noticeable. "That's where she scratched me when I tried to help her. That's what they used against me. Marks I got trying to help her."

Ransom sighed. "Do you have any idea *why* Laura Shay would've lied about the rape?"

There was a long silence. It was the first time Ben had come close to showing any sort of emotion. When he spoke, his voice sounded hollow, as if the question was something that had haunted him throughout his years in jail. "No. I don't."

"Hmmm," Ransom replied. He put his index finger to his lips for a moment, then said, "Mr. Harvey, I need to ask you where you were last night."

"He was here with me," said Mrs. Harvey with a sudden burst of energy.

"All night?"

"Yes. All the whole night. He never went out."

"Don't, Momma," Ben said with quiet firmness. "I was here with her most of the night but I go out for walks. Long walks. By myself."

"My boy gets antsy, you see," Mrs. Harvey added apologetically.

"In the middle of the night?" Ransom asked.

"At all hours," said Ben. "I can't stand to be cooped up. I need to be out in the open air."

"I see," said Ransom without expression.

"Do you?"

Ransom looked at Ben, whose eyes still showed no emotion. "So you don't know whether or not anybody could've seen you during your walks."

At last Ben betrayed a hint of a smile. "If I knew that, I wouldn't have told you."

"Of course," Ransom said.

"What?" Mrs. Harvey looked at her son in confusion.

Ben said, "Momma, I wouldn't lie and say I'd been in here with you all last night. Somebody mighta seen me go out for my walk."

Mrs. Harvey put a hand to her mouth but didn't cry. She nodded to her son and looked away.

Ransom gazed at Harvey for a few moments. It was clear that he had spent a lot of time working on making himself unreadable while in prison, probably both from necessity and desire. But the difficulty in reading the young man troubled Ransom, more from a sense of fairness than anything else. He knew he could use Ben's cooperation in clearing him—if he needed clearing—but at

the same time he understood the lack of trust. After what
he'd been through, Ben would probably never trust again.

"Mr. Harvey, what did you do all that time you were
in jail?"

"Whatever I was told."

"Besides that," said Ransom with a smile. "I remember reading that you were planning on becoming a lawyer.
Did you continue that?"

"I studied what I could."

"Is that where you heard about DNA testing?"

"That and on TV. You know where I heard about it."

"Oh, yes," said Ransom, remembering the familiar TV
trial that he'd grown so sick of he refused to even recall
the initials. "I was just wondering... That testing is very
expensive, isn't it?"

"I guess it is," Ben said after hesitating. He sounded
as if he'd realized too late that there was some point to
the detective's questions that he hadn't been aware of at
first.

"How could you afford it?"

"My lawyer paid for it."

"Really?" Ransom said with genuine surprise. "Who
would that be?"

"John Livingston, same guy that defended me the first
time."

Out of the corner of his eye Ransom saw Gerald jot
down the name.

"That was very nice of him."

"Yes. It was."

A smile played about Ransom's lips as he narrowed his
eyes at the young man. After a long silence he suddenly
said, "Well, I think that's all for now." He was on his
feet before he'd finished the sentence, and Gerald wasn't

far behind. He was used to his partner's habit of suddenly closing the conversation.

Ben looked up at them with his poker face and made no move to rise. Instead he rested his elbows on the arm-rests and folded his hands. Mrs. Harvey got up from her chair with a little difficulty and cast a glance at her son that was both resigned and worried.

"I'll see you to the door," she said as she placed a delicate hand on Ransom's elbow.

Gerald held back for a moment as Mrs. Harvey and Ransom walked down the hallway to the door. He looked at Ben and said, "You're playing it all wrong, kid. That man you just blew off is your best friend."

"I ain't got no friends."

"Oh yes you do. My partner is your friend. Maybe your only friend. He thinks you're innocent. I don't think any-body else is going to, do you?"

With this he turned and followed the others to the door. Mrs. Harvey kept her voice low as she said, "My Ben is a good boy, Mr. Ransom. He didn't hurt that girl back eight years ago, and he wouldn't hurt her now."

Ransom looked back toward the room where Ben was still seated. He was all too familiar with the changes for the worse that a kid could go through in prison.

"I'm sure you're right, ma'am," he said as he opened the door. Gerald passed through, but Ransom paused as Mrs. Harvey laid a hand gently on his arm to stop him.

"Mr. Ransom, I couldn't bear it if my son went back to prison. All this time he's been gone and I knew he was innocent, I prayed to the Lord that my Ben would be released and the truth would come out."

Ransom was struck by the order in which she'd listed her pleas. He looked into her anxious eyes and said, "Mrs.

Harvey, I'm afraid you may get the answer to your prayers."

"WHERE TO NOW?" Gerald asked once they were back in the car.

"Gibson's Drugstore, I suppose," Ransom replied with a weary smile. "We'd better go ahead and talk to her co-workers."

The drive back to the far north side took even longer than the drive down had, interrupted only briefly by a stop for sandwiches that they ate on the way. Ransom couldn't help thinking that it would've been much more convenient to have taken care of questioning the staff at the store while they were in the neighborhood earlier, but there was an order to an investigation that it was never wise to ignore, especially in a case that had the potential for being high-profile. The first order of business was usually to inform the next of kin and note the reaction, so like it or not they were forced to drive the length of the city again to take the next step.

Gibson's was located a block north of Wilson on the corner of Broadway and Gray Street. Gerald was able to find an open parking space three doors up from the store. With his skill at parallel parking he deftly slipped the car into the space, then they climbed out and walked back to the store.

The building had been built sometime in the 1940s and looked every year of its age. The store took up the first third of the ground floor, with apartments making up the remaining two-thirds as well as the two floors above. The door to the store was cut at an angle across the corner of the building, which made it look almost as if it were made of building blocks from which some mischievous child had plucked out one of the supporting pieces.

A bell mounted on the upper corner of the door announced their entrance with a rusty clang. The interior of the store was crammed with shelving units on which the stock of over-the-counter drugs seemed to be dwindling. The light was low and the air was heavy, which gave Ransom the feeling that the whole place was full of a thin, oppressive mist. A long, low wooden counter ran half the length of the west wall, where two young women were huddled in conversation. One was brunette and the other blond, and neither of them looked as if she'd reached her twentieth birthday. They glanced up when the detectives came in, but almost immediately resumed their intense exchange in lowered voices.

The detectives made their way around the shelves to the counter. The girls didn't stop talking until Ransom came to a halt directly in front of them.

"Is Mr. Gibson here?"

The girls glanced at each other, then the brunette said, "No. He went home for the day." A rather large wad of gum crackled between her teeth as she spoke.

"I'm Detective Ransom and this is Detective White," he said, flashing his badge at them. "Did Mr. Gibson tell you we'd be talking to you?"

The moment he introduced himself, the girls froze like two deer tensing at an unfamiliar sound in the forest. They glanced at each other again, then the blond said tentatively, "He said you might."

"You are…?"

"My name's Sue," said the blond, "and this is Betty."

"There's another young woman working here, I believe?"

"Oh, yeah. Janet. But she's on vacation this week."

"Hmm," said Ransom. "Mr. Gibson must be terribly shorthanded this week."

"We don't have a lot of customers. And he wasn't expecting none of us to get killed," Betty replied with an impish grin.

"Can we ask you about Laura?"

"Sure. Go ahead," said Betty.

"I guess," Sue replied faintly.

"Is there somewhere we can talk to you without being interrupted by customers?"

"Customers!" Betty exclaimed with a snap of her gum.

"There's Mr. Gibson's office," Sue offered.

Betty grimaced. "One of us will have to keep out here in case any 'customers' show up."

Ransom smiled. "Then maybe we could talk to you one at a time."

Betty grinned broadly. "Sure, slick."

Sue looked at Betty, her expression showing that she was aware an exchange was taking place that was going over her head. Apparently the one part she did get was that they were going to be interviewed separately, an idea she didn't appear to relish.

Sue led them to the back of the store, past a pharmacy department that was being used for storage.

"Mr. Gibson doesn't employ a pharmacist?" Ransom asked.

"He used to. He couldn't afford it anymore, though. People that live in this neighborhood have to go someplace where they can get drugs cheaper."

"What about insurance?"

"Most of them don't have any, and don't qualify for Medicaid."

She led them through a curtained doorway into the back room, and they saw immediately why Betty had produced her sardonic grin when Sue had referred to it as an office. It was little more than a stock room with a desk pushed against the wall by the door. The one small window was just to the left of the back door and so begrimed that one could hardly tell it was daylight outside.

Sue sat on the wobbly desk chair whose foam rubber was popping through a tear in the seat. Gerald stood leaning against a pile of boxes and Ransom sat on the desk overlooking the young woman. As it turned out, she was very little help. She hadn't worked at the store very long, and apparently kept pretty much to herself, though it wasn't by choice.

"The other girls—Laura and Betty, and even Janet—they're pretty close, I think. At least, they talk to each other a lot. They don't talk to me very much. I don't think I'm their type."

"What type is that?" Ransom asked.

She turned her doleful eyes up at him and said, "Interesting. I guess I'm not very interesting to them."

Ransom could sympathize with the other girls. Although he didn't like the idea of anybody being purposely excluded from a close-knit family, Sue was so lifeless in manner that he could almost feel the energy being leeched out of his body.

She was able to provide them with one useful bit of information, though. When Ransom asked if she knew whether or not Laura had had any friends, boys or otherwise, Sue replied, "Well, I don't really know. She didn't talk to me any more than she had to. But I heard her—when she and Betty were gabbing—I heard her talk about a man named Earl sometimes. I got the feeling he was going with her. But I don't really know. I only heard a little bit. And if they ever noticed me listening, they would move away from me."

Ransom was silent for a moment, then said, "Well, when we came in it looked like you were having quite a conversation with Betty. Maybe now that Laura's gone, she'll pay you a bit more attention.''

Sue looked up at him. ''Janet will be back soon.''

Ransom thanked her and asked her to send Betty back to them. Sue agreed to this request with all the enthusiasm of the terminally downtrodden, and disappeared back into the store.

''Still awake?'' Ransom said to Gerald.

''Just barely,'' he replied. He looked as if Ransom had startled him back to consciousness.

It was only a few seconds before Betty came through the curtains. She marched into the back room and threw herself down on the chair with the air of someone who dared anyone to challenge her.

''Well, Betty, did you consider Laura a friend?''

She folded her arms across her chest and smiled at him. The tail end of her chewing gum stuck out from between her teeth. ''Yeah, I guess.''

''You don't seem very upset about her murder.''

''That's 'cause it's so cool. I never knew anybody that got killed before.''

Ransom smiled inwardly. He thought the young woman might prove to be difficult to question, but he couldn't help liking her rather rustic straightforwardness. At least she seemed to restore some energy to the room.

''It's anything but cool,'' he said soberly, making it a point to hide his amusement. ''It's a very serious business.''

''Whatever you say.'' She produced a frown. ''I'll cry at the funeral. I promise.''

''What can you tell me about her friends? Her *other* friends.''

She shrugged. ''Nothing. She didn't have any that I know of.''

"Really?" said Ransom, raising an eyebrow. "Not even boyfriends?"

"Uh-uh," Betty replied with an emphatic shake of her head.

"She didn't have *any* boyfriends?"

Betty sighed dramatically. "I *told* you."

Ransom waited, then said, "What about Earl?"

Betty's mouth dropped open, almost allowing the wad of gum to flip out. It hung for a moment behind her teeth before she rescued it by continuing her noisy chewing. She laughed loudly.

"Who told you about that? The mouse?"

"The mouse?"

"Suzie Homemaker," she replied derisively. "The mouse. That's what me and Laura called her."

Ransom shrugged. "She mentioned hearing the name."

The grin returned to Betty's face. Her eyes were lit with amusement. "But I'll bet she didn't tell you who he is, did she? 'Cause she didn't know."

"Well?"

Betty sat back in the chair, which creaked and popped as if it might explode from the pressure of its unrestrained occupant. "It's a name she came up with."

"A name? Then Earl wasn't a real person?"

"Oh, he was real, all right. Earl is our boss, Gibson."

Ransom glanced over at Gerald, who returned a puzzled look.

"I believe Mr. Gibson's name is Bill—William—isn't it?"

"Course it is. Why do you think she called him Earl?"

"I'm sorry, you've lost me."

"It was a game, don't you see? I mean between Laura and me. She told me she always used to do this. See, I never really saw her much outside of work, so we always had to talk about stuff here. So she made up a name for Gibson—Earl—so she could talk about him here, right under his nose, and he wouldn't even know it was him we were talking about.''

"Ah! I see," said Ransom, smiling.

"So whenever she wanted to tell me what he was doing, or what he was like on one of their nights together, she just called him Earl.''

"He never caught on?''

"Him? No, he's dumb as scratch. He even once heard us talking about Earl and he got jealous. He didn't say anything, but you could tell. Jealous of himself! Can you beat that?''

"So Mr. Gibson was jealous of Laura?''

Betty grimaced and gave a dismissive wave of her hand. "Not *jealous* jealous. You know what I mean? He was steamed, but he'd never do anything to anybody. He's too much of a mouse.''

"A mouse. Is everyone a mouse?''

"Most people," Betty replied with a slight nod. But she said it in such a way that made it clear that she didn't include him in the category. He was flattered.

"So what did she tell you about her relationship with Gibson?''

"Usual boring story. Wife doesn't understand him. Didn't want to take advantage of Laura, but she was so nice, yadda yadda yadda. Huh! Doesn't want to take advantage but sure didn't mind taking her to the sack. From what Laura told me, he was pretty good in the sack, too— wouldn't think it to look at him, but I guess it stands to reason. Most of them tired husbands are good at it as long as it's with somebody else besides their wives. Christ, Laura told me stories—''

She broke off abruptly and an expression of intense

distress came over her. Apparently in the middle of her remembrances, she realized that this "cool" murder was going to alter her own life. She didn't say anything. She didn't cry, either.

"Do you want a minute?" said Ransom, noting the change.

"No," she replied irritably. "I'm fine."

"You know," he continued after a long pause, "I met Mr. Gibson this morning, and he doesn't seem...well, I'm rather surprised that someone like Laura would go for him."

"Who said she went for him? She just kind of went *with* him."

"Do you have any idea why?"

Betty shrugged. "He took her out. She didn't have anybody else. Men, I mean. I think she could've done better, but she was kind of...I don't know...I don't think she thought she deserved any better."

"Did they have any problems?"

"Problems?"

"Well, you mentioned that he was jealous. Did they fight at all?"

Betty heaved a disgusted sigh. "Jeez, will you get off that jealous crap? He wasn't really jealous. How the hell could he be? He's the one with the wife. And no, they didn't fight. He was too much of a mouse, and she didn't give enough of a damn to fight with him. Why would they have problems? They both got what they wanted."

Ransom looked at her for a moment. "Sometimes people want more."

"Not Laura. Not from him."

"From anyone else?"

"Didn't have anybody else. Like I told you."

Ransom sighed. "Do you have any idea whether or not Mrs. Gibson knew about his relationship with Laura?"

Betty let out a derisive 'huh'! "Who would think *he'd* be screwing around? And his wife's a mouse!"

"SHE SURE DOESN'T THINK much of her boss, or her friend," Gerald said once they were back out on the street.

"Or anyone else, for that matter," said Ransom. "I found her quite refreshing."

Gerald laughed. "Refreshing?"

Ransom shrugged. "She was honest."

When they arrived back at Area Headquarters, Ransom stopped at Newman's office to give him a quick rundown of what they'd done so far. When he finished, Newman said, "So basically we have nothing."

"Gerald is busy hurrying everybody up," said Ransom in a tone that implied his response should be unnecessary.

"What about phone records?"

"She didn't have a phone."

"Christ! What was she living in, the Dark Ages?"

Ransom replied. "No, I believe she was living in poverty."

Newman grimaced. "Jesus, this is just what we need," he said as he sat back in his chair and ran his fingers through his greasy salt-and-pepper hair. "And the media's already on to it. I've been getting questions all day. People are very itchy about this." Newman accompanied this statement with a glance toward the ceiling to indicate that he was referring to forces on high within the department, rather than the general public. He leaned forward and rested his elbows on the desk. "Look, Ransom, I don't have to tell you to be careful, be thorough, and by the book…" Another glance upward showed that exactly which book he was talking about might depend on which

floor your office was located. "But be more so, will
you?"

Ransom offered his superior a smile that did anything
but inspire confidence. "Certainly."

"I'm not kidding!"

"Have I ever done anything that wasn't by the book?"
Newman curled his lips. "Not so's you'd notice."

WHEN RANSOM GOT back to his office, he looked up John
Livingston and found a listing for him with a LaSalle
Street address located in the Loop. He dialed the number
and after two rings the phone was answered by an effi-
cient-sounding young woman who rattled off the names
of the partners so quickly that they sounded like one word.
He identified himself and asked to speak to Mr. Livingston. The woman informed him that Livingston was in
court that afternoon and was not expected in the office
until morning.

"I'll need to talk to him in the morning," said Ransom.
When the woman hesitated, he added, "Tell him it's
about a murder investigation involving one of his clients."

"I'm sure Mr. Livingston will be able to see you," the
woman replied briskly, as if the circumstances weren't the
least bit unusual.

Ransom asked her to repeat the name of the firm—
slowly—and he wrote the names down, then hung up.

Not long after that Gerald appeared in the doorway. He
found his partner fondly rolling an unlit cigar between his
first two fingers and his thumb.

"I called both the crime lab and the coroner. We'll have
everything we need first thing in the morning."

Ransom raised an eyebrow. "Everything?"

"What there is to have."

Ransom gazed at the cigar for a few moments as he continued to roll it in silence. Finally he said, ''Would you call John Quincy Adams High School?''

Gerald's mouth dropped slightly. ''What for?''

''Ben Harvey and Laura Shay were in homeroom together. I want to know who the teacher was. I want to talk to someone who knew them.''

''You mean someone who knew them eight years ago?''

''Um-hmm.''

There was a long silence, then Gerald said, ''Uh, Jer...'' He stopped and Ransom raised his eyebrows. Gerald wrestled with himself for a few seconds, then, thinking better of what he had been about to say, shrugged and left the office. He didn't look particularly happy.

FIVE

"SHAY MADE headlines just a few days ago when Ben Harvey, the man she accused of raping her eight years ago, was released from prison after DNA testing proved his innocence."

A picture of a young Ben Harvey, cribbed from a yearbook, was flashed on the screen. Emily clucked her tongue. He appeared to be such a guileless, open-faced boy, happy and looking forward to the future. He didn't look at all like the type of boy who would commit a violent attack. But then, she reminded herself, if people wore their criminal intentions on their faces, the world would be a much safer place.

Emily was sitting in the living room directly across from the console television set that looked almost as antique as the rest of the furniture. She wasn't one for watching much television, but she did like to catch the news. It wasn't as accurate or thorough as a newspaper report, but it was more immediate.

"Harvey was released from prison earlier this week..." A tape rolled of Harvey and his lawyer in the prison parking lot, cutting their way through a group of reporters on hand for the event. It put Emily in mind of Christ walking through the angry mob who'd just a moment earlier intended to throw him off a cliff.

"When asked how he felt about Laura Shay, his accuser, Harvey said..."

They cut to a shot of Ben looking over the roof of the

car. *"Those people have taken up enough of my life. I'm not gonna give them any more."*

The camera cut back to the reporter, a young Chinese woman standing in front of Laura Shay's apartment building.

"No word yet from the police as to whether or not Harvey is considered a suspect..."

The reporter continued to prattle. Emily shook her head. The difference between the yearbook picture and the recent videotape was startling and tragic. The boy who had once looked so open was now a man whose eyes looked as hard as the steel bars behind which he'd been confined. Emily believed in justice, swift and sure, but this miscarriage of justice was enough to bring one up short. How cruel could the system be if it would cause such a change in a promising youth who'd been wrongly accused? And what had caused that miscarriage? And was it a different kind of justice that the accuser was now dead?

Emily shook her head again. On the news they'd switched back from the reporter to the anchor, who was still saying something about the murder. Above his left shoulder they had frozen a picture of Ben Harvey as he'd spoken to reporters. *There's such deadness in his eyes,* Emily thought.

When Ransom arrived that evening he found Emily still sitting in the living room. The television was switched off and as he came into the room she laid aside the tattered edition of *The Merchant of Venice* she'd been reading. She was in her usual place in the easy chair, beside which was a small circular table on which she kept her current reading material and her omnipresent cup of tea.

The living room of Emily's house had always struck Ransom as an anomaly: it was filled with overstuffed furniture of the kind he always associated with the elderly, and was decorated in earth tones, choices that had suited Emily's long-deceased husband. But the room contained some curiously feminine touches, such as the lamp with the tan shade from which dangled an even row of prisms. The couch had been re-covered since Ransom had known her, but she still maintained the color scheme by having it done in a tan corduroy fabric, albeit in a lighter tone than its predecessor. Ransom found the room comfortable, but not as comfortable as the kitchen.

"Where's Lynn?" he asked as he took a seat on the couch.

"She's run home to pick up her mail and fetch a few things. She'll be back directly."

"Oh," he said absently, then fell silent, though the intensity of his thoughts was manifested in the speed with which he was drumming his fingers on the arm of the couch.

"Is there something on your mind?" Emily asked with a glint in her eye that showed that she already knew the answer.

Ransom sighed. "I worked on a case today that I'm sure is going to be…a bother." He added the last two words with a dismissive wave of his hand. "Laura Shay's murder."

"Really?" Emily said with a gusto that almost approached being unseemly. Ransom had learned over time that Emily's interest in crime was born purely of a fascination with the workings of the human mind and a knowledge of the mind that grew from seventy-odd years of experience with her fellow man. But even though her motives were pure, this case had already been too fraught with public interest for Ransom's liking.

"My dear Emily," he said with a coy smile, "your eagerness is absolutely shocking."

"Oh, tosh!" she replied. It was the closest she ever came to an expletive. "You're much too cynical to ever be shocked." She adjusted herself primly in her seat and said, "You know, earlier I was watching a news report on the murder, but I had no idea you'd been assigned to it."

He sighed again. "I wish she'd had the good grace to get killed on the south side where she grew up."

"Jeremy!" Emily exclaimed with Victorian surprise.

"Sorry, I'm just tired. And cases that get media attention are always liable to be a circus."

"I suppose that's true," Emily replied thoughtfully. "The one report I watched very clearly implicated Ben Harvey in the murder—something they managed to do without even being able to say that he's actually a suspect."

Ransom tightened his lips in disgust. "Just as I thought."

"Well," said Emily, taking a deep breath and raising her thin eyebrows, "do you think he had anything to do with it?"

"There's no evidence of it yet. We'll probably know more tomorrow morning. But I did go out and talk to him."

"Did you? And how did he seem to you?"

"Like a man who's still behind bars."

Emily nodded. "Yes…yes, even from the little they showed of him on the news, he looked very much as if his life were over, instead of as if his life were just beginning. I suppose in time he could choose to move beyond this horrible thing that happened to him, but even if he did, he'd probably never be completely free of it."

They fell silent for a moment, both lost in their own thoughts. Ransom knew that Emily was right: it was a choice. Harvey had to choose to leave the past behind and go on with his life. But the sad fact was that it still wasn't as simple as that. Most likely he'd have to spend his whole life choosing to leave the past behind. He looked over at Emily. She was staring off into the distance, a puzzled frown on her face.

"Emily?"

She shook her head. "Oh, I'm sorry, Jeremy, I just... why do I keep thinking of *The Merchant of Venice?*"

"Probably because you're reading it."

"No, it's not that...." Her voice trailed off, and after a few seconds she raised the index finger of her right hand as if requesting a moment's pause, then recited, "'The villainy you teach me I will execute, and it shall go hard but I will better the instruction.'" She lowered her hand.

Ransom smiled. "Shakespeare for every occasion."

"But pertinent, don't you think? I understand that the only thing a criminal learns in prison is how to be a better criminal. I wonder what effect it would have on an innocent?"

"So you're still plumping for revenge."

She shook her head briskly. She was obviously frustrated with herself. "I don't know what to think. I know what Ben Harvey *says,* but I find it hard to believe that he wouldn't at least be *thinking* about revenge."

Ransom smiled again. "Would you have been happier if he said he wanted to kill Laura Shay?"

"It would at least be understandable."

"Well, if it makes you feel any better," Ransom said with a sigh, "having met him I believe that he's very angry. And I think he's trying very hard to control it."

"Ah!" Emily replied with a satisfied tilt of her head. "And how did he react to the news of the murder?"

"Very coolly. He was being careful to not react in any

visible way. He freely admits he has no alibi, even though his mother was willing to lie for him and say he was in all night. But I don't know how many people could actually *prove* where they were over the course of an entire night anyway.'' He paused for a moment, then added, ''In a way I got the impression that he was issuing me some sort of challenge.''

''Oh?'' said Emily, her interest piqued.

Ransom nodded. ''Yes, but I don't know whether it was a challenge to find him innocent or...''

Emily raised her thin eyebrows. ''Or?''

''Or to catch him.''

Emily thought about this for a moment, then said, ''Perhaps he was just challenging you to be a better detective than the ones that put him away in the first place.''

''Emily, I don't know that their investigation was at all negligent. I would be willing to guess that it wasn't. But it doesn't matter in this case. If the crime lab is unable to come up with anything, then we won't have any evidence against him or anyone else.''

''What about the neighbors?''

''The night shift is canvassing the building, but I don't hold out much hope. In a neighborhood like that people tend to not see anything even if they've seen it. And the murder was probably pretty quiet. If you take someone by surprise, slip something around the throat and tighten it fast enough, I don't think there'd be a lot of noise.''

''Oh, Jeremy, that's terrible!''

''It happens quite a bit.''

''No, that's not what I mean,'' Emily said as she folded her hands in her lap. ''Of course the girl's murder is a shame and it would be terrible if it couldn't be solved, but I was thinking of poor Ben Harvey.''

''Yes?''

"Well, he's already spent many years imprisoned for a crime he didn't commit."

"That's not going to happen this time," Ransom replied evenly. His manner was a bit more terse than it ordinarily would have been with Emily.

"I'm not saying *that*. I know there's no chance of his being railroaded with you looking into it." She said this matter-of-factly, without the least hint of flattery. She trusted Ransom's veracity enough to believe it to be true. "But if there isn't enough evidence to solve the case, Mr. Harvey will be worse off than he was before."

"How so?"

"He's already being vilified rather openly in the press. If not vilified, then convicted by inference. If the murderer isn't caught, people will go on believing that he is a killer who simply got away with it. His friends may support him, if he has any. In fact, most of them are probably sure to support him, given how much he's already suffered. But the doubt will always be there. He could end up more imprisoned than he was before."

She gave her lap a gentle double pat with her folded hands. To anyone who didn't know her, it might have merely seemed the quaint gesture of an older woman, but Ransom knew that it signaled her indignation at the thought of injustice.

"Oh, I do *hope* he's not guilty!" she said.

THE LATE NEWS was pretty much just a replay of the earlier report, with the single additional fact that nobody in the building had heard or seen anything, just as Ransom had predicted.

Emily was in her easy chair and Lynn had returned earlier and was seated across from her on the couch, holding a half-empty cup and saucer on her lap. Lynn was

only half aware of the droning voice of the newscaster.
The brief visit to her own home had brought back a flood
of memories of life with her partner, Maggie. The memories were all still painful, and although nobody would
expect otherwise so soon after the death, she had higher
expectations of herself. She knew that she had to learn to
be easier on herself, that she needed to let those feelings
reign for a while and give herself the latitude to grieve.
But it was not within her nature to be so lenient on herself.
She recognized that probably her greatest struggle in this
would be to learn to give herself a break.

She lifted the cup to her lips, feeling as if she were in
a trance, and took a sip of the tea, which had cooled to
tepid. This roused her in time to hear the reporter say,
apparently for the hundredth time that day, *"When asked
how he felt about his accuser, Harvey said…"*

Cut to the tape of Harvey looking over the roof of his
car. *"Those people have taken up enough of my life. I'm
not gonna give them any more."*

Emily suddenly leaned forward in her chair, her eyes
alive with interest and her face alert.

"Emily? What is it?"

"That's very interesting," Emily said quietly, apparently to herself. "Now, why didn't I notice it before?"

Lynn glanced at the television, where the anchor was
engaging in some mindless banter with the weatherman
before handing over the reins to him.

"Emily?"

SIX

THE NEXT MORNING Gerald reported the coroner's findings.

"Just what we thought," he said, dropping a sheet on Ransom's desk. "She was strangled."

Ransom gave an ironic smile. "How nice that we have a coroner to tell us things we already know."

"She died sometime overnight, at least a few hours before she was found. But look at this." He tapped one particular entry with his index finger.

Ransom let out a low whistle. "Blood alcohol level was extremely high."

"Yeah," said Gerald. "She was blind drunk."

Ransom looked up at him, his eyes curious and incisive. He picked up a pencil and began to tap it against the paper. "Blind drunk. Hmm. I wonder how accurate a description that is."

Gerald stood by silently for a moment. He had long since become accustomed to allowing his partner to lose himself temporarily in his own private musings. When he thought it had gone on long enough, he said, "The crime lab came up with next to nothing. Only one recent set of prints besides the girl's, probably belonging to Bill Gibson."

"Probably?" said Ransom, pausing in his pencil tapping.

"They were on the doorknobs, inside and out. The lab ran them through AFIS. They didn't match anyone."

"Ah," Ransom replied with a thoughtful smile.

AFIS, the Automated Fingerprint Identification System used by the Chicago Police Department, could quickly identify fingerprints providing that the prints belonged to someone who already had a record in Chicago. While the failure of AFIS to identify the second set of prints left the detectives with a question, the one thing it did prove was that the prints didn't belong to Ben Harvey.

Gerald sat on the battered leatherette couch that abutted the left wall of Ransom's office. Ransom contemplated the information for a few moments, still holding the pencil suspended above the desktop.

"Do you want to question Gibson again?" Gerald asked.

Ransom didn't respond for a few seconds. Then he dropped the pencil and heaved a weary sigh. "Well, we know that he went into the apartment, so the prints were found where we would expect to find them. If he killed her and then came back to 'find' the body, then he had plenty of time to fix up an alibi with his wife before we even found out about the death. But why would he do that?"

"What?" said Gerald, not sure to which part of his hypothesis Ransom was referring.

"Why would he bother making a pretense of finding the body? It would've been much safer to just leave it there and let somebody else find it. There really wouldn't have been anything to connect him with the murder except his relationship with her. And..."

He allowed his voice to trail off and leaned back in his chair. It was another one of those occasions when Gerald found himself being forced into the role of Watson to Ransom's Holmes. It was one of the few aspects of Ransom's personality that Gerald found truly annoying: that every now and then he enjoyed having his "brilliance" prompted.

With a barely audible sigh, Gerald said, "And what?"

"And...I know that it's very unscientific, but I thought he was genuine. I thought he was genuinely shocked to find the body."

"So did I," Gerald concurred, purposely giving it enough emphasis to signify that he was approving of his partner's theory. He almost laughed out loud at the sudden, canny look on Ransom's face as realization of Gerald's gentle needling broke through.

Ransom smiled and said, "Thank you, Gerald."

"So, what do you want to do?"

"Did you locate the homeroom teacher?"

"Yes. The school identified her, but she's retired now. I got her address from Pershing Road."

"Good," said Ransom. Then he folded his hands on the desk and narrowed his eyes as if all the information they had so far was suspended in the air before him. After a moment he said, "Timing, timing, timing! That's the problem here. I still think Harvey's release and Shay's murder are cause and effect, whether or not Harvey killed her. But if he didn't, then the actual cause has to be something else."

"The rape."

"Exactly. We're going to have to go back and find out who raped that girl eight years ago."

Gerald stared blankly at Ransom for a moment. "If they couldn't get it right back then, how can we after all this time?"

Ransom smiled. "First we have to find out why they didn't get it right before."

THEIR FIRST STOP on the road into the past was LaSalle Street. In the Loop, LaSalle is a concrete canyon running

south from the river until it is cut off abruptly at Jackson
Boulevard by the Board of Trade building. John Livingston's office was in one of the buildings a couple of
blocks south of City Hall. Rather than park illegally and
block traffic, they decided to park at the end of the alley
that bisected the street two doors down from the building
to which they were going.

Ransom was pleased to find that Livingston's firm had
taken up residence in one of the older, more ornate buildings that had escaped being torn down in recent years
to make way for taller structures. The detectives went
through the revolving door, which was heavily weighted
and hard to push so that the effort it took to get into the
building gave visitors a feeling of portent. The lobby was
spacious and lined ceiling to floor with black marble.
Light was provided by huge *faux* art deco wall sconces
mounted at regular intervals along both walls, and by four
modest crystal chandeliers that hung far overhead.

"Good God!" said Gerald, stopping in his tracks.

"It is impressive, isn't it?" Ransom said.

"His name's Livingston, right?" said Gerald as they
approached the building directory.

Ransom nodded. "The firm's name is Fenner, Pratt,
Abernathie and Livingston."

They located the name quickly—mainly because it was
long enough to stand out on the directory—and headed
around the corner into a hallway lined on both sides with
elevators. As with the main lobby, this hallway had marble walls and floors, and each elevator door was polished
brass embossed with Chinese dragons that looked as if
they were coming together in battle when the elevator
doors closed. The bank of elevators on the left served the
fortieth floor, where the firm was located.

As they stood waiting for an elevator to arrive, Gerald frowned at the doors.

"Why dragons?" he murmured.

"It was a more elegant time," Ransom replied with a slight smile.

Gerald sighed. "I feel like I'm in a movie theater."

A pair of dragons slid apart, their frozen faces displaying no surprise at the sudden end of their conflict before disappearing into the walls. The detectives stepped into the elevator and Gerald pressed the button for the fortieth floor. The doors closed and the elevator slid upward quietly. It seemed only a few seconds before the doors reopened and the detectives stepped out.

There was no marble here, but elegance still prevailed. The carpet was a dark plush that looked almost new, and the walls were paneled with oak.

"My, my, my, Mr. Livingston must be doing well," said Ransom.

The law firm occupied a suite of offices, the door to which was located just to the right of the elevators. Ransom led the way through the door into an enormous reception area replete with several matching armchairs clustered around a semicircular credenza. Opposite this, the receptionist sat behind a large, curved desk on which there was little more than a multiline phone. The obligatory computer rested on a return on the receptionist's left.

The receptionist was a striking woman with long blond hair tied at the back of her neck with a black ribbon. She wore a knee-length, dark blue silk dress with a thin black belt tied loosely around the waist. She beamed a smile at the detectives and said, "May I help you?" Her tone was a perfect mix of polite inquiry and puzzlement at their unexpected appearance. Ransom recognized her as the woman he'd spoken to on the phone.

"We're here to see John Livingston," said Ransom. "Detectives Ransom and White."

He was impressed with the woman's equilibrium. There wasn't the slightest glitch in her pleasant, professional expression.

"Oh, yes. Would you have a seat? I'll tell Mr. Livingston you're here."

Ransom and Gerald each took a seat on the chairs by the credenza. Much to Ransom's surprise, instead of using the phone, the receptionist got up and headed down the hall to the right. The carpet was so thick that her departure was done in complete silence. It gave the impression that the woman was spiriting herself away.

Gerald whispered, "I feel like I'm in a library."

It was only a matter of moments before the receptionist reappeared and said, "Would you gentlemen please follow me?"

She led them down a long hallway lined with solid oak doors. Ransom marveled at the difference between this building and the more modern office buildings that shared the street. There was nothing flimsy about this place, and the basic solidity of the surroundings was probably very reassuring to potential clients.

The receptionist stopped at the last door at the end of the hall, gave a short double knock, and entered without waiting for an answer.

The office was as impressive as the rest of the suite. It was immaculate, except for the faint smell of cigarette smoke that tinged the air. There were no ashtrays in evidence, so Ransom suspected that the minor vice was something to which potential clients were not to be subjected. On the right, the entire wall was made up of shelves filled with heavy tomes. To the left was a grouping of soft chairs around a low table, presumably for whatever informal discussions might be held in this formal setting. At the far end of the room was the most prominent piece of furniture, a massive mahogany desk polished to a luster that reflected the ceiling lights.

John Livingston was seated behind the desk in a high-backed chair of wine-colored leather. He rose as they entered.

"Mr. Livingston," said the receptionist as she crossed the room, "this is Detective Ransom and Detective White."

Livingston was about thirty-five years old. He was dressed in the obligatory three-piece blue suit, white shirt, and dark tie. His dark brown hair was combed back but not slicked down. His eyes were narrow, which made him appear to be pondering something important whether or not he really was. It was a physical attribute that had proven to be a great asset in his work. Juries tended to think that he was full of insight, and his clients were fortunate in that he really was. If he had any drawbacks, it was that he looked young enough to be inexperienced. But if any prosecutors ever made the mistake of thinking that, it was a mistake they made only once.

Ransom thought that perhaps it was his youthful appearance that accounted for the firm occupying suites in this particular building. If the rest of the firm was this young, these austere surroundings would certainly add an air of stability.

The receptionist stood by while Livingston rose from his chair, reached across the desk, and shook their hands.

"Gentlemen," he said as he did this. "Please, be seated."

The detectives sat in the two leather chairs that faced the desk.

"Would you gentlemen like some coffee or tea?" the receptionist asked.

"No, thank you," said Ransom. Gerald shook his head.

The receptionist then glided out of the room without a sound or another word to her employer. Apparently she was well enough acquainted with his needs that she didn't have to ask.

Livingston sat back in his chair and made a point of contemplating the detectives for a moment before speaking.

"I can't say that I'm pleased to see you," he said at last, "nor can I say I was pleased to hear that you'd talked to my client."

"Oh. He's told you about our little visit already," said Ransom with a slight tilt of his head.

"My client has had very unfortunate experiences with the police and the criminal justice system. He thought it advisable to consult with his attorney after being questioned by the police. Of course, he should have done it *before* talking to you." He paused for effect, then added with calculated nonchalance, "I understand that you didn't inform him of his rights."

Ransom smiled. "Then you should understand that I didn't arrest him, either."

"But you questioned him."

"I asked him where he was the night before last. Mr. Harvey seemed to take great pride in the fact that he couldn't account for his time."

The coolness with which he delivered this news greatly irritated the lawyer, who was taking pains to hide his aggravation.

Livingston leaned forward and said, "Is my client a suspect?"

"Under the circumstances," said Ransom, "I think that would be obvious."

Livingston sat back in his chair, resting his palms against the edge of the desk. He eyed Ransom for a few moments. He recognized the detective as a formidable opponent with the admiration that only a truly clever man could bestow on an adversary.

"Under the circumstances," said Livingston, purposely approximating Ransom's calm tone, "I'm not quite sure why you wanted to talk to me. I'm sure you've heard of client confidentiality."

"Oh, I'm not interested in anything confidential. In fact, at the moment I'm not really interested in who killed Laura Shay."

The lawyer almost betrayed his surprise. He counted himself fortunate that he caught himself just in time.

"You're not?" he asked placidly.

Ransom shook his head slowly. "No. I'm interested in who raped her."

Livingston's face clouded over.

"Why?"

"Because the rape seems to have set in motion something that eight years later ended in her death. It was a life-altering event for two people. Since Mr. Harvey didn't commit the rape, then there was also a third person whose life was affected. I want to find out who that person is."

Livingston stared at him for a moment. Though Ransom had chosen his words carefully, the implication of what he was saying didn't escape the lawyer. Although he wasn't used to being unsure of himself, he was beginning to wonder just how much he should cooperate. Then again, he thought to himself, most of the information regarding the rape case was a matter of public record.

"So you see," said Ransom after giving him some time to think about it, "I would like to know who really raped Laura Shay."

"I'd like to know that myself," Livingston replied with a deep sigh.

Ransom's right eyebrow slid upward. "Then you don't?"

"Of course I don't. How would I?"

"I don't know..." said Ransom, calmly spreading his hands, palm upward. "I thought perhaps lawyers sometimes had their own ideas about who committed a crime— just like detectives do."

This seemed to placate Livingston somewhat, although it was clear from his expression that he didn't trust Ransom at all. Gerald, who it had been agreed beforehand would not take notes on this occasion, gently dug his nails into the arms of his chair at this point to divert himself from laughing or even smiling. There were times when he really enjoyed his partner's tactics.

"As a matter of fact," Livingston said, "we do have our instincts. But I have no idea who raped that girl, and I don't think Ben does, either. The only thing I knew was that he didn't do it, so I did my best to defend him."

"Really?" said Ransom, allowing some genuine surprise to seep into his voice. He adjusted himself in his chair, then slid his right leg over his left and said, "How, exactly, did that come about?"

"What?"

"Well, you don't maintain offices in this building by taking on charity cases. How on earth did you end up defending Ben Harvey in the first place?"

Livingston sighed. "I was a public defender back then. I was assigned."

"And you thought he was not guilty?"

"I *knew* he wasn't guilty. Just like you said. You get a feeling for it. Public defenders see the dregs of humanity. You get a feel for who's telling the truth and who isn't."

"So this certainty of yours was a feeling," said Ransom with no inflection.

"The outcome has borne out my 'feelings,'" the lawyer replied with a superior smile. Ransom inclined his head once in acknowledgment. "When you're on an investigation, don't you know whether or not somebody's telling you the truth?"

"Sometimes."

"It's the same with a lawyer, particularly a public defender. You develop a sense for whether or not someone's telling you the truth. In fact, the truth is easier to spot because you so seldom hear it. It sticks out. But I think that even without that sense, I would've known Ben was honest. You should've seen him back then. He was young, naive, and completely out of his depth. I don't think he knew much about the world at all. And he was in shock. He walked through the whole process in a daze, like he couldn't believe it was happening. The guilty ones don't do that. They may profess their innocence every time they open their mouths, but they *know* they're guilty, so they believe what's happening to them."

"Hmm..." said Ransom. He folded his hands on his knee, cocked his head to one side, and considered this. He appeared to agree with the assessment. After a few moments he said, "Is that why you paid for the DNA test?"

There was a beat before Livingston said, "Ben told you that, did he?"

Ransom gave a single nod.

"Then you *did* ask more than just his whereabouts the night before last."

Ransom shrugged. "I was just curious."

Livingston looked at him for a minute before responding. He seemed to be trying to decide whether to answer the question or mount a protest. He finally sighed and said, "Yes. That was why. As you know, DNA testing got all over the media during the Simpson trial. I got dozens of letters from inmates I defended in the past, asking me to have DNA tests run. Ben was one of the people who wrote to me." The lawyer stopped and smiled to himself. "I'd forgotten about him. That's what happens, you know. Once they're in jail, most people forget them."

"But Ben Harvey was the only one for whom you actually had the test run."

The smile vanished. "Even I can't afford to pay for tests for everyone. Frankly, most of the others were probably guilty. They think because one person got off, they all can. They think just maybe a DNA test will muddy up the facts enough to get them out. They don't know that the test would bury most of them. But as I said, I *knew* that Ben was innocent, so I thought the test would prove it. And yes, I footed the bill. Ben has said he will pay me back someday, and he probably will—that's the kind of kid he is. But it's unnecessary. I felt bad enough about what happened to him when I was trying to defend him. The price of the test may take some of the sting out of that loss."

Ransom recrossed his legs and took a deep breath. "Why was it so easy to railroad Mr. Harvey into jail?"

"Because there was some evidence, and because he's black. And he had a record."

"Did he, now? I thought he was supposed to have been an exemplary young man."

"Except for one night. He went for a ride with a friend in the friend's 'new car.' What he didn't know was that the friend had actually 'borrowed' the car without permission of the owner. Had Ben been white, anyone concerned would've considered that joyriding or just stupidity. He would've gotten a stern lecture and been sent home. But he was black, so he got the whole nine yards, which included a suspended sentence and a record. That was enough to allow the DA to present Ben to the court as a criminal. A jury is predisposed to believe that anyone with a record, no matter how trivial, is guilty before the trial even starts. Especially if he's black."

"'I never was more convinced of anything in my life, than I am that that boy will come to be hung,'" Ransom muttered.

"Huh?"

"Nothing," said Ransom, shaking his head. "You just reminded me of something I read. Why don't we deal with the evidence and leave the rest aside?" His tone was designed to let the lawyer know that he felt they could forgo the social commentary for the moment.

Livingston said, "The girl went to the hospital after the rape. They examined her and found bits of skin and blood under her fingernails. The blood type matched Ben's, and of course the scratches on his face were obvious."

"How did he explain that?"

"He saw her on the street. She'd been beaten up and was a mess. In Ben's words, she was 'in a state.' He offered to help her, to take her home, and she attacked him. He ended up scarred for life for his troubles." Livingston paused there, apparently wanting the full meaning of this to sink in. "And there was a helpful neighbor who testified that he saw them grappling outside his home. Unfortunately for Ben, it was dark and the neighbor couldn't tell whether or not Shay was already disheveled—which is, of course, what Ben swore.''

''Is that all?''

''And the hospital examination found semen, both inside her and in her panties.''

''I see,'' Ransom said, sitting back in his seat.

The lawyer nodded. ''The semen was proof of rape, and the scratches were 'proof' that Ben attacked her. That was enough back then. Today we automatically test the semen to see whether or not it matches the accused. And that's exactly what we did. We went back to the evidence and tested the dried semen in the panties, and Ben was exonerated.''

Ransom thought for a moment, then said, ''Mr. Livingston, why do you think Laura Shay accused your client?''

Livingston seemed to freeze for a split second, like a single frame of film that had inexplicably come to a halt in the projector before proceeding. ''I don't know,'' he said evenly.

Ransom felt there was quite a bit more than the lawyer was saying. Even though Livingston's face seemed almost cast in stone, Ransom believed he could read a wealth of suppressed information there. Either the lawyer had some idea and was unwilling to speculate, or he had no idea and wished he did.

''Since Mr. Harvey readily admitted that Laura Shay was 'in a state' when he saw her, is it possible that she mistakenly identified him because of the trauma?'' Ransom offered this in an attempt to draw the lawyer out. There was a flicker in Livingston's eyes. It was apparent that he was trying to control his anger.

''Oh, that young lady *knew* what she was doing, all right.''

''Really,'' said Ransom, raising an eyebrow.

"Oh, yes!"

"What makes you think that? Instinct?"

"If that's what you want to call it. When she testified, she recited her answers like she had learned them off a blackboard. And she kept looking across the court at Ben, then looking away."

"Is that unusual?"

"To look away? No. To look at him in the first place, I think so. In my experience, the victim usually tries to avoid looking at the attacker at all until they're asked to identify them."

"And you have no idea who actually attacked her."

Livingston shook his head. "My job is to poke holes in the evidence. The police's job is to find out who really did it."

Ransom smiled. "Touché."

Livingston looked down at the top of his desk for a moment. The desk was so highly polished that he could see himself in it. He looked as if he weren't quite sure he liked what he saw at that moment. It was a rare moment of relenting for a man who, like Ransom, tended to use direct eye contact as a weapon. After some consideration he said, "But...well, I suppose it wouldn't do any harm now. To be perfectly frank, I thought maybe her father had done it."

"Her father?" Ransom said after a beat. In the back of his mind he remembered Mrs. Shay's apparent distaste for the relationship between father and daughter. Could this have been the cause?

"On what do you base that observation?"

"He was an alcoholic," Livingston explained, "and the doctor who examined Laura after the rape told me that Shay seemed a little reluctant at first to let Laura talk to the police. She thought maybe that was why."

"The doctor was...?"

"Dr. Hutchins. Beverly Hutchins. A very capable woman. Very observant."

"Hmm. Was there any other reason you thought the father might be guilty?"

"He was a drunk..."

There was a lengthy pause during which Ransom waited with carefully controlled anticipation. The lawyer had rested his elbows on the desk and made a temple of his fingers, and his eyes stared out through the space between the two detectives. Ransom felt certain that there was more to come. When he felt he'd waited long enough, he prompted Livingston with a simple, "Yes?"

Livingston looked at Ransom and said, "And I didn't like him. I probably shouldn't admit to something like that, but I just didn't like George Shay." He sounded as if he were loath to make such an admission, but he couldn't have known that was exactly the kind of assessment that Ransom would find the most trustworthy.

"Why is that?" Ransom asked.

Livingston sighed. "Because he seemed very anxious that the trial be over quickly and that Ben would get put away."

Ransom gave a noncommittal shrug. "I would think it would be natural for a father to be worried about the effect the trial would have on his daughter and want it over as soon as possible."

"Oh, no," Livingston replied with a disdainful smile, "I don't think he was worried about his daughter at all."

"WHAT DO you think?" said Gerald once they were back in the car.

Ransom took a deep drag on his cigar, watching the tip

to make sure it was properly lit, then stuck the lighter back into the dashboard.

"I think we're treading water. We have too many questions."

"The biggest one is who committed the rape," said Gerald.

Ransom shook his head. "No, the most important question is why did the girl lie about who committed the rape. I have a feeling that if we could get the answer to that one, we could solve the whole thing in a hurry."

"Well, if her father was the one who did it, it could explain why she lied. Except I wouldn't think he would take her to the hospital afterwards."

Ransom waved this off. "Parents who abuse their children do that all the time, although they normally lie about what caused the harm." He paused and tapped an ash out the window. "There probably was no way to hide the fact that she'd been raped once she was in the hospital."

"Well, that makes sense, then," said Gerald.

"What does?"

"Suppose Shay beat and then raped his daughter. Then he has to take her to the hospital. If she's like most abuse victims, she goes along with him when he lies about what happened to her. And at the hospital doctors know she's been raped, so the Shays lie about who did it."

Ransom thought about this for a few moments in silence, then shook his head and said with frustration, "No, no, no, it just doesn't work. Harvey said that when he saw Laura she was on her way home...although, I suppose if her father raped her, he didn't have to do it at home."

Gerald added, "If your father raped you, would home be the first place you would go?"

"No, but I also think that the hospital would be the last place I would go."

"Yeah." Gerald paused, then added, "I wonder how badly hurt she was."

They fell silent for a few moments, each going over the possibilities in their minds.

Ransom sighed. "You know, if Shay attacked his own daughter, we have an even bigger problem. Since he's dead, it would mean that the murder didn't have anything to do with the rape."

Gerald rested his hands on the steering wheel and looked down at them pensively. He then turned to Ransom and said, "That's not exactly true."

Ransom looked back at him and raised an eyebrow. Gerald continued, "It would mean that Harvey is the only one we know of who had a reason to kill her."

Ransom flashed an unreadable smile and said, "Accepted. Now, I suppose we'd better talk to Dr. Hutchins. Maybe she can help clear up the business about the father."

He flipped open his cell phone and called information for the number of St. Mary's Hospital, then called the hospital. He was fortunate on two counts: Dr. Hutchins was still on staff, and she was working that day. He had the operator page her, and within a couple of minutes had her on the phone.

"Dr. Hutchins," she said with hurried formality.

"Doctor, this is Detective Ransom. I'm investigating the murder of Laura Shay."

"Ah…" she replied, slowing down noticeably. "Yes, I heard about that."

"We're on our way out to your neighborhood, and we'd like to talk to you."

"Certainly, but it's my clinic day, so you'll have to make it fast."

She didn't offer any explanation for what clinic day

might mean, but she did give him directions on how to find her once he had arrived at the hospital. He thanked her, then disconnected and stuck the phone back into his pocket.

Gerald started the car and they headed for the expressway. Once they had passed through the remainder of the downtown area and had gotten connected with the Dan Ryan, the way was pretty clear, or as clear as the Ryan ever was. They were just about to exit onto 95th Street when Ransom's cell phone emitted the none-too-gentle chirping noise that he found very annoying. He pulled it from his pocket, flipped it open, and said, "Ransom."

"Jeremy? Hello? Is that you?"

He smiled. Emily always managed to sound tentative over the phone, as if she didn't quite trust it to deliver her voice.

"Yes, Emily."

"I hate to interrupt you. I know how busy you must be…"

"It's all right. At the moment I'm just sitting here. We're driving out to the south side."

"Oh! Then Detective White is with you. Please give him my regards."

With elaborate patience, Ransom covered the tiny holes that served for a mouthpiece and intoned, "Emily sends her regards."

Gerald smiled more at Ransom's irritation than at the message. He said lightly, "Tell her I said thank you."

"Detective White sends the same," he said into the phone, with a glance at Gerald. "Now, Emily, I know you didn't call just to chat."

"Yes, well, Jeremy, Lynn and I were watching the news last night, and we saw that young man who's involved in your investigation. Ben Harvey."

There was a loud crackle over the phone as Gerald made the turn from the exit ramp onto 95th Street. Ransom exhaled testily and turned his head to see if that would clear the static. On her end, Emily gave an admonishing glance at her receiver as if it had finally lived down to her expectations. When the crackling stopped, Emily said, "Hello? Are you there?"

"Yes. Sorry. What were you saying?"

She explained to him what Ben Harvey had said and why she thought it was important. Ransom wasn't too sure he agreed, but he knew that if Emily thought it meaningful enough to call him, then he'd have to give it some consideration. Ordinarily he wouldn't have questioned Emily's observations or the conclusions she drew from them, because the only time he had done that she had proven to be right. But on this occasion he wasn't too pleased with what he was hearing. Like Gerald, Emily seemed to be of the opinion (no matter how much faith she professed to have in Ransom's talents) that Ben Harvey might be connected to the murder. But whether or not he was able to disguise the fact from Gerald, he was a bit stung that his partner so obviously thought that he wasn't giving full enough attention to Ben Harvey. It didn't help to realize that Emily, no matter how judiciously she might be sharing her observations, seemed to think so, too.

"That might just have been a figure of speech," he said.

"That's possible, but doesn't it strike you as curious?"

"Possibly."

"Are you going to question that young man again?"

"Probably. Eventually."

There was a momentary pause which Ransom took as silent reproof. Then Emily said, "Well, perhaps when you do, you can ask him about it."

They said their good-byes, then Ransom snapped the phone shut and stuck it back in his pocket.

"Well," he said with a sigh, "it seems everybody knows how the investigation should go better than I do."

Gerald thought better of responding.

They continued along 95th Street to Western Avenue. St. Mary's Hospital was located about four blocks west of Western. When they reached it, Gerald steered the car into the driveway and followed it around to the parking lot behind the building.

"Hutchins said the clinic is at the back of the hospital at the far end of the lot," said Ransom. "Over there."

Gerald made a wide sweep around the perimeter of the lot and found a spot as close as he could to the boxlike addition that jutted off the back of the building. The hospital proper had been built in the 1950s. It was fifteen stories of gray stone. At the top of each corner, just below the roof, there were huge, imposing granite angels with massive wings and outspread hands. They looked down on those entering the hospital as if offering protection and prayer for the sick and suffering.

Although great care had gone into making the clinic fit in with the general design of the hospital, including using the same type of stone and carving statues of cherubs that served as tiny cousins to the angels above, it was obvious that the clinic was a much later addition. The stone was not yet nearly as weathered as that of the main building. Over the entrance the words ST. MARY'S CLINIC had been chiseled.

Ransom gave an involuntary shudder as they entered the clinic, not because he had an aversion to hospitals but because it unexpectedly brought back a rush of memories of Emily's hospitalization and the uncertainty he'd suffered at the time.

With Gerald close behind, Ransom followed Dr. Hutchins's directions and went down the short hallway to the reception desk in the middle of the waiting room. The room was so crammed with people it looked like steerage in a boat full of immigrants. Shoddily clothed children were crying while their harried parents tried to quiet them, and other, unaccompanied adults sat scowling or half dozing. There was one man who looked close to the brink of death, wedged in a corner seat and slumping slightly over the arm of his chair. The worried creases across his forehead made it look as if the noise in the room just might push him the rest of the way over.

"I'm here to see Dr. Hutchins," Ransom said to the woman behind the desk.

"So's everyone," the woman replied without looking up. "Name?" Though it was still fairly early in the day, she sounded as if she'd already put in ten hours and was anticipating ten more.

"Detective Ransom."

The woman looked up and her eyes widened. "Oh, yes. Dr. Hutchins said to expect you. This way."

She came out from behind the desk and led them down a hallway lined with examining rooms, all of which were occupied, to a tiny office. There was a small metal desk with a chair behind it, and two chairs for visitors in front. The desk and the metal bookshelf behind it were both cluttered with papers.

"Have a seat," said the woman. "I'll tell the doctor you're here."

She left them, not bothering to close the door. It was only a couple of minutes before Hutchins entered the office and closed the door. The detectives rose from their chairs, introduced themselves, shook hands with the doctor, and then resumed their seats.

Hutchins crossed behind the desk and sat down. She was still a very handsome woman, though the rigors of her job had made her prematurely gray, and there were more lines on her face than Ransom would have expected to find in a woman who didn't look like she'd reached forty yet.

"Thank you for seeing us," said Ransom.

"As you can see, I don't have a lot of time." She pushed the papers out of her way. "Paperwork. Bane of my existence. Insurance is bad enough, Medicaid is hell."

"I take it most of these people are poor."

"That's the whole function of this clinic. It's for the poor. I'm in internal medicine in the hospital, but I give one day a week to the clinic."

"That's very good of you," Ransom said sincerely.

The doctor shrugged. "Health care shouldn't only be for the rich. Now, pardon me if I rush you, but what can I do for you?" She folded her hands and rested them on the clear space she'd made on the desk.

"As you said on the phone, you've already heard about Laura Shay's murder. Do you remember much about the night she was brought to the hospital?"

"Sure do."

"Really? It was a long time ago, and you've seen a lot of people since then." He gestured in the direction of the waiting room.

"Oh, I'm not likely to forget it," Hutchins replied with a smile. "It was the first time I had to testify about a case."

"You testified? I didn't know that."

She nodded. "Oh, yes. Just about her condition and the procedure for taking care of specimens—evidence, to you guys."

"And what was her condition?"

"She was in shock, I guess you'd call it. Couldn't get much of a response from her about anything. Not until the police showed up. Then all she'd say was that she wanted to go home."

"Was she badly hurt?"

Hutchins pursed her lips and shook her head slowly. "Not really. Bruises, cuts, that sort of thing. Nothing life-threatening."

"Not badly enough that she *had* to come to the hospital?"

"No, not really."

"Any idea why she came here, then?"

Hutchins sighed. "Well, I assumed that since she was raped she wanted to get checked out and have the evidence preserved."

Ransom paused and examined the doctor for a moment. She was exactly as Livingston had described her. She seemed quite competent and straightforward.

"Doctor, there's something I don't understand."

"Yes?"

"We spoke with John Livingston, Ben Harvey's lawyer, and he said that he half suspected that George Shay, Laura's father, might have been the one that attacked her, although he readily admitted that he felt that way more out of a dislike for the man than anything else. But he also told us that you'd said something about that, too."

Her expression changed when Ransom mentioned the father, as if she were already aware of where Ransom was heading.

"Yes, I did mention it when Mr. Livingston talked to me at the time."

Ransom smiled. "But I can't imagine that you had the same reason as Livingston for considering the possibility."

Hutchins sighed again. "No. Well, actually, it was Livingston who broached the subject to begin with, but it wasn't the first time the idea had occurred to me. You see a lot of horrible things when you're working ER, and not all of them are medical. I've seen my share of the results of abuse."

"And that's the way Laura Shay looked to you?"

She shook her head. "Not really. I'll tell you, Mr. Ransom, Mr. Shay was very solicitous of his daughter, which is something you often see in abusers when they bring their victims to the hospital. But you see that in people when their loved ones are hurt, too."

"But if Laura didn't really *have* to come here—if her wounds weren't life-threatening—do you think Mr. Shay would've brought her if he'd done it?"

"That's just the thing. That wasn't what made me think he might've been the one that did it. It was something else…" Her voice trailed off, and the expression on her face mirrored her puzzlement as she brought the incident back to mind.

"Yes?"

"It was the way he acted when the police got here. I really got the impression that he was worried about the police talking to her."

"But that doesn't make any sense."

"I know, I know," said Hutchins, throwing up her hands. "If he didn't want her to talk to the police, there was no reason for him to bring her in. There was no need for evidence. Like I said, it was just an impression. Not a lot to go on and not something you could take to court."

"Couldn't he have just been worried that it might upset his daughter to be questioned at that time?"

Hutchins looked doubtful. "I guess that could be the

case, but..." She stopped and shook her head. "Like I said, it was just an impression."

"WHERE IS THIS homeroom teacher?" said Ransom once they were back in the car.

Gerald reached in his jacket pocket and pulled out his notebook. He flipped through several pages and stopped when he found what he was looking for. "Her name is Nora Brown. She lives in a place called the Lawn Villa. I guess that's an apartment building. It's in Oak Lawn. Not far."

They drove down 95th Street to Cicero, then turned right. About halfway down the block they found Lawn Villa. Once they'd parked they walked back to the building. Ransom had to smile. Apparently Lawn Villa derived its name from the suburb rather than the landscaping, because there was a barely-two-foot-wide tract of grass surrounding the building like a narrow green moat.

The building itself was a recent addition to the area, not more than ten years old from the look of it, and immaculately cared for. It was twenty stories tall and from the second floor up there were several rows of gleaming, uniform windows. On the first floor on both sides of the entrance, there were long windows, tinted so that the occupants could see out without passersby being able to see in. The only drawback Ransom could see to the place was that the facade had been done in a shiny brick in a shade of yellow that he always thought looked bilious.

Just to the right of the entrance was a small brass plaque, polished to a shine, that read:

LAWN VILLA
A COMMUNITY FOR SENIORS

"A retirement home by any other name..." Ransom intoned as they went through the door.

The interior of the building was so startling that the detectives stopped just inside the door. Rather than the standard, dull lobby, they were faced with an atrium that was brightly lit by a skylight. Two cagelike elevators slunk down the far side and came to rest in a garden of tropical plants. The doors to the apartments were on balconies that ran the inner circumference of each floor.

The atrium was a bustle of activity. To the left was a commissary that seemed to be doing a great amount of business, and to the right was a dining room where the staff was setting tables, presumably preparing for the first seating for lunch. A group of children was standing in front of the garden at the bottom of the elevators, and a man who looked to be about thirty was facing them, waving his arms and leading them through a medley of songs by Rodgers and Hammerstein. Several of the residents sat on folding chairs listening to the music, while more of them were on the balconies, enjoying the concert from the comfort of their individual perches.

"May I help you gentlemen?"

This offer came from a woman sitting behind a desk on which a large nameplate identified her as the concierge. She was thin, with a small nose and tight lips, and her hair was dark gray with lighter streaks of gray woven through it, and pulled back and pinned at the back of her head. But Ransom thought that her most striking feature was her eyes: they were dark blue and very hard, peering at him over a pair of half-glasses held in place by a silver chain. He got the feeling that the hardness was reserved for questionable visitors.

"Yes," he said cordially. "We're here to see Nora Brown."

"Mrs. Brown?" the woman replied with an inclination of her head to indicate that she knew the lady in question but was still in doubt as to their business with her. "Is she expecting you?" She put her hand on the phone and stared at Ransom as if whom she decided to call depended on what she thought of his answer.

"Yes," he said with a smile, "we called ahead."

Her hand tightened on the receiver. "Who may I say is calling?"

Ransom's eyes narrowed. "You may say the gentlemen that she is expecting are calling."

The woman hesitated for a moment. She looked as if she would have liked to detain them a bit longer, but when her eyes shifted away from Ransom's steady gaze, it was apparent that she had remembered she couldn't afford to offend the welcome guests of the residents. She snatched the receiver from its cradle, dialed, and then waited.

"Mrs. Brown?" she said crisply. "There are two gentlemen here to see you.... All right, I'll send them up."

She replaced the receiver and pointed across the atrium. "The elevators are over there. Mrs. Brown lives in apartment five-oh-two. She is expecting you." She added this last in a tone that implied that wonders would never cease.

"Thank you," said Ransom with a nod.

As they crossed the atrium Gerald said, "I wish you'd stop doing that."

"What?" Ransom asked innocently.

"George Sanders."

"Very good, Gerald," he replied with a laugh.

They skirted the singing children, who were just beginning a spirited rendition of "The Surrey with the Fringe on Top," and caught one of the elevators just before the doors closed. Ransom looked down at the scene below as the elevator swept upward.

"You know, I can think of very little that would be more depressing than spending my waning years being serenaded by an endless stream of Von Trapp family children."

Gerald glanced down at the rapidly diminishing youngsters. "I think it's kind of nice."

Ransom looked at him for a moment, then said, "There are times, Gerald, when you frighten me."

The elevator stopped at the fifth floor. The detectives got off and found a small sign indicating that apartments 500 through 510 were to the right. They quickly located 502, and the door was open before Gerald had even completed giving it a knock.

They were met by a woman who didn't look old enough to be living in a retirement home. Her hair was light brown and brushed back over her ears, and the only wrinkles on her face were at the corners of her eyes and mouth. She was wearing a knee-length, light tan cotton dress that was a bit lightweight for Chicago's changeable spring weather. Then again, the building was self-sufficient enough that she probably didn't have to go anywhere if she didn't want to.

"Mrs. Brown?" said Ransom tentatively.

She greeted them with a broad smile. "Yes. Detectives? Come on in. You'll have to excuse me. The place is a mess," she explained unnecessarily, since her apartment was spotless, "but I wasn't expecting any company today. I haven't had very much time to clean since you called."

"This is a very nice apartment," said Ransom.

"Thank you. Have a seat."

She motioned to a small couch that sat facing an identical one across a coffee table.

"So," she said as she sat opposite them, "which is which?"

"My name is Ransom. This is my partner, Detective White."

"I'm pleased to meet you."

"Yes..." Ransom said slowly. "You'll pardon my saying this, but you don't look like you belong here."

"Hmm?" Nora replied with a pleased smile.

"You seem much too young."

"Thank you, Mr. Ransom, but I can assure you that I'm 'of age.'"

"Why did you decide to live here?"

"You wouldn't believe it, but I'm tired," she said, laughing.

"Tired?"

She nodded. "Oh, yes. I raised two children of my own. I worked almost all my life. I was thirty years at John Q—that's what we called the high school for short. I took care of my kids, my husband till he died, and all those other kids at school. So when it came time for me to retire a couple of years ago, I decided it was time for me to be taken care of."

Ransom smiled. "I see."

"I'm tired of taking care of everything, you see. And here I don't have to do a damn thing if I don't want to. They have maid service, and laundry service, and all the meals are prepared. That was a must, because I cooked too damn many meals during my lifetime already. They'll deliver the things from the commissary if you want. I never even have to leave the building and look at the blasted world if I don't want to." She laughed again. It was, Ransom thought, a very carefree laugh. "You have no idea how much just taking care of daily business takes out of you." She paused, then added in a confidential tone, "But best of all, I don't have to worry about my kids moving back home with me. Do you think that makes me irresponsible?''

"No," Ransom replied. "I would say you've probably earned the right to live the way you want."

"Thank you." There was a pause, and Nora's smile faded a bit. "But you haven't come here to talk about me and my situation, have you."

"No, ma'am. You know why we're here."

The remainder of Nora's smile disappeared. "Yes. Mr. White told me on the phone. Poor Laura." Ransom expected her to provide more in the way of a eulogy for the dead girl, but although Nora looked sad about the death, there was a blank quality in her expression that showed she was at a loss to find any more kind words to say. She looked up at Ransom and said, "But I don't know how I can help you. I haven't seen or heard of Laura since she graduated high school."

"Actually," said Ransom, "it's her high school days we're interested in. We'd liked to know what was going on with her the year that the rape occurred."

Nora sighed and absently combed the hair back over her right ear with her fingers. "I've been thinking about it ever since I heard she was murdered. It doesn't seem possible. It didn't seem possible then. It was such a terrible time. Nearly tore the school in half."

"I believe the school is in an unusual situation," Ransom interjected. "Very racially mixed."

"Half and half we used to say back then. It's more black now." She said this without emphasis, merely stating it as fact.

"We haven't been able to find out much about Laura Shay. She doesn't seem to have been very close to anyone. What was she like back then?"

"Needy."

"Needy?" Ransom repeated, raising an eyebrow. "Not poor?"

Nora's smile returned. "You're a sharp one, aren't you? If you'd been in my class you would've given me a run for my money. Yes, she was poor, but she was needy, too. I guess you know what I mean."

"Go on."

"She was one of those people who needed attention, needed affection, you name it. I don't think she got much of anything at home."

"I've met her mother," Ransom said in a tone of commiseration. He thought that Nora would respond best to this—not that she appeared to need much drawing out.

"Oh, yes," Nora said with a roll of her eyes, "her parents were a prize. They turned Laura into one of those kids who can never get enough."

"Of what?"

"Of anything." Nora stopped and thought for a moment, then shook her head sadly. "You know what they say about those people who were in concentration camps in the war? They say that some of them, when they were rescued, they'd been starved for so long that they gorged themselves when they first got out, and they died as a result. That's sad, isn't it? Everybody needs food to live, and it was withheld from them for so long that when they finally got hold of some, it killed them."

She stopped again and looked down at her hands. She seemed for a time to be lost in her memories, and Ransom decided not to interrupt her for a while.

He finally broke the silence by saying, "And that's how you thought of Laura Shay?"

Nora looked up at him. "Yeah. Starving. Only with her it was almost worse. All that need was so obvious I think it drove most people away from her. That type of thing usually does. People don't like to feel like they're going to be eaten alive."

"Well, did she have *any* friends? That's the kind of information we really need."

Nora sighed. "Yes, she had some girlfriends. Not close. Mostly poor, like her." She paused for a moment, then added, "Oh, but she did have one close girlfriend for a while. Alice Condon. She got married since school to a boy named Marc Peters."

Gerald jotted down the names.

"You seem pleased about that," said Ransom, noting her broad smile.

"You see? I *am* an old lady! I'm smiling because they were sweethearts in high school. It was kind of sweet. And there was Ruby Hawkins. She was another girl that Alice hung around with, I think. As far as I know, she hasn't married."

"How about boyfriends?"

"Boyfriends?"

"Did Laura have any boyfriends?"

For the first time Nora hesitated. She looked from Ransom to Gerald, who was holding his pencil over his notebook in anticipation of receiving some names. Nora looked back at Ransom and said, "Well, I wouldn't really know what she did outside of school."

"You must've heard things. You heard about Alice and Ruby."

Nora blinked once. "The students don't talk to the teachers about such things as boyfriends."

It occurred to Ransom that the former teacher was choosing her words very carefully. He took that as evidence that she had a belief in honesty that wouldn't allow her a direct lie, but would accept evasion.

"How about the teachers? Did they talk of such things?"

Nora stiffened. "I don't think many teachers would think it was right to gossip about the students' private lives."

Once again Ransom found the response very carefully worded. He decided to let it go.

"How about Ben Harvey? What can you tell me about him?"

Nora's face lit up, though Ransom wondered at first whether it was because she truly liked Ben or was just relieved to change the subject.

"Ben was a teacher's dream: a student who wanted to learn. He was always eager and never any trouble to anybody." She stopped and her face clouded over. "I saw him on the news. Such a change."

"Did he have anything to do with Nora? Were they close?"

"Not that I saw. I don't think they had much to do with each other." She seemed happy to be able to answer the question directly.

Ransom took a deep breath. "What did you think when you heard about the rape?"

"I thought she—" Nora began quickly, then stopped herself. Her face had flushed with anger and her features sharpened.

Ransom cocked his head to one side and said, "You thought she what, Mrs. Brown? Lied?"

Nora didn't answer. She looked as if she were mentally kicking herself for her outburst.

Ransom's eyebrows slid upward as he said, "Could it be you thought she deserved it?"

Nora looked up. Her eyes were wide and her cheeks turned deep red. "No, of course not. Nobody deserves to be raped. I was going to say that I didn't think Ben was capable of it.'' Her words had the empty ring of someone grasping for an excuse.

But you said "she," thought Ransom. He decided to help her out of her dilemma.

"So you thought she was lying."

"Yes," Nora replied. She looked relieved and the redness started to fade.

"Very interesting," said Ransom, touching the tips of his fingers together.

His tone caused Nora to look over at him. She had the uncomfortable feeling that he was referring to her reaction rather than her explanation. She would have been more uncomfortable to learn that she was right.

"Well, Mrs. Brown," Ransom said as he rose, "I don't think we need to trouble you any further."

Gerald got up and stuck his notebook back in his pocket, then the detectives headed for the door. Nora sat for a moment lost in thought. She looked a bit older than she had when they'd arrived. Then she remembered her hostess duties, rose quickly from her couch, and went over to the door to let them out.

"I hope I was some help to you." She sounded completely bewildered, as if she didn't understand what had just happened but was somehow certain that it wasn't very good.

"You've been a great help," Ransom replied.

Gerald went through the door and Ransom started to follow, but stopped just as he was crossing the threshold and turned back to Nora.

"Oh, one other thing. When Laura was your student, did you ever notice any signs that she might have been abused?"

Nora's eyes widened. "You mean by...you mean at home?"

"Wherever."

Nora stared at him for a few seconds, then shook her head. "No. Neglected, yes. Abused, no. I would've reported it."

Ransom smiled and passed through the doorway.

ON THEIR WAY BACK to the car Gerald called information for Alice Peters's and Ruby Hawkins's numbers, then made quick calls to both of them.

"Ms. Hawkins says she's leaving for work in an hour, so if we want to talk to her we'll have to go there now. Peters said she'll be home all day."

"Where does Hawkins live?"

"Blue Island."

"And Peters?"

"Not far from the school."

The eyes of the concierge followed them as they crossed the atrium and exited the building. Once they were out on the street, Gerald said, "Well, Mrs. Brown wasn't much help. Why did you..." His voice trailed off as he tried to find the proper word.

"Antagonize her?" Ransom offered with a smile.

"I guess. Why did you do that?"

"Because I honestly thought she was about to say that Laura Shay had it coming to her when she was raped— or something of that sort—and she caught herself in time."

"Yeah, but she wouldn't have meant that."

"Wouldn't she?" They'd reached the car and came to a stop on opposite sides of it, looking at each other across the roof. "Laura's mother said something very interesting to us yesterday."

"Yeah?"

"She said that before Laura got herself raped things weren't very good."

Gerald looked at him for a moment, irritated once again that there was apparently something Ransom was seeing that he was missing.

"So?"

Ransom sighed. "She said *she got herself raped.*" He paused for emphasis, then added, "Now, don't you think that's an unusual view for a mother to take of her daughter's attack?"

SEVEN

IT WAS NOT LONG after phoning Ransom that Emily and Lynn embarked on the new project of cleaning all of Emily's cut crystal. This required Lynn to climb a stepstool and lift the pieces down carefully, one by one, from the top shelves of the kitchen cabinets. There was a punch bowl and cups, brandy snifters, Old Fashioneds, and tall glasses, as well as several vases of various shapes and sizes. By the time Lynn had retrieved all the pieces and arranged them on both sides of the sink, the kitchen counter looked like a sea of inverted icicles. She then filled the left tub of the sink with warm, soapy water and left the faucet running into the right tub to rinse off each piece after washing it.

A cloth had been laid on the kitchen table to soak up the excess water from the glassware as Lynn set them within Emily's reach. Emily then dried them with one of the yellow-checked kitchen towels. Each piece of glass brought with it a remembrance of her husband who had passed away long ago and the friends who had made gifts of these things to them.

"My goodness," said Lynn as she lowered the punch bowl into the soapy water, "you must've been one hell of a hostess."

"What?" Emily said, looking up. She'd been drying a small, simple bud vase and trying to remember who had given it to her, so it was a few seconds before she realized what Lynn had just said. When she saw the punch bowl she said, "Oh! No, I'm afraid we were never much for big parties. We were the type of people who just had a few friends over now and then. I think it's much nicer that way, don't you?''

''You know,'' said Lynn, unconsciously avoiding the question, ''I don't think you ever told me your husband's name.''

Emily smiled at the reflection of herself in the vase. ''Albert. He's been gone...oh, it's been well over ten years now.''

Lynn bent down into the task of running the cloth into the grooves on the outside of the bowl. Years of neglect had left a yellowish film on the glass that she was finding difficult, but not impossible, to remove.

After a long silence Lynn said, ''Do you still miss him?''

Emily set the vase upside down on the cloth to let the residual moisture drain out. She folded her hands on the table and sighed. ''Do I still miss him?'' she said reflectively. ''I still think of him every day. We were married for over thirty years, you know. I still love him. So in that sense, I suppose you could say that I miss him. But I think that missing someone might be part of our desire to keep things from changing. And they always do. Somewhere along the line resignation sets in, and you understand that things will never be the same. After that, the sense of loss can become a sense of gain.''

Emily heard a sniff, and looked up just in time to see Lynn wiping the back of her wrist across her cheek.

''Gain?'' said Lynn, her voice faltering.

''Yes,'' Emily replied gently. ''Once the pain had had some time to soften, I found myself able to think more of what Albert brought to my life rather than what the loss had cost me.''

Lynn tried to focus her concentration on the bowl.

"Sort of like trying to make some good come out of something bad." She said this without rancor, but it was evident from her tone that she didn't much like the idea.

Emily shook her head, which loosened a strand of gray from the bun she had pinned at the back. "No, not at all. It's just a natural progression. No human being can go on in pain forever. We couldn't stand it. The pain *has* to lessen eventually."

Lynn rubbed the inside of the bowl with the dishrag, then held it up in the light that streamed in through the window over the sink. Satisfied with the results, she dipped it once more into the water for good measure, then transferred it to the other sink and started rinsing it off.

"Does it bother you going through all these things again? They must remind you of your husband."

"Bother me?" Emily said more brightly. "No. In fact they're bringing back some pleasant memories. I'm not given to brooding." She stopped for a moment and her eyebrows knit together. "Brooding...I wonder why I keep thinking of brooding..."

"Probably because of that murder case that your resident detective is working on. What did he say when you called him?"

Emily smiled. "I don't think he took my little idea very seriously."

Lynn looked over at her and pursed her lips. "Then he's not very bright."

Emily clucked her tongue with amusement and said, "Jeremy is very bright, but I think it may be possible for him to be blinded by his sense of justice."

"What do you mean?" said Lynn, her eyes widening with surprise.

"He's a great believer in justice," Emily explained, her admiration obvious, "probably even more so than me.

And he knows that a great injustice was done to that young man, Ben Harvey. I think Jeremy may hope to find justice for that boy who was put in jail so many years ago. But…''

Lynn stopped in the act of turning the bowl over under the running water and looked over at Emily.

"But?"

Emily turned toward Lynn. Her eyes had lost their momentary vacancy and took on a sharpness with which Lynn wasn't completely familiar. "But the boy who went into prison was not the same person who came out."

Lynn gazed at her for a few moments with her eyebrows raised. Then she completed her rinsing and brought the bowl over to the table and set it down in front of Emily.

"This is a beautiful piece."

Emily pursed her lips. "It's far too ornate for my taste. I can only remember once that we ever used it."

Lynn shrugged. "It's probably worth a lot. It's an antique."

"So am I," said Emily with a twinkle in her eye, "but I like to think I'm a bit more useful."

"SHE WAS TRASH," said Ruby Hawkins as she tilted her head and threaded the wire of a jade earring through the tiny hole in her left earlobe. Her hair was very short and had been straightened so that it fit her head like a helmet. Once she'd completed her task she straightened up and brushed at the skirt of her navy blue suit as if she were aware of some lint that was invisible to the naked eye. Underneath the jacket she wore a white blouse with a narrow ruffle down the front.

Although she was dressed impeccably, her apartment gave Ransom the impression that whatever she did for a living, she wasn't exactly affluent. It was a very small efficiency apartment, just off Greenwood in Blue Island. There were a few pieces of inexpensive but serviceable furniture and a Pullman kitchen.

Her assessment of Laura Shay would have sounded harsh had it not been accompanied by her broad smile and sparkling brown eyes. "There! What was I saying? Oh, yeah. Laura was trash."

"You liked her," said Ransom with a smile.

"Of course I did. I was a teenager."

Ransom laughed. "Do you care to expand on that?"

"I think you know what I mean."

She glanced at herself in a mirror that hung on the wall next to the front door and ran her right pinkie along the ridge of her lips, which were covered with a muted purple gloss.

"You considered her a friend?"

Ruby hesitated. "Up to a point."

"Hmm," said Ransom thoughtfully. "Would that point have been the rape?"

Ruby turned and faced him, her smile waning just a bit. "That's not what I meant. *That* was something else. What I meant was, Laura was the type of girl who talked a lot about herself but never really told you anything. I don't know if you understand what I mean."

"Why don't you explain it to me?"

Ruby sighed deeply. "Well, she would tell you all about some guy she slept with, but when she was done you didn't feel like she'd told you something personal. That make sense?"

Ransom nodded. "But you still considered her a friend."

"Like you said, I liked her," Ruby replied, the smile returning.

"And did all that end when the rape occurred?"

As quickly as the smile had returned, it disappeared. "That changed everything, everywhere, every which way."

"How so?"

"When Laura named Ben, it was like battle lines were drawn. The school was like a war zone. I would have stayed friends with her, because color never did mean much to me, but I couldn't. Everything went crazy. It was pretty much the way you'd expect, with black folks think-ing he was innocent and white folks thinking he was guilty, but I didn't know what to do. I didn't think she would've named Ben if he wasn't guilty, and I don't care what color someone is, if you rape somebody, you should go to jail. But my other friends, they acted like if I stayed friends with her I was turning my back on my own peo-ple."

"And it was easier to turn your back on Laura."

Gerald looked over at his partner. Although this had been said in a nonjudgmental tone, Gerald was surprised at Ransom's choice of words.

Ruby appeared to be surprised, too. Her large eyes nar-rowed. "It was a hard time to be holding the weight of the world on my shoulders, Mr. Ransom. I was young, and I didn't know whether or not I'd end up with a school full of black folks who weren't talking to me. Do you have any idea what that would have been like?"

"I'm sorry," Ransom said sincerely. "I didn't mean that the way it sounded."

"It's all right," she replied, the hardness around her mouth softening. "And you're wrong, anyway. I didn't have to turn my back on Laura. After the rape, she didn't come around anymore."

"Did you miss her?"

"I suppose I would have if I'd had time to think about it. There was too much going on back then. And I had a boyfriend pretty steady, so I didn't have a lot of time for her anyway." She stopped and a reminiscent gleam appeared in her eyes. "Thomas. I haven't thought about him in a long time. He was *fine*. Lots of class. Lots of style. I thought he was the one. Damn near broke my heart when he turned up gay."

Ransom laughed. Since Gerald was accustomed to keeping unobtrusively in the background, he merely smiled into his notebook.

"You said Laura was trash. What exactly do you mean?"

"Trash," Ruby replied with a shrug. "Slept with any boy, even though you'd hardly thought it to look at her. She didn't keep herself up nice. She always looked like she would end up in a trailer park. I don't know why boys would have anything to do with her, but I guess you men really will go with anything that'll let you in there."

"I understand there are some men like that," Ransom replied wryly. "But you still liked her."

"She was fun. Always talking about boys."

"Did she ever get specific about any of her boyfriends?"

"I don't think I'd call them boyfriends," Ruby said. "I don't think any of them lasted long enough to be called that. But no, she didn't usually give out names, if that's what you mean."

"Well, did she ever tell you of anyone in particular?"

Ruby folded her arms and looked at him quizzically. "What do you mean? Any of those boys she slept with, they wouldn't have raped her, would they?"

Ransom shrugged. "Most women know their attackers."

She sucked in her lips and thought about that for a minute. Finally, she said, "No, not that I can remember, really. But if you had to track down all those boys, you sure would have a lot of work ahead of you."

Ransom said, "If she was that free with herself, Im surprised you would let her around your boyfriend, no matter how he turned out."

"Oh, Laura never would've had anything to do with Thomas. She was a friend. She wouldn't have gone after anybody with a girlfriend."

"Even though she was trash?"

"She was trash with standards," Ruby replied, laughing.

Ransom's forehead creased with puzzlement. "You know, that's very odd, because when she was killed, she was having an affair with a married man."

Ruby's smile vanished and her lips tightened. She looked not as if she didn't believe this, but as if she found it disturbing. She shook her head and uttered a "tsk." "That's a shame. She must've changed from when I knew her. But that happens when somebody gets raped. It changes a woman."

Ransom considered this for a moment, then said, "Miss Hawkins, do you know if Laura ever had a boyfriend? Anybody she *did* talk about?"

Ruby was silent, her eyes narrowing as if she were peering into the past. Then suddenly she took a deep breath and said, "Oh, yeah, there was Tony. She talked about him sometimes. Thought he was nice and handsome. But nobody else that I remember."

"Do you know who Tony was?"

She shook her head. "There was a thousand people in our graduating class, Mr. Ransom. I didn't know everybody. And I don't think she ever even said if he went to our school.''

"Hmm," Ransom said. After a few seconds he asked, "Did she ever talk about her parents?"

"Her parents?" Ruby replied, her face a mask of complete surprise. "Not much to talk about there."

"Oh?"

"Have you met them?"

"I've met the mother. The father is dead."

"Oh. Well, if you met Mrs. Shay, then you know what I mean. Back when we were in school, well, if Laura was on her way to the trailer park, her momma and daddy were already there, if you know what I mean."

Gerald glanced up at her with a puzzled frown as if he didn't quite understand what all this talk of trailer parks was about.

"No, what do you mean?" said Ransom.

"Just they were drunks. Laura drank, too, but not so much. And she didn't talk about her parents hardly at all. She didn't like to."

"So you wouldn't know if they...hurt her."

"Hurt her?" Ruby said, her eyes narrowing. "You mean like hit her and such? I don't think so. I don't think they paid enough attention to her to do something like that!"

"WELL, IT SEEMS THAT the idea of Laura's father as the attacker is just a washout," said Ransom as they drove back down Western Avenue on their way to the Peterses' house.

"Why?"

"I think her friends would have known if she were being abused, don't you? Or at least suspected. But nobody, including her homeroom teacher, thinks that she was abused. And Mrs. Brown at least said she would have reported it if she had noticed any signs of abuse. And I believe it.''

"Maybe the rape was the first time," Gerald suggested.

"At that late date? From what I understand, abuse in the family begins much earlier than senior year of high school.''

"I guess.''

"But there's still Alice Peters. Maybe she knows something about it.''

Alice and Marc Peters lived just off Western Avenue on 107th Street. The street was lined with houses on plots large enough to make the owners feel like they owned a bit of land, but close-set enough to be claustrophobic. The Peterses' house was at the far end of the block. It was red brick with a prominent chimney running down the front so that it looked as if it had been built first, then shoved in sideways between two other houses.

The front walk was a lazy "S" bordered on both sides with recently turned earth. Apparently the Peterses lined the walk with flowers during the warmer months, and were preparing to plant. The walk led to a small, enclosed porch that jutted off the side of the house like an architectural wart.

Gerald pressed the doorbell, and the door was opened almost immediately by a young woman with short blond hair and a pair of glasses with black plastic frames. She had an hourglass figure, although most of the sand had run to the bottom, and was wearing a neutral rag-knit sweater and a pair of dark blue jeans.

"I was watching for you," she said. "I hope you're the detectives.''

She sounded more excited than Ransom thought was seemly given the circumstances of their visit.

"I'm Detective Ransom. This is Detective White."

"Come in, come in!"

The front door opened directly into the living room. The chimney that was so prominently featured on the outside of the house was necessitated by a fireplace, disproportionately large in comparison to the rest of the room, on the wall to the right. On the mantelpiece there were several pictures of children as well as a gold-framed, posed photo of Alice and her husband at their wedding. The furniture was a tasteful, sedate mixture of earth tones in styles that Ransom thought might be more appropriate to a middle-aged couple.

Alice closed the door behind them and smiled when she noticed Ransom eyeing the fireplace. "That's the reason we bought the place—well, that and the price. This is what they call a starter home, which means it's all you can afford. It wasn't very expensive because it looks so stupid from the outside. It looks like the other houses were built around it, doesn't it? But they weren't. This one came later. But I didn't mind because I really love the fireplace."

Her gaze was fixed on the grate, which was swept clean. From the light in her eyes it was apparent that she was enjoying memories of evenings by the fire.

"That's what it's supposed to be about," she said suddenly to herself.

"I beg your pardon?" said Ransom.

"Oh! Nothing. I'm sorry. Look, would you mind if we talked in the kitchen? I was sorting laundry, and I'd like to get it finished while the kids are down."

"How many children do you have?" Ransom asked as Alice led the detectives down a long hallway that went through the dining room and into the kitchen.

"Three: Jamie, Bobby, and Rebecca. Jamie's the eldest.

He's four. All three of them are upstairs taking a nap. I was trying to get some work done while I had the chance. When they get up, they'll want to eat and it'll be pandemonium.''

The kitchen was painted yellow and there was a row of wooden cabinets over the sink. The varnish on the cabinets was worn away in spots. The floor was covered with ancient linoleum that was off-white with multicolored speckles. There was a table and chairs shoved up against the wall on the left. One of the chairs was pulled out, and beside it was a huge wicker hamper. Two small piles of clothing of widely varying sizes were on the floor in front of the chair. Alice sat down and with a careless wave of her hand motioned the detectives to two other chairs. Gerald took out his notebook and laid it on the table.

"I really hope you'll forgive me, but I have to get this done. I can't tell you how many loads of wash I have to do every week. I don't even want to think about it."

"That's quite all right," said Ransom with a smile.

"How did you find out about me? How did you know I was Laura's friend?"

"We visited Nora Brown. She told us."

"Nora Brown?" Alice said, pausing and looking up at him. She searched her memory for a moment, then suddenly her expression cleared. "Oh! So you got to see 'old lady Brown,''' she said, apostrophizing the appellation. "How's she doing?"

"She doesn't seem very old."

"She never did, really. Only to teenagers. You know how it is."

"Hmm."

Alice had drawn a handful of clothes from the hamper. She laid them in her lap and was in the process of extracting a white T-shirt from the jumble when she was struck by his tone. She looked up at him again.

"I probably shouldn't sound so excited. I'm sorry, but I've never been questioned by the police before, and I'm here all day long with the kids, so any sort of talk with another adult is really welcome here..." She tapped her chest with her index finger. "Even if it's about something...terrible."

"I understand."

"It's terrible about Laura. I couldn't believe it when I heard it on the news. You don't expect to turn on the TV and hear about someone you knew being murdered. It was a shock. I even cried." As she said this several different emotions traveled across her face like passing clouds, as if she were reliving a series of events in a matter of seconds.

"You considered her a friend?" Ransom asked.

Alice resumed her sorting as she replied. "I did at one time. But I haven't seen or heard from her for years."

"What was she like?"

Alice paused with a single red sock in her hand and smiled. "She was the type of girl that your mother wouldn't want you to be around." She tossed the sock in the pile of colors and reached into the hamper for another batch.

"Your mother didn't want you to be around Laura?" said Ransom.

Alice shook her head. "Oh, no. She thought Laura was a bad influence. She used to say that if you hung around someone like Laura, she'd end up ruining your life...or something like that."

Ransom smiled. "And did you agree?"

Alice stopped again and dropped her hands into her lap, giving herself time to think about this. She sighed deeply and said, "Probably. Laura was dangerous, in a way. Things happened to her—and I don't mean good things. But I think that was because she was the type of girl who took risks. So to somebody like me she was really interesting."

"Risks?" said Ransom, raising his right eyebrow.

Alice looked him in the eye, then turned away, laughing as she blushed. "I'm a good Catholic girl, Mr. Ransom. I've had three kids in four years, which should give you an idea of how good I am."

Gerald paused in his note taking and coughed into his hand.

"And Laura wasn't?"

Alice pursed her lips. She looked as if she were considering exactly how openly she should answer that question. She shook her head and said, "No, she wasn't."

"She was promiscuous?"

"Yeah. I think that's one of the reasons my mother didn't want me around her. Mothers can sense that sort of thing, you know? I don't know how else she could've known. But I *liked* Laura. She was so different from me, you know what I mean?" Alice stopped and looked down at the floor, lost in some reflection. After a while she sighed again. "I guess I had sort of a sheltered life, compared to some people."

"Compared to Laura, you mean," said Ransom kindly.

Alice smiled. "Yeah. I think she was the first girl I knew who actually admitted to having sex. I mean, she was always *careful*. She told me that she never had sex without making the guy use a *condom*." She stopped and her cheeks reddened. "My mother would probably die if she ever heard me say that word. Anyway, Laura even showed me how they worked. On a banana." She paused again and smiled to herself. "You know, even though my

mother never liked me having anything to do her, learning
stuff like that from her made me feel...I don't know, it
made me feel better. Do you know what I mean?''

"Yes..." said Ransom slowly. He did understand how
gaining knowledge of that sort might be a relief to a
young person.

Alice laughed. "You don't sound too sure."

Ransom smiled. "To be perfectly frank, I sometimes
fear that some of the things we learn diminish us."

Alice's eyes widened, and she stared at him for several
seconds before she once again broke into a smile. "You
sound like my mother."

"She must be a very sensible woman," he replied
frankly. He cleared his throat, then continued. "Did Laura
ever talk about her parents?"

"Sure...well, not a lot. But she did sometimes."

"Were there problems?"

Alice laughed. "What teenager doesn't have problems
with their parents?"

Ransom gave a nod. "That's true. But I was wondering
if there might have been any problems that were...out of
the ordinary."

Alice looked at him with an expression so quizzical it
was almost comical. "Out of the ordinary? No. She...I
think she liked her dad a lot, and she wasn't crazy about
her mother. But...I don't know what you mean."

Ransom gazed at the young woman's open countenance
for a moment, assessing her. He decided that, as innocent
as she appeared to be, if there had been any abuse, she
probably would have known what he was talking about.
At last he said, "I wasn't thinking of anything in particular. I just wondered what their relationship was like."

"Same as everybody else's with their parents, I suppose," Alice replied.

Ransom paused, took a deep breath, then said, "Now, what can you tell me about Laura Shay's rape?"

"What?" said Alice, startled. The jumble of clothes on her lap rolled over her knees and onto the floor. There was a beat before she realized they'd fallen, and she bent down to retrieve them.

"I don't know anything about it. Why would I?" She straightened up with the clothes in hand.

"Well, you were Laura's friend. We thought she might have told you about it."

Alice shook her head and laid her hand on top of the clothes on her lap. "We were sort of close until that happened. After that, Laura didn't talk a whole lot and never about what happened. I thought it was terrible at the time, because it changed her so much. And then there was Ben."

"You knew Ben?"

She nodded. "Oh, yeah. He was a really nice boy. I really liked him. Then this happened and…I couldn't believe it at the time…I didn't want to believe it, but, well, you never know, do you?"

Ransom's expression hardened and his eyes grew more narrow. The abbreviated smile that played about his lips would have worried anyone who knew him. "You never know *what,* Mrs. Peters?"

Alice looked at him and blinked. After a moment her face turned beet red all the way down to the roots of her hair, and she looked away from him. She absently picked at the clothes as she said, "I meant you never know what will happen." She raised her eyes to his and the redness started to dissipate as she added sincerely, "But I was very glad when I heard that he was innocent. I was sorry for all he went through, but to finally be proven innocent, that must mean *something,* doesn't it?"

"Yes," Ransom replied without expression, "it means something. So Laura never told you anything about the rape—who *really* did it."

"No," Alice replied, her face so blank that Ransom had to believe she was telling the truth. "If she had told me that, I would've come forward."

Ransom shifted in his seat, crossed one leg over the other, and rested an arm on the table. "Mrs. Peters, now that you know that Ben wasn't the rapist, do you have any idea who it might have been?"

"No, none at all. It could've been anybody, couldn't it?" She shook her head without removing her eyes from his. "I mean, honestly, I don't think...you have to remember that I really did like Laura, so don't get me wrong when I say this, but I don't think anybody needed to force themselves on her. The way she talked, she was pretty...she did it a lot."

Ransom replied coolly, "But then, of course, that's not what rape is all about, is it?"

"What?" Once again Alice looked startled and her cheeks reddened. Ransom was somewhat mollified to see that she'd been speaking out of innocence. She said, "No, I guess not."

"Was she close to any boys? Was she seeing anyone at the time?"

Alice shook her head, and looked relieved that they'd moved on. "Not really. She dated a lot. Mostly guys who...well, wanted something, I guess."

"Anyone special?"

"No."

"Did she talk about anyone in particular?" Ransom asked with less patience. For being Laura's best friend, Alice didn't seem to know very much about her.

Alice sat looking down at the floor for a few moments, thinking about this. "Not really…"

Ransom waited, then said, "What about Tony?"

Her features relaxed and a smile spread across her face. "Oh, yeah! She used to talk about Tony a lot."

"Did you know who this Tony was?"

"Not really…Tony Thornton, I think. At least…well, I was sure it was Tony Thornton, because he was the only Tony we knew. He was a friend of my husband's, sort of. She had a big-time crush on him." She stopped and her smile abated. "But he wasn't her boyfriend. He never would've had anything to do with anyone like Laura. Tony was top of the hill."

Ransom elevated his right eyebrow. "Excuse me?"

"Oh," Alice laughed, "'top of the hill.' It's an expression we use around here. You've seen Lynnwood Avenue, right?"

"Yes."

"It runs for about a mile at the foot of a hill. Well, on Lynnwood, the other side of the school, that's lower class, I guess you'd call it. And over here where we live is middle class. But along the top of the hill, that's the only place in this whole area where there are mansions. So people with money, we call them 'top of the hill.' Tony was one of them. He lived in a huge house on the hill right by One Hundred and Seventh Place. Marc—my husband—used to live right down the street from him."

Ransom gave her an impressed tilt of the head. "Your husband was top of the hill?"

"Yeah. But his parents felt he should make his own way in the world. And that's exactly what he's been doing. Not like Tony. His parents always gave him everything. Still do, for all I know." When Alice spoke of her husband, her voice was full of pride, but there was a tinge of envy added when she spoke of Thornton, as if, as proud as she might be of her husband, she wouldn't have minded being given everything.

Ransom sat for a few moments in thoughtful silence, then sighed and said, "So you have no idea who might've raped Laura. After the incident, the two of you weren't as close?"

"We couldn't be."

"Why was that?"

"Because she went away."

This arrested Ransom's attention. Gerald, who had left off taking notes during Alice's explanation of "top of the hill," noted his partner's reaction and tightened his fingers around his pencil.

"She went away?" Ransom repeated.

"Yes." Alice nodded and looked at Ransom as if she couldn't understand his reaction. "Yeah. She went away to school."

"To college?" Ransom asked, his brow deeply furrowed.

"Yeah. Out in California. Only, as it turned out, she was only gone for a couple of semesters. I don't know why. I think her family ran out of money. And she went through an awfully hard time." She stopped abruptly and looked from Ransom to Gerald, then back again. Her cheeks flushed once again and she glanced down at the floor. "It's not nice to talk about. It's like I said, really awful things seemed to happen to her all the time."

Without changing expression, Ransom said, "I'm sorry, Mrs. Peters, but I don't know what you're talking about."

"Well, I think money was only part of the reason she

came back home. The other part was...while she was out there...she had a miscarriage.''

Gerald stopped writing in midsentence and looked at the young woman in surprise. Ransom, on the other hand, was careful not to allow what he was thinking to transfer to his face.

"Laura Shay was pregnant?" Ransom asked evenly.

"Uh-huh. I think that was part of the reason her parents decided to send her to college out west. I don't think they wanted her to have the baby here. In fact, I don't think they wanted her to have it at all.''

"So...it was the product of the rape?"

"Yeah. Like I told you, Laura was careful with the guys she slept with. That's why they knew it had to be from the rape.''

Ransom paused for a moment, then he allowed himself a curious half-smile. "But even if you're careful, there can always be mishaps.''

Alice looked uncertain. It was clear that her education at Laura's hands hadn't been very extensive. Ransom thought with an inward smile that it was a good thing that Alice was a good girl. She said, "I don't know about that. All I know is, she was sure it was from the rape. She did tell me that much. Then she went out west and by the time she got back, I was gone. I went downstate to Urbana. I never did see her again.''

"I see," Ransom said absently. He didn't appear to be paying attention. He suddenly looked at Alice incisively and said, "And you're sure that she had a miscarriage?"

"What else would she have done?" Alice said in a tone that showed she was fully aware of the alternatives and horrified at the thought.

Ransom shrugged lightly. "She was attacked. Most people would've understood if she didn't want the baby.''

"Oh, but she did," Alice said forcefully.

"She did what?"

"She *did* want the baby. That much I know."

"WAIT...WAIT," said Ransom, holding out a hand to stop Gerald in the act of starting the car. He reached into his pocket and extracted a cigar, which he lit with a match from a stray book he found in his jacket. At that point he didn't have the patience to wait for the dashboard lighter.

"What are we waiting for?" Gerald asked, still leaning forward with his hand on the ignition.

"I want to smoke this," Ransom replied with a wave of his cigar, "and we don't have that far to go."

"Where are we going?"

Ransom turned slowly to face his partner and said, "We need to talk to Mrs. Shay."

"We've already done that."

"In light of what we've just learned, we need to talk to her again."

Gerald sat back in his seat and sighed heavily, his gaze traveling out through the windshield. The right side of Ransom's mouth curled upward.

"Something the matter, Gerald?"

"Well, we're spending an awful lot of time on this rape, and I can't see that it's getting us anywhere."

"Can't you?"

"No. I can't. I mean, I still think it's more likely that she was killed by somebody in her present, like that druggist, Gibson. He had a key to her apartment."

"And he has a wife who gives him an alibi."

"So she was lying."

Ransom curled the other side of his mouth. "There's always that possibility."

Gerald continued, "Or she could've been killed by anyone else who knew her recently, a friend or an enemy."

"If she had any," Ransom interjected wryly.

"Well, maybe if we were spending more time looking into that instead of looking into the past, we might find somebody."

"We did talk to her coworkers, and the neighborhood was canvassed. None of us came up with anything."

Gerald sighed with exasperation. "That doesn't mean we shouldn't go on in that direction. Look, Jer, I agree with you that the murder might have something to do with the rape. But if that's the case, then the only person we know of who would have a reason to kill her is Ben Harvey."

"I'm not ruling him out."

"You're not?" It was unusual for Gerald to challenge Ransom's thinking, but in this case he felt compelled to do it, even though it made him uncomfortable, not only because of the tension it might cause but because his partner was usually right. And there was always the possibility that since Ransom didn't like to have his reasoning questioned, he was apt to become more nettlesome than usual. But that turned out to be an unrealized result.

"No, I'm not," Ransom replied with a heavy sigh. "Although I admit I would be disappointed to find that Harvey was the killer. But what are we supposed to do with him? He admits that he doesn't have an alibi. Are we supposed to verify that he doesn't have one?"

After a slight pause, Gerald laughed. "You got me there."

There was a brief silence during which Ransom thoughtfully puffed on his cigar while staring out the window.

"No," he said at last, tapping a long ash out the window, "I'm convinced that what happened eight years ago has some bearing on Laura Shay's murder—something other than the fact that Ben Harvey was available to do it. Mrs. Peters just raised a couple of very interesting questions, and I think that Mrs. Shay is probably the only person who can answer them."

"Two questions?" Gerald asked, furrowing his brow.

"Yes. Where did someone who was known to be poor suddenly come up with the money to send their daughter to college in California...?" Ransom let his voice trail off suggestively.

Gerald looked at him for a moment. Suddenly, his face went whiter than usual and he slapped his forehead with his palm. "Oh, jeez. Blackmail."

"Um-hmm," said Ransom with a nod. "And the other question is, why did Laura want to keep the baby?"

EIGHT

WHEN MIRANDA SHAY opened the door, she was wearing the same floral flannel that she'd worn on their first visit. In fact, it had grown so dingy that it looked as if she'd been wearing it *since* their first visit. The little sprigs of flowers looked as if they were wilting against the graying background. The whites of her eyes were shot through with red, and she blinked at Ransom a few times, apparently in an attempt to focus them.

"Oh, it's you," she said as she fixed her eyes on him. The aroma of gin emanated from her like musk. "What do you want?"

"We'd just like to ask you a few more questions," said Ransom with a smile that mixed malevolence and charm.

"Questions? I don't want any more questions. Why aren't you out there arresting that boy that killed my girl?" She swayed a little, and with some difficulty reached out her hand and grasped the doorjamb for support.

Ransom cocked his head slightly to one side, like a bird scrutinizing its prey. "We'll just take a few minutes of your time."

Through her haze Shay was able to comprehend that despite the detective's nonaggressive tone, this was not being offered as a request. She rolled her eyes, an action that almost sent her reeling backward, then pushed herself away from the doorjamb and walked back into the house.

Ransom glanced at Gerald and said, "Don't mind if I do," then followed her in.

Gerald smiled and shook his head as he crossed the threshold and closed the door.

No attempt was being made now to hide the bottles from them, although in Shay's current state, Ransom would've been surprised if she even noticed the two gin bottles that stuck out from underneath the love seat. There was a third bottle, half-empty, wedged between the cushions. Shay wavered for a moment before dropping down onto the left side of the seat, and wrapped her hand around the neck of the bottle as if it were a lifeline. Ransom once again pulled the wooden chair up in front of her, and Gerald took a seat in the corner and opened his notebook.

Shay raised her left wrist to her forehead and held it there for a few seconds before swiping it across her brow. ''What do you want now?'' she asked wearily.

Ransom smoothly crossed his legs, folded his hands in his lap, and said, ''Mrs. Shay, do you have any money?''

Shay gaped at him in astonishment, then with one barking laugh said, ''What? You gotta be kidding! What, you want a loan?''

''No,'' Ransom replied with a shake of his head. ''I'm merely inquiring into your financial situation.''

She swept her arms outward, encompassing the whole room. The action sent dust motes into a crazy dance in the single stream of light that poured through an opening in the drapes. ''Oh, sure. You can see just by all the expensive crap I have here that I'm rollin' in money. Course I don't have any money. Don't you have eyes?''

''Did you ever?'' Ransom asked, unfazed.

''I told you before, my husband never got anything. He always said, 'Oh, honey, you just watch me. I'm going places.' He never went any further than that goddamn canning company. Squandered everything he had trying to get more.''

She stopped and leaned back against the seat. The effort at sarcasm had allowed her a moment of clarity that drained away once she'd said her piece. Ransom sat looking at her long enough to pierce through the alcoholic fog and cause her some discomfort.

"What is it?" she demanded when she could take it no longer. "What're you asking about that for?"

Ransom sighed, then said, "I just think that's very odd."

"What is? That we didn't have any money? You got a funny way of putting things."

He smiled. "No, I think it's odd that someone so chronically poor was able to send their daughter away to college."

"What?" Shay replied after a pause. Her belligerent expression had melted into fear before freezing in place.

"I said it was odd that you found the money to send Laura to college. However did you do it?"

Gerald smiled down at his notebook, recognizing that his partner was enjoying himself.

Shay remained frozen for a minute before forcing herself to reply. "Saved up. We saved up for a while."

Ransom elevated his right eyebrow. "Even while your husband was squandering all your money?"

Shay swallowed hard and said, "Yeah. I made him save up."

"Really." Ransom sat for a moment, purposely looking as if he was giving this idea due consideration. Then he said, "I wonder how far back bank records go. Gerald, do you think they go back that far?"

"I don't know," Gerald replied without looking up.

It was a gambit with very little risk involved on Ransom's part: he knew that bank records would not go back almost a decade, but he was counting on Mrs. Shay not knowing it. And it proved successful. Despite her level of inebriation, Shay looked for a moment like a trapped animal. Then suddenly her face relaxed and she smiled.

"Who says I kept the money in a bank?"

Ransom raised his right eyebrow and said, "Surely you didn't keep all that money around the house? A college fund? With an unreliable husband on hand?"

Shay offered no reply. She simply stared at him, still retaining her superior smile.

"Well, we'll let that pass for now," said Ransom at last.

Though Shay's stance had been one of defiance, she was visibly relieved. She pulled the bottle of gin from between the cushions and took a drink, then wedged the bottle back in place.

"Now," said Ransom, taking a deep breath, "what happened?"

"What?" Shay tried to refocus her eyes.

"I understand that Laura only lasted a couple of semesters at college. What happened? Why did she come home?"

There was another pause before Shay responded. "Money ran out."

"Really?" Ransom said, contriving to look bewildered.

"Yeah."

"Didn't you know how much school was going to cost before you sent her there?"

Shay looked confused. "We didn't…I didn't…I guess we just didn't realize it was going to be so expensive."

Ransom looked at her for a moment, then clucked his tongue. "Well, that was very poor planning, don't you think?"

Shay recoiled angrily. "I already told you how my husband was about money."

"Yes, you did. You said he was always scheming." He stopped and gave an apologetic nod. "I'm sorry, you said he was always 'planning,' or that he always had ideas. Something like that."

"Yeah…" Shay leaned back against the seat again, eyeing Ransom as if she'd just discovered he had fangs. "Look, that was all a long time ago. What does all that have to do with Laura getting killed?"

Ransom narrowed his eyes at the woman and said, "That's what I'd like to know."

Shay stared back at him for a few seconds before going on the attack. "You already know who killed her: that Ben Harvey! Why the hell don't you go arrest him?"

"If Mr. Harvey is guilty that's exactly what I will do."

She was still glaring at him, but there was a hesitancy about her expression that Ransom believed stemmed from fear. "You mean, you really don't think he did it?"

"I don't know, Mrs. Shay. But you keep going back to Ben Harvey, don't you?"

"So what?" she said with a dismissive swat at the air.

"So, it would seem that even *you* think your daughter's murder has something to do with what happened eight years ago."

"I don't think…I don't think…" She searched for the words, then shook her head angrily. "I don't know what to think!"

Ransom recrossed his legs, then refolded his hands. "Where did the money come from, Mrs. Shay?"

Her face remained stony, but tears appeared in her eyes, apparently against her will. "I already told you."

Ransom nodded. "That you saved up a college fund and kept it…where? In an empty coffee can? That you sent your daughter away to college not knowing that you only had money for a couple of semesters?"

She looked down at the floor, unable to tolerate Ransom's unwavering gaze any more. "My husband…" She paused and released a single, sarcastic laugh. "He always had ideas."

"And what was his idea, Mrs. Shay?"

She looked back up at him. "I don't know what you're talking about."

Ransom leaned in toward her. The gin on her breath was almost overpowering. "I can tell you what *I* think."

"I don't care what you think," she replied, giving another angry swat at the air and narrowly missing Ransom's nose.

He leaned back in his chair and heaved a heavy sigh. "Do you know who really raped your daughter?"

"Laura always said it was Ben Harvey."

Ransom closed his eyes for a moment, then opened them. "You understand that now that it's known that Ben Harvey wasn't the rapist, it's possible that there's someone else who might have a motive to kill her."

"Who?" Shay spouted, her eyes widening so that she looked and sounded like an owl.

Ransom shrugged. "The press is very interested in Laura's story. It could be that whoever it was that really attacked her is in some danger."

Shay looked at him for a moment. Unaccountably, her expression lightened and something of her old cunning returned. "You think . . ." she began, then stopped herself. "Laura always said it was Ben Harvey."

"Yes," said Ransom, sounding more weary by the minute. "I know what she said to her friends and the police and the court and to everybody else. I'm fully aware of what she said. Now I want to know who really did it."

Shay came close to smiling. "I only know what she said."

If Ransom had actually had fangs, they would've shown themselves at that point. His lips grew thinner and his smile more ominous. "I see," he said with a slight inclination of his head. He started to rise, but suddenly checked himself as if a new thought had just occurred to him, and sat back down.

"Oh, by the way, I was terribly sorry to hear about the baby."

A row of greasy creases formed across Shay's forehead. "What baby? What're you talking about?"

Ransom manufactured his bewildered look once again. "Why, Laura's baby, of course. I understood that she had a miscarriage."

Shay's eyebrows came together. She looked as if she was seriously weighing what to say next. Despite her alcoholic sense of invincibility, she was painfully aware that Ransom had already caught her out once in the matter of the money, and now she couldn't tell if he was trying to do it again. She wondered if he'd mentioned the miscarriage because he really believed that that was what happened, or because he knew the truth and saw another chance to trip her up. In the end she decided the safest route was the truth, or at least part of it.

"Didn't have a miscarriage," she blurted out.

"Oh?"

"No. She had an abortion. She got pregnant by that rape. You think she would've wanted to keep the baby?"

Ransom smiled. "Oddly enough, that's exactly what I think."

Shay sat back as if she'd been slapped, and the look of shock on her face furthered the impression. Her mind went blank for a moment, then flooded with the idea that she'd somehow walked into a trap again.

"Why the hell would you think that?" she protested. "Why the hell would she want to keep that baby?"

"Why indeed," Ransom replied calmly. "And yet, that's what we were told."

"Well, whoever told you that is a liar!" Shay shot back, her face flushing with anger. "We told Laura she—" She stopped again, and after a stunned moment looked down at the floor.

"You told her what?" Ransom said sharply.

"Nothing! We didn't tell her nothing! And I've said all I'm gonna say to you." She grabbed the bottle of gin and took a couple of swallows. "Now go on! You get out!"

Ransom's smile broadened. "Certainly, Mrs. Shay. Gerald?"

The detectives rose simultaneously and went to the door, leaving Shay glaring at them from the love seat, her fist still clutching the neck of the bottle.

Ransom paused by the door and said, "Oh, one more thing. Which college did your daughter attend?"

Shay blinked once and said, "University of California. That was it. In Los Angeles."

"Thank you, Mrs. Shay," he replied with a genial nod. "We'll be seeing you."

"SHE *KNOWS*, Gerald," said Ransom in a tone of complete disgust as they went quickly down Shay's front walk to the car. "She knows who raped her daughter and probably who murdered her."

"You don't know that," Gerald countered.

"If she knows who raped her daughter, then she knows who the killer is."

"That's an awfully big if. Who's to say that Laura

didn't tell her parents it was Harvey that raped her? Maybe she did. Maybe *she* was the one hiding something. If that's so, then her mother really doesn't know who it was."

Ransom stopped in his tracks just as he reached the car, turned, and gave Gerald his most withering look. "She *has* to know where the money came from."

Gerald hesitated, then said, "Well, maybe she has another reason for not telling us where they got the money."

"Oh, I'm sure of that," said Ransom wryly as he opened the passenger door and dropped into his seat.

Gerald used the brief moment he was out of view as he rounded the back of the car to roll his eyes at his partner's stubbornness. As he climbed in behind the wheel he said, "Even if what you think is true, even if Shay knows who the rapist was, that doesn't mean he's the murderer. And even if he is the killer, we don't have anything. The crime lab didn't come up with anything."

"He'd be the only other one we know of with a motive," said Ransom with increasing irritation. "Fear of discovery."

"The only other one we *know* of," Gerald replied with emphasis. "Other than Harvey."

"Perhaps," Ransom said, taking a cigar from the pack in his pocket, "but I believe we should keep going with what we *do* know."

"What's that?"

The cellophane wrapper crackled as Ransom rolled the cigar between his fingers. "We know that the man who attacked Laura Shay eight years ago didn't pay for his crime…at least legally. We have to find him."

Gerald's caterpillarlike eyebrows moved closer together. "What do you mean, legally?"

Ransom turned to him and with an ironically curled lip

replied, "This whole thing hinges on the fact that George Shay was always scheming on how to make money. I think he finally found a way."

"What do you mean?" said Gerald.

"I think," said Ransom, finally unwrapping the cigar, "that George Shay took his daughter's rape and tried to make a killing off of it."

"Jesus Christ!" Gerald exclaimed, turning away to the windshield. As the father of two girls, Gerald didn't want to believe that any parent would be capable of something so repellent. The trouble was that he'd been in Violent Crimes for so long that he didn't really doubt it. Nothing about human nature surprised him.

"We need to go talk to Ben Harvey again."

"Harvey?" Gerald said with genuine surprise. "Why?"

Ransom smiled at himself. "Because of that phone call from Emily. She noticed something that I didn't think was important. I should've known better."

NINE

IT MIGHT HAVE BEEN his imagination, but to Ransom, Louisa Street, particularly the block on which the Harveys lived, seemed to be darkening with anticipation, as if clouds of suspicion were gathering and blocking out the sun. A solitary news van was parked across the street from the Harveys' house. Ransom hadn't expected any of the media to still be present. He knew they would have converged on Harvey the day before, but he figured by now they would have been off and running after whatever story they could find to supersede yesterday's sensation. And he was never too happy with the presence of the media. He felt himself fortunate that the occasion rarely arose, since the press tended to pick and choose their tragedies in a way that was incomprehensible to him. The few times he'd conducted an investigation that garnered media interest, he was usually able to assiduously avoid contact with them. But it looked as if this was going to be one of those exceptions.

Gerald parked in front of the house, and he and Ransom climbed out of the car. Before Ransom had even closed his door, a young Asian woman leaped out of the van and hurried across the street toward them.

"'Scuse me! 'Scuse me!" she called before she reached them. "Are you the detectives on the Shay murder? You'd be Detective Ransom, right?"

She came to a stop in front of him, uncomfortably close. She was no more than five feet tall and had long black hair. Her eyelids were painted with a dark blue eye shadow that looked like smudges on her very pale skin. Ransom looked over her shoulder at the van. A young man holding a video camera was poised just inside the side door, and looked ready to rush to the scene on signal.

"What makes you think we're the detectives?" Ransom said with a smile.

"Come on, Mr. Ransom. You kind of stand out in this neighborhood."

"So do you, but I wouldn't take you for a detective."

"Besides, I've seen you before."

"Have you, now?"

"I'd like to get an interview with you, on camera. Find out how the case is going."

As she said this she motioned to the cameraman to join them. He had only set one foot onto the street before he was arrested by the look he received from Ransom.

"I don't think so, Miss..." He raised a questioning eyebrow.

The reporter frowned at not being recognized. "Kwan," she said flatly. "Natalie Kwan."

"I don't think so, Miss Kwan. I'm here to do a job." He and Gerald started to walk toward the house, and Natalie followed along.

"So, how *is* the case going?"

"Don't you have a grieving family to badger?" Ransom said wearily.

She laughed. "Not in this case. Laura Shay doesn't seem to have been very popular, does she? None of her neighbors had anything to do with her." She paused for a moment and glanced at him to see if he'd respond, if not in word, then by expression. She was met with a slightly twisted lip. "Of course, her coworkers knew her, but not very well."

Ransom shrugged. "Some people prefer to be left alone."

The sarcasm wasn't lost on the reporter, but she continued, undaunted. "Do you think Ben Harvey murdered her?"

"Surely you don't expect me to answer something like that," Ransom replied in a tone meant to reflect that he felt like he was dealing with a tiresome child.

"You don't have any other suspects, do you?"

"Other than whom?"

"Other than Ben Harvey, of course."

"Did someone say that Mr. Harvey is a suspect?"

"It stands to reason. Why else would you be here? Are you going to make an arrest?" There was an avidity in her tone that showed that she was delighted at the prospect. If Ransom was going to make an arrest, she would have been right to hang around. And she would have a real coup, because none of the rival stations were on the scene.

They had progressed halfway up the Harvey's front walk. Ransom stopped and faced the young woman. "I hate to disappoint you, but I'm just here to ask questions. That's my job."

"Oh. Like mine," she replied with a coy smile.

Ransom almost laughed, but restrained himself. He didn't want to let the reporter know that he found her amusing. "Mine have a purpose," he said lightly. Then he cocked his head and leaned toward her as he said, "Are you supposed to be on private property? The owners might complain to the police." He managed to say this as if he were speaking to a lowly servant who'd stepped outside her place.

"Oh!" Kwan said, putting a hand over her mouth and feigning embarrassment. "So solly!" She bowed twice to him in an imitation of a stereotype of her heritage, and then walked away. As the detectives approached the door, they heard the reporter loudly chastising her cameraman for failing to join her in terms that would have made the proverbial sailor blush.

"Ah," said Ransom as Gerald pressed the doorbell, "the freedom of the press."

When Ben Harvey opened the door, the expression on his face was even less welcoming than before, if that was possible. Though he faced Ransom, he gave a sidelong glance toward the street. His eyes locked for a second on the van, then swiveled back to the detectives.

"Yes?"

"Mr. Harvey, we'd like to ask you a few more questions."

"So?"

Ransom looked at him for a moment before answering. Then with a meaningful glance in the direction of the van he said, "Don't you think it would be better to do it inside?"

Ben waited for a full minute before stepping aside and letting them pass, then he closed the door and followed them into the living room.

"My momma's asleep," he said in a cautionary tone.

Ransom smiled. "I wasn't planning to raise my voice."

They stood for a moment in an uncomfortable cluster in the center of the room. Ben was defiantly determined not to offer any hospitality, and Ransom was equally determined not to mind.

"We don't need to sit." His tone was calculated to make Ben feel foolish, but Ben didn't give any indication that he was feeling anything. Ransom continued. "We won't be here long. I just wanted to ask you about your little press conference."

This caught Ben off guard. Despite himself he furrowed his dark brown. "I didn't give any press conference."

"I'm talking about when you were released from prison. You were met outside by reporters."

"I didn't talk to them."

"Not really, but you did say one thing to them. When you were asked how you felt about Laura Shay, you said, 'Those people have taken up enough of my life.' Now what exactly did you mean by that?"

The momentary confusion on Ben's face transformed back into a blank wall. Though he didn't give the appearance of it, Ransom could sense that Ben was relieved. "I meant just what I said. What else do you think I coulda meant? Seems obvious to me."

Ransom smiled. "Oh, I don't mean the part about having your time taken up. That's perfectly understandable. I meant what did you mean when you said 'those people.'"

Ben stared back at Ransom without changing expressions. After a pause he said, "It was just a way of talking."

"Hmm," said Ransom doubtfully. "It's an expression that means more than one person. I think if I'd been asked that question, I would've said *she's* taken up enough of my life."

"It was just a way of talking," Ben repeated. His voice still held no emotion, but it now seemed as if it were taking an effort to remain that way.

"You know, Mr. Harvey, if I were in your position—"

"You're not," Ben exclaimed so suddenly and so angrily that it took both detectives by surprise. The flash of anger that passed across his face disappeared quickly.

"As I was about to say," Ransom continued, "if I were in your position I would think that Laura Shay was the one responsible for my imprisonment...but I wouldn't think anyone else was involved, necessarily, unless I had reason to.''

Ben had regained his composure and settled back into his icy stoicism. Ransom could barely see the vein on his forehead pulsate. Though Ransom had felt strongly about the injustice this man had suffered, Ben's insistence on not helping them in what amounted to his own defense was beginning to get to the detective. He closed his eyes and took a deep, calming breath, which he exhaled slowly and silently. ''Do you have any reason to believe that someone besides Laura was involved in railroading you into prison?''

''You mean besides the police?''

Ransom couldn't help but smile. ''Yes, I mean besides the police. Did you ever think there was someone else involved?''

There was a long pause during which Ben didn't move. Then he took a step back that placed him directly in front of his mother's chair. He sank down into it, like a man in a dream, and after a moment all of the stoniness melted from his face like a wax statue being held too close to a flame. His lower lip drooped and began to tremble. For the first time, he came close to resembling the boy in the yearbook picture.

''Eight years, all that time I been locked up I been trying to figure it out. I knew somebody had to know I was innocent, because *I* sure as hell knew I didn't do it, but I didn't know why they wouldn't come out and say so. I couldn't figure out why...'' Tears flooded his eyes and coursed down his cheeks as if years of anger and frustration were pouring out of him. ''I couldn't figure out why Laura had lied about me.'' He stopped and looked up at Ransom. ''I thought she liked me. But I figured somebody...somebody else got her to do it. I couldn't think why else she would lie. I figured somebody else had to know what happened. Whoever really raped her, he had to know."

Ransom looked down into the young face that had been spoiled by one horrible incident, and although he was usually very closemouthed about his cases, at least until they were solved, he felt compelled to offer the young man something to ease the suffering he'd gone through.

"I think you're right, Ben. Somebody else did know about it. Of course, whoever raped her knew. And I believe her parents did, too."

"Her parents?" Ben said, blinking away tears.

"I think they had something to do with her lying."

"But why? Why me? Why would they want her to lie?"

Ransom had definite ideas about that, but wasn't about to share them. "I don't know why yet," he said after a pause, "but I'm going to find out."

WHEN THEY ARRIVED BACK at Area Headquarters, Gerald went off to begin the tiresome task of phoning to confirm the few verifiable facts they'd managed to uncover. Ransom stopped at Newman's office to brief him on what they had so far. Ordinarily he wouldn't have sought out his "superior" in such a manner to give him a report, since he didn't relish the feeling of having to answer to anyone. But he knew that if he didn't in this case, Newman would surely come to him and demand a report, which Ransom would like even less. Newman was unhappy with the lack of progress, but given the notoriety of the case, he refrained from making the usual noises about how they should hurry up and bring the case to a close. He knew it was important that the case they ended up with against the murderer was airtight, with no possible chance of a mistake. Another error in the matter of Laura Shay was likely to bring down the wrath of the top brass and the media in equal measures. So all that was left for him to tell Ransom was that he should be as quick as he could, but it was more important that he be *right*.

As a result, Ransom left the meeting feeling much more uplifted than he'd expected. He almost felt as if he had the room to pursue the case at his own pace—not that he wouldn't have done that anyway.

He then went back to his office and, while waiting for Gerald to finish the telephone legwork, spent his time poring over the record of Ben Harvey's arrest and conviction. Everything struck him as being pretty straightforward, with one exception, so he decided to talk to the detective who'd handled the case. A quick call to Personnel informed him that Margaret Collins, the detective who'd questioned Laura Shay the morning after the rape, had gone on maternity leave five years ago and never come back. Personnel supplied him with her current phone number.

"Is this Margaret Collins?" he said into the receiver.

"Yes?" There was an appealing huskiness to the voice.

"This is Detective Jeremy Ransom."

"Oh, Christ!" she exclaimed, although she sounded amused. "I was wondering if I'd get a call."

"You know why I'm calling, then?"

There was a soft sucking sound, followed by a sharp exhale. Ransom smiled. Collins was a smoker.

"The Shay thing, of course. Ever since I saw it on the news, I had a feeling I'd hear from somebody. What do you need? And make it snappy, will you? I have a house full of kids here."

"I was just wondering about one thing," Ransom said.

"I understand from the report that Laura Shay was questioned on the night of the rape, but an arrest wasn't made until the next morning. Why was that?"

"According to the officers that talked to her," Collins proceeded, reverting to a more professional tone, "she was unresponsive. They couldn't get anything out of her. Not unusual after being attacked like that."

"And her father?"

"Drunk," Collins replied flatly. It was clear she spared little sympathy for people who overindulged.

"So you were sent to question her the next morning."

"Yeah. Me and my partner talked to her, and that's when she told us who did it."

There was something in the former detective's tone that caught Ransom's attention. "And did you think she was telling the truth?"

Collins responded with a short, cynical laugh. "The truth? I suppose."

"What do you mean?"

"I got a four-year-old daughter, you know. She likes to learn little rhymes—Mother Goose and crap like that. You know how she sounds when she recites them? Just like that Shay girl did when she told us her story."

"What about Ben Harvey? What was his story?"

"You got the report there," Collins replied. "He said he saw her walking down the street, he tried to help her, she scratched his face and ran away."

"Hmm," said Ransom. After a pause, he said, "How did Harvey seem to you?"

"Seem?"

"Did he seem genuine?"

"Genuine!" Collins said with a throaty laugh. "Yeah, you could say that. He acted like he didn't know what was happening to him. Which is funny, because the Shay girl acted like she knew *exactly* what was happening to *her*."

Ransom sighed. "Did you think *he* was telling you the truth?"

"You know how it is, Ransom," Collins said, pausing to take another drag on her cigarette. "After a while, nobody sounds like they're telling the truth."

Ransom smiled to himself. "Is that why you decided to 'retire'?"

Collins laughed. "You got it. When I got pregnant, I intended to come back to the force after my leave was over. But once I had a kid I didn't want to do it anymore. Too much risk of infection, if you know what I mean!"

SOON AFTER Ransom had ended the call, Gerald came into the office and plopped down on the old Naugahyde couch that was kept pushed up against the wall to the left of the door.

"Well," he said with a sigh, "Laura Shay *did* attend college for two semesters, then dropped out. No explanation of why."

Ransom sat back in his chair and stared at his partner for a minute, then pulled out a cigar and lit it. "That really is a surprise," he said as he expelled a stream of smoke.

"Why?"

"Somehow, with my Victorian sensibilities, I thought maybe she'd been sent out west to have the abortion and the school story was used to cover the truth."

"Why would Mrs. Shay lie about something that would be so easy to check?"

Ransom curled his lip and said, "She hardly seemed in any condition to think something like that through."

"Does it make any difference?"

Ransom raised his right eyebrow, signaling to Gerald to explain further.

"Well, does it make any difference if they blackmailed the rapist and used the money to send her out west to school or for an abortion, or both?"

"I really don't know," Ransom replied with frustration. He sat for a while lost in thought, taking an occasional puff from his cigar and blowing the smoke toward the ceiling. Gerald rose from the couch and crossed to the window to the right of Ransom's desk. He opened the window a few inches, then returned to his seat.

Ransom finally straightened himself in his chair and said, "I think we're going to have to track down Tony Thornton."

"Tony Thornton?" Gerald repeated. From the puzzled look on his face it was evident that he couldn't quite remember where he'd heard the name. "You mean the guy that Laura supposedly had a crush on in high school? Why?"

"Relax, Gerald." Ransom took another drag from the cigar and then, in deference to his partner, released the smoke in the direction of the window. "I realize it may seem way off the mark, but it's not, really, if you give it some thought. He's the only one remotely connected with this case who's believed to have money."

"*Remotely* connected," Gerald pointed out.

"Granted. But the connection wasn't so remote at the time. She knew him when she was raped. Or at least Alice Peters believed she did."

"But the rapist still could've been anyone," Gerald replied with increasing emphasis. "It could've been anyone in the neighborhood."

"Oh, not just anyone. In order for blackmail to have occurred at all, Laura had to know her attacker. And she or her father had to know him well enough to have some idea how he was financially situated.''

"But they could've found that out later."

Ransom shook his head. "No. They had to know. Once again, because of timing. Laura accused Harvey the morning after she was raped. That means the fix was put in literally overnight."

"It still could've been anybody in the neighborhood. Just from where these people live they could tell who had a lot of money and who didn't. Just from where their houses were."

Ransom smiled as he recalled Alice's name for the wealthy of the neighborhood. "That's true. And there may be no real link at all between Laura Shay and Tony Thornton. But I keep thinking of how many people—including Mrs. Shay—seem to think that Laura got what she deserved when she was attacked."

Gerald shrugged. "That could just be because she was 'loose,' like Alice Peters said."

"Yes, but suppose it was something else. Suppose Laura acted on her crush, and went after Thornton. Maybe that's what her mother meant when she said 'she got herself raped.'''

After a pause, Gerald said, "You know, if I 'supposed' like that you'd be down my throat in a minute."

Ransom sat back in his chair, took a drag from the cigar, and blew the smoke toward the window. "That's because, my dear Gerald, when you do it, it's conjecture. When I do it, it's a working hypothesis."

Gerald laughed.

"If nothing else, we should talk to him because he knew Laura. If *he* wasn't involved with her, maybe he knows who was."

Tony Thornton didn't prove difficult to locate. After obtaining the number from the phone company, Gerald called and spoke to Mary Thornton, Tony's wife. She informed him that her husband was away on business and wouldn't be back until late that night, then pointed out that he was a very busy man.

"When did he leave?" Gerald asked.

"Yesterday morning," Mary replied crisply. "It's just a short trip this time."

Gerald made a note that Thornton had left town the morning after the murder.

"Will he be in his office tomorrow morning?"

"No. He'll be here at home, if you insist on seeing him."

Gerald smiled as he hung up the phone. He almost wished that Mrs. Thornton was the one they'd be questioning. Ransom would have loved that.

Lynn opened the door to greet Ransom just as he came onto the small, screened-in porch that fronted Emily's house. It was an unnecessary gesture, since he had his own key, but Lynn had spotted him through the living room window as he came up the front walk and thought it might be nice to have a word with him alone.

"How's she doing?" Ransom said as Lynn closed the door.

"She's fine. She's so concerned about me that she's letting me do everything, so she's getting to take it easy."

Ransom chuckled lightly. "So you've managed to accomplish something that I couldn't do even by taking her away on holiday."

"Well, yes," Lynn replied, a shadow crossing her usually bright face, "but I wish it hadn't taken..."

"Oh, I'm sorry," Ransom said gently. "I didn't mean that. I wasn't thinking."

"It's all right," Lynn said. "I knew what you meant."

"And how are *you* doing?" he asked as she led him down the hall to the kitchen.

"Me?" Lynn said with a light laugh. "I'm a mess."

"I don't believe that."

"Then, Mr. Detective, you're slipping."

Ransom checked his step for a moment. Though she'd said this in jest, he was painfully aware that Gerald wasn't exactly in agreement with the course he was pursuing in the investigation, and he'd also gotten the impression that Emily wasn't, either. More than anything, Emily's good opinion had come to mean a great deal to him, and it was a bit unnerving to find himself even slightly out of sync with her. It came close to making him wonder if Lynn's light joke was true. He followed Lynn into the kitchen, where they found Emily setting the table for dinner.

As they ate, Ransom filled them in on the progress of the investigation. Emily listened intently between her birdlike bites of food, while Lynn's attention appeared to be rooted in another dimension.

"Alice Peters seems to have been a wealth of information," said Emily. "What did you think of her?"

"Of all the people we've questioned so far, she seems the most sincere."

Emily replied with a "hmm" and thought about that for a moment before saying vaguely, "Yes...I suppose... that's true."

"What? Do you think there's some reason to doubt her?"

"Oh, no. I'm sure you're right. I was just thinking about Alice Peters's mother."

"Her mother?" Ransom said, raising an eyebrow.

"Yes. You said that her mother said something to the effect that having contact with someone like Laura would end up ruining one's life. Mothers often have a sixth sense about things like that, you know. And it certainly looks as if Alice's mother has been proven correct."

Ransom assented reluctantly. "She seems to have ruined some people. But she *was* raped."

"Oh, yes, I'm not discounting that," Emily said, "but Alice's mother sensed that bad influence before the attack occurred. But I do understand Alice's fascination with Laura. I think it was something like the way some people are fascinated by fire. And that can be dangerous, too."

"Yes, Emily," Ransom replied with a smile.

Emily lost herself in thought for a moment. "So you believe that Mr. Shay tried to blackmail the man who raped his daughter," she said with a cluck of her tongue to demonstrate how distasteful an idea she found this.

Ransom stopped in the act of cutting a piece of beef with his fork and looked up at her. "You don't think that's plausible?"

"On the contrary," Emily said solemnly, "I believe it's quite possible. Only…" Her voice trailed off and her gaze traveled over his shoulder.

"Only what?" Ransom said, feeling another sting to his pride at the thought that once again his theory was being challenged.

Emily adjusted herself in her chair and folded her hands in front of her plate. "Only it doesn't explain why the money was cut off."

Ransom looked back at her across the table, his face blank. "I don't know what you mean."

"Yes, well, say that you're correct that Mr. Shay attempted blackmail. On the surface it looks as if he was successful because he got the money to send Laura out to

California to college. But Laura returned almost immediately, which would indicate that the money was cut off.''

Ransom looked down at his plate of half-eaten food and pursed his lips, mulling this over. "Either that," he said with a sigh, "or I'm completely wrong and the Shays actually did save the money and really were such bad planners that they didn't realize how quickly the money would run out."

"Oh, don't be silly," Emily said with a wave of her hand, casting a curious look at him.

"You haven't met Mrs. Shay, Emily. She's strictly a lower-class, Dickensian character. That family certainly made a mess of their lives, somehow. And Mrs. Shay is very, very bitter about it." He paused for a moment, then added, "Gerald doesn't want to believe that a father would try to make money off of his daughter's attack."

Emily smiled benignantly. "That's because Detective White is a decent human being." She cocked her head and her eyes became more penetrating. "But he does believe it, doesn't he?"

Ransom hesitated for a second before answering. "Yes, I think he does."

Emily shifted in her seat and then said reassuringly, "I'm sure you're not wrong about the blackmail business. It certainly fits the circumstances, and I can't think of anything else that would. I just think that the fact that the money stopped flowing is another interesting wrinkle." She absently brushed her hand lightly against her cheek, then picked up her utensils and ate a few small bites of potato while they silently gave this some consideration. "You know," she added at last, "it's rather like Shylock, isn't it?"

"What is?"

"Well, Shylock tried to make a killing and ended up losing everything he had. It sounds as if Mr. Shay did much the same thing."

"I thought you were casting Ben Harvey in the role of Shylock."

"As I said," Emily replied primly, although there was a twinkle in her eye, "there's a bit of Shylock in all of us." She refolded her hands on the table and leaned toward him. "Now, do you think that Laura Shay really was as much like her father as Mrs. Shay would have you believe?"

"I have no reason to doubt it. Mrs. Shay seemed to resent the fact. Why do you ask?"

Emily raised her thin gray eyebrows knowingly.

Ransom laughed. "I think you're trying to tell me something, Emily."

She smiled broadly. "Only that if it's true, it strikes me that it could be very significant."

All amusement drained from Ransom's face. "Oh, my God!"

"Exactly," Emily said, sitting back in her chair and once again taking up her utensils.

"What?" Lynn said, Ransom's exclamation apparently having broken her reverie. "What's the matter?"

"Blackmail," Ransom said, mentally castigating himself for not having thought of it before.

"If all of your suppositions are correct, and Mr. Shay tried to blackmail the rapist, perhaps Laura saw Mr. Harvey's release as an opportunity to try it on for herself, so to speak."

Lynn blinked. "You mean this girl might have tried to blackmail the man who raped her?"

Emily nodded. "She was in a perfect position to do so. All she had to do was let the truth come out—and she certainly had an interested audience—and even if the case couldn't be prosecuted now, she could be sure to ruin the man's life. And if that's true, then she didn't just pose a vague threat to the rapist, she posed a very real threat.''

Though the ebb in Ransom's confidence had been only slight, this explanation, which furthered his theory, caused a renewed flow. "I wish to God that silly girl had had a telephone.''

"Why?''

"If she tried blackmail, she had to contact her mark somehow. And I'm assuming that she was smart enough not to put her demands in writing. She must've called whoever it was. If she only had a phone we might have a record of who she called.''

"What about pay phones?'' Lynn suggested.

Ransom shook his head. "Even if we could figure out where she made a call from, they don't keep records of calls from pay phones.''

They ate in silence for a few minutes. Then he turned to Emily and said, "Oh, by the way, I did go back and talk to Ben Harvey as you suggested.''

"Yes?'' said Emily, looking up with interest.

"Of course, you were right. At first he insisted that when he said 'those people' it was just a slip of the tongue, but after a while he broke down and admitted that all along he'd believed that Laura wasn't the only one responsible for his ending up in prison. He had no idea why, but he felt it wasn't just her.''

"Now, that strikes me as very significant,'' Emily replied after a thoughtful pause. Ransom noticed her posture stiffen as it always did when she spoke of Harvey. "Of course it stands to reason, since he knew that Laura was lying, and she had to have a reason to do so, there had to have been at least one other person who was in it with her: her attacker. And I don't think Mr. Harvey would need a lot of imagination to guess the reason.''

Ransom sighed wearily. ''I don't think he ever imagined that Laura's parents were involved.''

Emily's expression grew more grave. She shook her head. ''A very, very dirty business.''

''I hope that once the truth comes out it will help Harvey to get beyond everything that has happened to him.''

''I don't think the truth will help him very much in that respect,'' said Emily, once again folding her hands. ''If what you believe is true, Mr. Harvey was sold into prison. I hardly think that that knowledge will provide him much consolation.'' She paused and looked across the table at Ransom, the blue of her eyes deepening with intensity. ''The only thing that would help him would be if he made a conscious decision to leave his sorrow behind and go on with his life.''

Lynn shot a glance at Emily, who had raised a cup of tea to her lips and was taking a reflective sip from it. Lynn hesitated for a moment, then continued eating.

MIRANDA SHAY had long since passed the sour stage of soddenness and had gone on to the trancelike phase of someone who has gotten drunk too early and stayed awake too long. She hadn't moved from the love seat since the detectives had left her, although she had slumped down so that her chin rested on her chest, which made her look like a marionette that had been carelessly tossed aside.

A deep darkness had settled into the living room, the only illumination being provided by the television set that continued to flicker impotently in the corner where it had always stood. The ten o'clock news was on, and she was thankful that there was only brief mention of her daughter's murder. But it was enough to remind her of all the trouble Laura had caused during her lifetime. She spared a single, coarse laugh at the thought that she should have expected Laura to cause as much trouble in death.

Her mind went back to the night of the rape and the scene that had taken place right in this living room. Laura had come home, her clothes torn and her body cut and bruised, and told them that she'd been attacked and who had done it. Mrs. Shay remembered the fury that George, her husband, had expressed when he heard Laura's story, and how he vowed he would have the boy locked up. There had been a great deal of relish in George Shay's eyes at the thought of the humiliation he would bring down on one of the neighborhood's most prominent families. The years of financial stagnation and disappointment Shay had suffered had left the scars necessary to take delight in someone else's downfall, no matter what it cost his own daughter. He had spent nearly half an hour yelling at the top of his lungs about how he would drag them through the dirt before he took his nearly hysterical daughter to the hospital to be examined and treated. But he hadn't been in a fury when they returned home.

Mrs. Shay could still remember the look on her husband's face, the low cunning with which she'd become so familiar, synonymous with the hatching of one of his "brilliant" schemes. He looked as if the spirit of the devil himself had entered into him. She was afraid she knew what was coming. And then he explained his plan to her.

She listened at first with a mother's indignation, not so much because of what he was intending to do with his daughter's tragedy but because after all the years of George's failed plans, she had no faith that this one would succeed. And she even offered a lame protest about their daughter's honor. But loath as she was to admit it, she inwardly thought that for once her husband might have hit on something, and she stood by him while he made the call.

The memory of that call brought Mrs. Shay back to the present: it was that call that ended up ruining them all, and eventually caused the current mess. She laughed again. Yes, it was exactly like all of her husband's other plans, all come to nothing. Only this one had been worse. They ended up penniless, and after George saw the outcome of his plans and realized what he'd done to his daughter, he couldn't bear it. He spent what was left of his life drinking himself to death—not that it took him that long.

Mrs. Shay lay there for a few more minutes, nursing her grievances with as much grace as she'd nursed the bottle of gin. She thought sadly that the past had given her nothing but a daughter who didn't love her and a husband who was a loser. Now even they were gone and there didn't appear to be any prospects for her life to change in the future. And now she was being hounded by those detectives as well, who thought she knew more than she was telling. It had almost been fun keeping it from them. She managed a hard smile as she reminded herself that she *did* know more than she was telling. But her smile faded quickly. It wasn't out of simple stubbornness or malice that she had refused to tell that Detective Ransom the identity of the rapist, but out of a deeply ingrained sense of self-preservation. The upper hand that they had held all those years ago had quickly turned and come down on them with a merciless slap, leaving them without means or recourse. And now she didn't know if there was still any danger for her in what had happened; the whole thing had been over and done with so long ago. How was she or anyone else to know that they would eventually find out that Ben Harvey was innocent and that Laura's death would rake the whole thing up again? It wasn't *her* fault.

Her head lolled to the side at the thought of the police coming back again and again until they got what they wanted. The police didn't believe that Ben Harvey was the murderer...and it would probably be harder to convince them he was guilty this time. This time...

It was as this thought came to her that the full import of what was happening entered her gin-soaked mind. The police *didn't* think that Ben was the killer. That's why they wanted to know the identity of the rapist. And she knew it. She alone knew it.

Miranda struggled to straighten herself up in her seat, her eyes wide with excitement. Eight years ago, along with the rest of her family, she'd been paid for her silence, only to have it backfire. She'd then found herself in the position of risking danger to herself if she talked. This time that danger was gone. All she had to do was utter the name to the detectives, and the man who'd screwed them over so completely would be ruined.

With some difficulty she hauled herself off the love seat and wavered her way to the small table in the corner on which she kept the phone. She picked up the receiver, unmindful of the new danger she was risking.

TEN

THE FIRST THING the next morning Ransom and Gerald set out for Tony Thornton's home. Thornton had eschewed the tight-knit, close community of the southwest side, where he'd grown up in the unparalleled elegance enjoyed only by the families who could afford the "top of the hill." He chose instead to live in a luxury high-rise condominium on North Avenue at the south end of Lincoln Park.

Despite himself, Ransom was impressed that Thornton had not chosen to live in one of the many new high rises constantly springing up around the city, buildings that Ransom viewed as atrocities that drew the kind of residents who couldn't bear the thought of living in a space that had already been occupied by someone else, mindless of the fact that their new homes, going for hundreds of thousands of dollars, were held together by spit and paste. Thornton had instead moved his young family into a stately building, decades old, with ornate patterns chiseled into its exterior and granite grates across the lower halves of the windows. The building stood midblock, and its presence was so impressive and imposing it seemed like a majestic masthead to the whole of Lincoln Park. Ransom smiled to himself, remembering that no matter how impressive the scene now appeared, the park had once been a graveyard.

There was a small crescent of a driveway for loading and unloading of residents in front of the entrance. Gerald pulled the car into it as far to the right as possible, leaving barely enough room for another car to squeeze through on the left. As the two of them climbed out of the car, a man of about fifty years came out of the door at a brisk pace. He was wearing a bright red cap with a black bill, and a matching coat that went down almost to his ankles. He said genially, "Excuse me, sir, but you can't park there." The gold buttons on his coat glinted in the sun, and he smiled ruefully as he spoke, revealing a gold tooth next to his left canine that looked as if it had been chosen to match the buttons.

"Yes, we can," said Ransom, flashing his badge at the man.

"Oh, my goodness!" he replied, his expression conveying that he couldn't imagine what business the police would have in his building.

"We're here to see Tony Thornton."

"Oh, dear, is anything the matter?"

Ransom produced his most unreadable smile and said, "We're just here for a chat."

"Well…" The doorman glanced at the car as if he would have liked to mount a further protest, but he apparently decided not to. "Step inside, please."

They followed the doorman into the vast expanse of a foyer. It had a spotless marble floor and rows of columns on both sides that were for decoration rather than support. There were floor-to-ceiling windows at opposite ends of the foyer, and light streamed through the tall bushes planted just outside, dappling the floor. It gave Ransom the feeling of being in an overly elaborate greenhouse. Gerald, on the other hand, slowly took in the surroundings with widened eyes, like a very young boy on his first visit to a museum. An engineer in a clean white jumpsuit was at the east end of the foyer slowly pushing a large machine across the floor, polishing the marble.

The doorman went to a mock-Grecian podium on which rested a telephone. He picked up the receiver and dialed a number. After waiting a few moments he said, "Yes? Mrs. Thornton? There are two gentlemen here to see Mr. Thornton." He didn't lay any particular stress on the word "gentlemen," but he managed to sound doubtful when he said it. He continued, "They *say* they're from the police." Here he infused a note of incredulity into his voice, meant to show the resident that he was sure the matter must be some silly mistake. After listening for a moment, he said, "Very well," and replaced the receiver. He then turned to the detectives and said with a smile, "Mrs. Thornton says you may go up. Suite ten-oh-two." He sounded as if he was impressed with the lady's largess. He preceded them across the foyer, held open the inner door for them, and stepped back with a half-smile that favored his gold tooth. As Ransom passed through the door, he was tempted to toss the man a nickel.

The lobby was covered with thick, wine-colored carpeting, immaculately clean. There were two elevators framed in festoons of grapevines with bulging fruit, all of which was painted white, and on each side of the elevator doors were identical, three-foot-high gilded statues of cats regally perched on spheres.

"You know," said Gerald as they waited, "we don't have any real reason to question Tony Thornton."

"I'm not going to question him, Gerald, I'm going to talk to him."

"We don't have any reason to do that, either. I mean, look at this place. Even if Laura knew him in high school, there's nothing to link him to her in the present."

"There's one thing," Ransom replied. "Money. Emily pointed something out to me last night that I hadn't con-

sidered." He paused and shook his head. "I really must
be slipping."

Gerald smiled. "Miss Emily is pretty smart."

Ransom returned a wry smile. "I like to think that I'm
not exactly ground beef."

"I didn't mean that," said Gerald, laughing.

"I never thought I'd see the day when I'd need Emily's
validation to bring my partner into agreement with me."

A seriousness had entered his tone that Gerald took as
a bad sign. He sighed with frustration.

The elevator arrived and the detectives stepped aside as
an elderly woman exited. She was wearing makeup so
thick it looked as if it had been applied with a roller. It
was apparently an attempt to recapture youth, but failed
miserably. The makeup had settled into her age lines, accentuating them instead of covering them up. Perched on
her head was a red wig whose color was far too even for
a woman of her age.

"God," said Ransom as the elevator doors slid shut,
"if you ever see me doing that, will you kindly shoot
me?"

"If I ever see you doing that, I'll ask for a new partner," Gerald replied as he pressed the button for the tenth
floor. "Now, what did Emily have to say?"

Ransom shot him a glance, none too pleased at the
thought that Gerald really *did* want his reasoning vali-
dated.

"She said that accepting that George Shay tried blackmail, it's possible that once the truth came out about Harvey's innocence, Laura might have tried some blackmail
herself."

Ransom had the satisfaction of seeing his partner's face
go blank with surprise, as if it had entered his head for
the first time that Ransom might have been right all along.

"And as I told you before," Ransom continued, "Thornton is the only one remotely connected—I know, remotely—with the case who's in a financial position to be blackmailed."

"Well, that would connect him in theory," Gerald said slowly, "but we don't have any *evidence* to connect him. So what reason are you going to give him for questioning him?"

Ransom smiled. "Background."

The elevator doors slid open with the sound of a single bell, and they stepped out into the hallway. The decorations were almost identical to those in the lobby, with the same thick carpeting and overly ornate carvings around the doorframes. There were only three doors, none of which were open in anticipation of their arrival. They quickly located the door marked 1002.

"A doorbell," said Ransom. "How quaint."

Gerald pressed the button and they waited.

After an interval long enough to convince Ransom that the Thorntons were purposely making them wait, the door was opened by a woman who looked to be in her mid-twenties, although she was done up like a society matron at least twenty years her senior. She had golden blond hair, heavily lacquered into place, lashes thick with mascara, and lips painted a pale red. She wore a tan dress with vertical stripes of metallic gold woven into the fabric.

Dry-clean-only for everyday wear, Ransom thought to himself.

"Yes?" she said, her tone communicating to them that they were neither expected nor welcome.

A mischievous smiled played about Ransom's lips. "We're here to see Tony Thornton. I'm Detective Ransom and this is Detective White. Would you announce us?"

She bristled at being addressed as the hired help. "I'm Mary Thornton," she announced, "Tony's wife."

"Oh," said Ransom, manufacturing an apologetic smile, "Would you tell him we're here, then?"

She looked at him for a moment before relenting and silently leading them into the apartment.

"Such a *young* woman," Ransom said under his breath.

Gerald stifled a laugh just before his jaw dropped open at the sight of the living room of the apartment. There was a ballroom sense of size and splendor to the living room. The floor was polished wood, the center of which was covered with a massive, expensive Oriental rug; in the middle of the high ceiling was a three-tiered crystal chandelier that resembled a wedding cake made of glass. Windows along the north wall looked out over the park, while the windows to the east showed the lake, only partially obscured by a building further down the street.

As with Alice and Marc Peters's house, the Thorntons' apartment contained furniture that Ransom would have expected to find in the home of a much older couple; but unlike the Peterses' home, here even the furniture reeked of money, so much so that Ransom wouldn't have been surprised to find that the posh sofa, the reproduction of a fainting couch, and the tastefully arranged groupings of comfortable chairs were stuffed with hundred-dollar bills rather than down or foam.

"Right this way, gentlemen. My husband is in his study." Mary Thornton looked pleased with the effect the living room had had, at least on Gerald, as she led them down a hallway on the right. There were three doors on either side of the hall, all closed against prying eyes. At the end of the hall was a swinging door that had been propped open to reveal the kitchen.

Mary stopped at the second door on the left and gave a double knock before entering.

"Come in," said a male voice from inside.

She opened the door and went into the room with the practiced efficiency of someone who is accustomed to bringing important clients in to meet her important husband. They found Tony Thornton crouching down and buttoning the coat of a little girl who looked to be about four years old and was a carbon copy of her mother, only without the hair spray and makeup.

"There you go, honey," Thornton said as he fastened the last button. "Mommy will drop you off at the center, all right?"

"Yes, Daddy," the girl replied dutifully, though she didn't look too happy about it.

Thornton rose and faced the detectives.

"These are the gentlemen who called late yesterday," his wife explained. Then she introduced them.

Tony Thornton was an impressive presence. He had an air of aristocracy that made him seem reserved beyond his years. It was a contrast to his wife, who seemed to be working at maturity. His hair was dark brown and combed straight back, his eyes were green, and he was wearing a tailored dark gray suit. When he reached out and shook hands with each detective in turn, Ransom registered the grip as firm and confident. It also crossed his mind that Tony Thornton might be the type of man he would enjoy disliking.

"Yes," Thornton said smoothly, "Mary told me you'd be stopping by."

At the sound of her name, Mary took the little girl's hand and said, "Come along, Amy. Daddy's busy and it's time for us to go, anyway."

She led Amy out into the hallway. The little girl shot

a forlorn glance over her shoulder at her father as he closed the door after them.

The room appeared to be a combination den and office with a large mahogany desk across one corner. Rows of books were shelved on one side of the room, but there was an entertainment center with a twenty-seven-inch television prominently displayed in a hutch in the middle of the books.

"I can't imagine what you gentlemen have to talk to me about," Thornton said as he crossed behind his desk. With an elegant sweep of his hand he motioned them to the chairs facing the desk. "But I'm certainly interested."

"You must've heard or read about the murder of Laura Shay," said Ransom once he was seated.

"Laura Shay?" Thornton tilted his head slightly and contrived to look puzzled. "I'm afraid I've been busy. I haven't seen much of the news the past few days."

"The past few days?" Ransom said, raising an eyebrow.

Thornton seemed to freeze for a split second, then said, "I'm sorry, I was assuming that you were talking about something that happened recently."

Ransom smiled. "Of course. Well, Laura Shay was murdered two nights ago. We understand that she went to high school with you."

"Laura Shay?" Thornton produced his puzzled expression again, allowing it to deepen, then suddenly broke into a smile. "Oh, Laura! Yes. Well, we went to the same high school at the same time. I wouldn't exactly say we went there together." He sat back and rested his arms on the arms of the chair, satisfied with his own answer.

"You did know her, then?"

The tone in which this question was asked caused a

momentary glitch in Thornton's calm. He noticed for the first time the small spiral notebook in Gerald's hand.

"What on earth are you doing?"

Gerald looked up. "Taking notes."

Thornton slowly transferred his gaze from Gerald to Ransom. "Am I being questioned?"

"No, no, no," Ransom replied smoothly. "We thought perhaps you could give us a little background about Miss Shay."

There was a pause before Thornton responded. "I don't know how I can help you. I knew who she was; I didn't *know* her."

"Well, nobody seems to have known her very well, so we need to get as much information about her as we can."

This didn't seem to mollify Thornton, particularly since Ransom's tone was anything but reassuring. However, he didn't protest any further.

"So, you did know her in high school."

"As I said, I knew who she was."

"Hmm. Have you seen her since then...or heard from her?"

"Good heavens, no! Why would I?" He sounded much less like the polished executive when he said this.

"No reason," Ransom replied with a nonchalant shrug. "I just thought that since you knew"—he stopped himself, smiled sheepishly, and continued—"I'm sorry, since she was one of your high school acquaintances, perhaps you'd seen something of her."

Thornton stared at him blankly for a moment. It gave Ransom a chance to assess the young man. Although Thornton exuded sophistication, there was something disingenuous about him that put Ransom in mind of a time when he'd had to question a company of actors. When dealing with them, he'd had to try to penetrate their theatrical facades to get some notion of what they were really thinking and feeling. Though Thornton wasn't an actor by profession, it crossed Ransom's mind that perhaps he was forced into playing a role simply by being a young man who was expected to act like an executive, no matter how unnaturally it might come to him. But whatever the reason, for Ransom there was no getting past the impression that Thornton was playing a role.

What came next did nothing to dispel that impression. Thornton made a show of letting his barrier down and leaned across the desk, lowering his voice and adopting the manner of someone having a man-to-man talk with another gentleman. To the detective, it seemed like a learned technique.

"You know," Thornton said, "I don't want to sound… like a snob, because I'm not. I don't look down on other people. However, that being said, Laura Shay and I didn't exactly run in the same circles, if you know what I mean. I don't know why you would think I had anything to do with her."

Ransom shrugged again. "Sometimes circles intersect. And no matter how different people are, we all have the same basic…needs."

Thornton's sleek forehead creased attractively. His expression was a comedy of bewilderment. "I'm sorry, you've really lost me."

"Never mind," Ransom said lightly. "So, you said you haven't had anything to do with Laura since high school, correct?"

"Not since or during. Like I said, we didn't run in the same circles."

"It's been a long time. Her circumstances might have changed."

"But according to the paper—" Thornton said before breaking off abruptly. His face flushed a deep crimson.

"Ah," said Ransom, "you *did* read about it."

Thornton sighed. "I'm sorry," he said, glancing down at the desk, then back up at the detective. "I didn't mean to mislead you, but I also didn't want anyone to think that I was at all interested in this matter."

"I don't believe anyone would have thought that just because you read about it in the newspaper."

Thornton sighed again and managed to look fittingly abashed. "I know, but just the fact that I went to high school with her—I mean, at the same time—brought *you* here, didn't it? I didn't want my name to become connected with this business just because I had the misfortune of graduating when I did."

"But why would anyone feel that way?"

"It doesn't matter what *anyone* thinks, only what my father thinks. He's very old-fashioned about the family name."

"Your father is...?"

"Mitchell Thornton. He's the owner of Thornton Investments, one of the oldest and most respected brokerage houses in Chicago." He managed to sound as if he were reading a prospectus when he said this. "In fact, I went to work for him when I graduated from college. If I brought any scandal to the family name—even by proxy—I think he'd disown me."

Thornton sounded as if he meant this figuratively, but there was definitely a note of anxiety in his delivery.

There was a pause before Ransom said, "As far as I know, there's no reason for you to be involved in a scandal, is there?"

"No." Thornton looked quite discomfited by the way Ransom had chosen his words.

"So," Ransom continued broadly, "as I said, what we're looking for is background. Since you say you didn't know Laura directly, can you tell me what you knew *of* her?"

"What do you mean?"

"Well, you knew who she was. How is that?"

Thornton's expression grew more incredulous. "We were in the same school. I heard about her."

"What did you hear?"

Thornton rested his elbows atop his desk and touched the tips of his fingers together. He pursed his lips for a moment, then said, "Gentlemen don't talk about that sort of thing."

"Were you a gentleman when you were a teenager?" Ransom asked with smile.

A flash of red washed over Thornton's face like a wave passing over sand. "No," he said ruefully, "I suppose I wasn't."

"So what did you hear about Laura?"

Thornton spoke slowly, as if to demonstrate that answering such a question was difficult because of his breeding. "I heard that she was...available."

"Hmm," Ransom said thoughtfully. "Was she available to you?"

"What?" He fought to retain some vestige of his facade, but he was losing the fight. "To me? I never would've had anything to do with someone like Laura Shay."

"I realize that under normal circumstances—"

"Under *any* circumstances. She was a—" He broke off just short of using a much more unflattering term than he'd chosen before.

"Yes?" said Ransom, raising an eyebrow.

Thornton looked away from him. "Just associating with

a girl like that could hurt your reputation. I mean, I realize that a lot of people don't think anything like reputation matters anymore, but it *does* matter. At least to people who have any sense at all. I come from a prominent family. I was brought up knowing what it meant to maintain respectability in a world where things like that have gone out of style."

Ransom found it curious that Thornton had averted his eyes while saying this. "At any cost?" he asked.

Thornton looked up at him. "What?"

"Do you feel the need to maintain your respectability at any cost?"

"I'm afraid I don't know what you mean," Thornton replied, trying to regain his composure but obviously frustrated with the train the conversation had taken. "If you don't do anything that's not respectable, there's never any problem."

Ransom smiled. "And yet, some of the most bizarre acts in the world have been performed by people who were raised with a very tight rein."

Thornton blinked at him, then sighed. "All right, all right. I suppose that's true. And all right, I did hear about Laura. But no, I didn't have anything to do with her." He sounded much more natural saying it this time. After a pause he added, "What I don't understand is why you would think I did?"

Ransom crossed his legs as he said, "Well, we had heard that during high school Laura had a rather intense crush on you."

"Really?" Thornton said with a slight smile. Apparently no matter what her reputation, he was pleased to have been found attractive. Suddenly the smile disappeared. "I suppose that's possible, but that doesn't have anything to do with me." He manufactured an embarrassed smile. "I mean, people get crushes on people they don't know all the time. Like movie stars."

"Hmm," said Ransom, narrowing his eyes at the young man. Thornton looked away and his face reddened again. This time the color lingered.

"So," said Ransom, uncrossing his legs and straightening up in his chair, "I assume that when you were in high school you heard about the attack on Laura."

"The rape? Yes, everybody did."

"What did you think about it?"

"What did I *think*?" Thornton repeated incredulously. "What *could* I think? It was a terrible thing."

"No, what I meant was, did you have any idea who did it?"

He shrugged. "I heard that black kid did it. He was arrested. Why would I think anything else?"

"I don't know," said Ransom with a sigh. "I thought perhaps your friends speculated about the case."

Thornton released a sardonic laugh. "My friends didn't know enough about it to speculate. And besides, that guy was arrested right away. Why would we think anybody else did it?"

"Tell me, did Alice and Marc Peters run in your circle?" Ransom asked.

"Alice and Marc? Yes. Sort of, I guess. I knew them better than some people, but I didn't know them that well."

"I just wondered, because Marc Peters was a neighbor of yours, and Alice was his girlfriend. And I understand that Alice knew Laura fairly well."

"Did she?" Thornton replied, the words ringing false. Ransom was sure that Thornton had been aware of the friendship, and that meant that there was a much closer connection to Laura than Thornton was willing to admit.

"My goodness," said Ransom with a smile, "you hardly knew anyone in high school, did you?"

Thornton's eyebrows came together. "I knew a lot of people, Mr. Ransom, just not the ones you're interested in. Sorry."

Ransom allowed a significant pause to lapse, during which he directed an intense gaze at Thornton, who continued to face the detective although he averted his eyes.

"You know, I find that very interesting," Ransom said at last.

"What?"

"That you didn't know that Laura Shay was enamored of you, even though she was close to people that you knew. That sort of thing has a way of getting around in high school."

Thornton had successfully regained his professional demeanor, but there was no disguising the fact that Ransom's persistence on this point was causing him some uncertainty. His face was blank but his brow was slightly furrowed, as if he wasn't even sure how confused he should be.

"Somebody might have mentioned it sometime," he said, "but I certainly don't remember it. It *was* a long time ago. And except for the fact that Alice befriended her for reasons nobody could understand, I had absolutely no contact with her."

Ransom gazed at him for a moment. Then a broad smile spread across his face.

"Well, that's that, then, isn't it?"

"I DON'T THINK that got us any further along," said Gerald as he turned the keys in the ignition. The doorman was standing just inside the outer lobby door, peering through the glass at them and looking greatly relieved that they were clearing the driveway. And they were leaving none too soon; an Audi, painted the shade of gold usually reserved for credit cards, was waiting in the entrance to the driveway for the detective's lower-class car to pull out. Either the owner hadn't wanted to risk a scratch trying to squeeze by, or he simply didn't want his expensive car to be seen too close to its poor cousin.

"He lied," said Ransom as he unwrapped a cigar.

"About having read about the murder in the paper, I know. But I think the reason he gave was pretty plausible, especially for someone with his background."

"I wasn't talking about that," said Ransom as he lit the cigar, taking a few short puffs to get it going.

"He lied about something else?" Gerald's expression was so perplexed it would've made Ransom laugh if he hadn't been so vexed.

"He lied about how well he knew those people—at least the Peterses. Perhaps even Laura."

"Where do you get that?"

Ransom looked at his partner as if he thought Gerald might be purposely being obtuse. "He slipped. He said that Alice Peters befriended Laura 'for reasons nobody could understand.' Obviously he was aware of the relationship, and it was much more a topic of conversation among his group than he would have us believe. Or he heard about it directly from the Peterses. Either way he lied about it."

"Well," Gerald offered tentatively, "that could be just more of what he told us before—that he wanted to distance himself from the whole thing. He admitted that."

"Not until I caught him in his first lie."

Gerald shrugged. "His explanation still makes sense."

"That he didn't want anyone to think he even *knew* Laura because it might hurt his family name?"

"Some people are like that. Besides, you know how the press is. And Thornton already knows that the murder has made news. Lots of people would be afraid of getting involved."

Ransom looked at him for a moment in silence before relenting. "Perhaps," he said, taking a drag from the cigar and releasing the smoke into the car. Gerald shot a significant glance at the passenger window, and Ransom rolled it down with an impatient sigh. It wasn't that he didn't care about Gerald's feelings; he simply didn't like to have his train of thought interrupted by mundane things, especially when he was frustrated. "But there's something else to consider: Thornton's explanation for lying to us also gives him a motive."

"For what?" Gerald exclaimed. "We don't have any evidence to show he's done anything at all."

"I realize that," Ransom snapped. "I was referring to the blackmail scenario. He has a father who would do anything to hush up scandal, and he had the money to pay off blackmail, both when the rape happened and now. If his father really is the ogre of respectability young Thornton would have us believe, and very protective of the family name, then that gives Tony a perfect motive for murder, if Laura chose to threaten his reputation now. The only thing is...oh, damn!"

He vigorously stubbed the cigar out in the ashtray, something he almost never did until they'd burned all the way down to the plastic tip. It was a sign that he was even more frustrated with the case than he'd let on.

"What's wrong?" Gerald asked.

"I keep coming back to the fact that the money given to the Shays—if they were indeed paid off—was stopped. Emily believes that that's the most important aspect of the whole thing and she's right. You know as well as I do that once a blackmailer has gotten hold of you, you're hooked for good.''

''So?''

''So why kill her now? Why didn't he just kill her then? Why the payoff, and why did it stop?'' He was silent for a few moments as Gerald steered the car through the small turnaround at the end of North Avenue and headed back to Area Headquarters. Though Ransom said nothing, he drummed his fingers loudly on the armrest. Finally he said, ''You know, Gerald, if we don't come up with some hard evidence, it's likely that whoever killed Laura Shay will go free...again.''

Gerald sighed. ''So far as we know, the only thing Tony Thornton is guilty of is being born rich. And you can't throw someone in jail for that.''

Ransom smiled. ''No. But I'd like to.''

ELEVEN

THE REMAINDER of the drive back to Area Headquarters was accomplished in almost complete silence. Although Ransom recognized that it wasn't unusual for the trail to run to a dead end, especially on a case in which the crime lab was unable to come up with anything, it was not something that a detective is likely to be pleased with. Especially someone like Ransom, who prided himself on being able to unravel the most complicated problem.

Gerald sat behind the wheel dividing his attention between the traffic and his own thoughts. Throughout the many cases they had handled together, Gerald had been able to remain confident in his partner's abilities. Even when he personally didn't understand Ransom's reasoning, he went along with him, painfully conscious of the fact that Ransom was almost always right. Now Gerald wasn't too sure, and it left him in the position of being at odds—at least mentally—with where Ransom was taking the investigation. But Gerald reminded himself that there had been other times when he truly believed Ransom to be way off the mark, only to find that he'd been right all along; and what Ransom believed had happened in this case was perfectly plausible. If only there were some concrete evidence on which to base it. The worst thing to Gerald's way of thinking was that if they indeed had on their hands a case that they were not destined to solve, he would find that fact much easier to accept than Ransom would. But Gerald also had the feeling that it would be easier for Ransom to accept a case being unsolved than to find out he was mistaken about it.

When they arrived back at Area, Ransom returned to his office without stopping to report to Newman, so he wasn't surprised when Newman appeared in his doorway just moments after he'd arrived. But he *was* surprised by Newman's demeanor. He looked like a jury foreman about to deliver a verdict with which he didn't agree. He slumped against the door as if his underpinnings had been removed, and swept an oily forelock off his face.

"Ransom, I've got some news for you that you're not gonna like."

"What's that?"

Newman sighed as if he was weary just thinking about what would come next. "Ben Harvey has been taken in for questioning."

"What?" Ransom exclaimed, rising from his chair. "By whom? This is *my* case."

Newman motioned for him to sit down, but Ransom didn't comply. "By Detective MacNamara."

"Who the hell is that?"

"He's with Area Two. South Side."

"The murder took place in our area. What in the hell are they doing questioning him there?"

"They're not investigating Laura Shay's murder. They're looking into the murder of her mother."

Ransom's anger quickly vanished and was replaced by genuine surprise. "Miranda Shay's been murdered? When?"

"MacNamara called to let us know. He knew we were handling the Laura Shay thing. Mrs. Shay was found this morning by the mail carrier." He paused, then added, "They'll be expecting us to share information with them. We do have information to share, don't we?"

Ransom lowered himself back into the old-fashioned wooden swivel chair behind his desk. "We don't have any evidence against Ben Harvey, no." He looked almost amused.

"Is there evidence against somebody else?"

Ransom spread his hands apologetically. "No."

"Dammit, Ransom, don't you have *anything* yet?"

"Just a lot of questions."

"You've got to be kidding me!"

"What would you like me to do, manufacture evidence?" Ransom replied calmly, though it was taking an effort.

"You know I don't mean that!" Newman had started to go red in the face. Ransom's reaction hadn't been anything like what he was expecting, and he was finding it very perplexing.

"Well, in lieu of evidence all we can do is question people and see if we come up with anything."

Newman gaped at him for a moment. Then a slight smile appeared. "Look, I know you. You must have some idea about it."

"Oh, I have plenty of ideas, but since even my partner seems to think I'm heading in the wrong direction, I'm certainly not going to share it with anyone outside of our area."

"I'm not outside the area," Newman said flatly.

Ransom pursed his lips for a moment, then smiled. "Of course you're not." He then explained to Newman the possibility of blackmail, both eight years ago and more recently. Newman listened without comment and, much to Ransom's surprise, didn't bluster when he'd finished the explanation.

"There's no proof of any of this?" Newman said after giving it some silent thought.

"None at all."

Newman glanced up at him. "Well, you don't have to sound so happy about it."

"I'm not happy about it. I'm not happy that I can't prove anything yet. Let's just say so far it's a theory that fits what's happened." He stopped and sighed deeply. "I suppose it's just as likely that Harvey killed both the women, but we don't have any proof of that, either. At least not in the daughter's case. But there's one thing to be happy about: now that there's been another murder, there's the possibility that there will be some evidence of something." He stopped again and smiled broadly. "Unless, of course, it's just a coincidence they were both murdered at this time."

Newman grimaced at him. "You're funny." He dropped a small sheet of paper, torn from a notepad, on Ransom's desk. "That's MacNamara's number."

Ransom picked it up and looked at it. Newman turned and walked out of the office, pausing in the doorway just long enough to say, "Cooperate," before disappearing.

Ransom returned his usual opaque smile, leaving Newman to wonder just how cooperative he would be with detectives from another area. But in reality, Ransom was excited. The fact that they'd brought Harvey in for questioning meant that at least at this early stage they were focusing their investigation on him, probably to the exclusion of everything else, so he didn't think there was much chance of their investigations intersecting for the moment.

He rested his hand on the telephone receiver for a few seconds, then snatched it off its cradle and dialed the number on the slip of paper. The phone rang four times before it was answered by a stereotypically gruff, cynical voice that said, "Violent Crimes. Dombey."

"Hello. This is Detective Ransom at Area Three. I'm calling Detective MacNamara."

"He's busy right now. Want me to have him call you?"

"No," Ransom replied steadily, "I want you to get him. I'm on the Laura Shay murder, and if he's busy questioning Ben Harvey, he'll most likely want to talk to me before he continues."

Dombey had emitted an understanding "Huh" when Ransom said the girl's name. When he finished, Dombey said, "Hold on. I'll see if I can interrupt him."

Ransom experienced a slight pang of sympathy for both of his fellow cops. He wouldn't want to be the one to interrupt an interrogation, any more than he'd want to be interrupted while questioning a suspect. But it was important.

As he expected, there was a lengthy interval before anyone returned to the phone. He could hear the familiar bustle of the squad room in the background, then the sound of the receiver being roughly retrieved from a wooden desktop.

"MacNamara." The voice was very deep. Ransom smiled at the thought of how Harvey was responding to this imperious tone. Most likely it would merely increase his defiance.

"This is Detective Ransom. I'm working on the Laura Shay murder."

"I know," MacNamara replied, amusement in his voice. "I've heard of you."

"You have?"

"I mean I been told you were on the other end of this."

"What happened?" Ransom asked.

"Mailman found her this morning. Mail slot's in the front door. When he was stuffing some sales catalogues through it, the door opened—it wasn't latched right—and there she was in the middle of the floor.''

"Strangled?"

"Yup. Looks like he used a piece of wire to do it. But it probably wasn't too hard to do. She looked like she was skunked when it happened."

"Sounds exactly the same as the daughter's murder. You said the front door was unlatched. Is that how the murderer got in?"

"No," MacNamara replied, his throat rattling. "Looks like he picked the lock on the back door."

"Was it a clumsy job?"

"Not really."

"Um-hmm," Ransom said with a sigh. "Do you have any evidence?"

"Not yet."

"Then what made you bring in Harvey?"

There was a smirk in MacNamara's voice when he replied. "We knew about the Laura Shay thing—the rape and the murder—so of course we went out and picked up this Ben Harvey character."

"Has he said anything?"

There was a pause before MacNamara said, "No. Not really. Not yet. Doesn't have an alibi, though. Says he doesn't need one. Cocky little son of a bitch. Sounds like he's making fun of us when he answers questions."

Ransom could sympathize. "So you really don't have anything to hold him on."

"We'll find something." He sounded as if he didn't like it being put quite that bluntly. "Tell you the truth, I'm surprised that you haven't brought this guy in already."

"There's no evidence against him," Ransom replied. "Nothing at the crime scene. No witnesses. Nothing to connect him with the murder except the obvious. But that's not enough.''

"Well,'' MacNamara said broadly, "maybe now he's killed somebody else, we'll get something on him.''

Ransom allowed a beat to pass before saying, "But you don't have any evidence.''

"You know we don't have anything back from the lab yet.''

"I don't think you will. The killer didn't leave any traces at Shay's apartment. If it's the same person, I doubt if he would be stupid enough to leave evidence at the scene after being so careful the first time.''

"Hmmph. He was probably just lucky. We'll find something. There ain't a test that's gonna get him off the hook this time.''

Ransom took a moment to control his temper, then said evenly, "He wasn't guilty of the rape, Detective.''

"So they say. But we'll get him on this.''

Everyone is so willing to believe that Harvey is guilty of something, Ransom thought to himself with disgust, *even though he was innocent of the rape and there's no evidence against him in the murders.* Once again he recalled the words from *Oliver Twist: "I never was more convinced of anything in my life, than I am that that boy will come to be hung."*

"Why would he kill Mrs. Shay?'' Ransom asked.

"Revenge,'' MacNamara said loudly, as if he thought Ransom might be a bit slow and raising his voice was the way to get through to him. "Revenge against the whole family for what happened to him.''

"Um-hmm,'' said Ransom, smiling into the receiver. "Well, it would seem his task is now finished.''

"Huh?''

"The whole family's dead. There's nobody else to kill."

"You call just to make jokes?"

"No, I wanted to know if you'd found out anything that would help in my investigation, because I've run into a wall," Ransom said with practiced nonchalance.

"Not yet," MacNamara said, sounding extremely satisfied, "but I'll let you know when we do. We'll get something on this son of a bitch."

I doubt that, thought Ransom. Then he said, "Oh, one thing. When you get Miranda Shay's phone records, will you fax me a copy?"

"Her phone records? What the hell would we need them for? We know who killed her. What you think? She called Harvey and asked him to come over to do her?"

"Just in case there's no other evidence," Ransom replied, managing to put a shrug in his voice. "And it might help with my investigation."

"All right, all right," said MacNamara. "I'll have my partner get them and send them to you. I don't see what good they'll do, but they couldn't hurt."

Ransom gave him the fax number, then they hung up.

"I heard about Mrs. Shay," said Gerald as he came into the office and flopped down on the couch. "You talk to Area Two yet?"

Ransom made a temple of his fingers. "I just got off the phone with a charming gentleman named MacNamara who has taken Ben Harvey in for questioning."

"Really?" said Gerald, trying to keep his face blank. "Do they have any reason to do that?"

"No more than we have, although Detective MacNamara seems to believe that his suspicions are certainties."

"Well, this could be the break we need. Maybe there'll be something to go on this time."

Ransom shot him a glance. Although he had been thinking the same thing not ten minutes earlier, he still took this as another sign that Gerald didn't think he was producing on this case. He swallowed his pride with some difficulty and said, "Yes, I'm hoping it'll turn something up for us. And I started by asking MacNamara to get us Mrs. Shay's phone records."

Gerald blinked. "What for?"

Ransom sat back in his chair and pulled out a cigar, which he unwrapped and lit as he explained.

"A long shot, I know, but there's too much coincidence connected to this whole thing. Harvey is released and Laura Shay is killed, which makes it look like cause and effect. Then Mrs. Shay is killed, which MacNamara believes is because Harvey is taking revenge on the whole family."

Gerald tilted his head slightly and frowned. "Well, I suppose that's possible, but it seems…hard to believe. I can imagine him killing the daughter for revenge, but the mother?"

Ransom produced a wry smile. "Thank you, Gerald. It's nice to know we agree on something. So, as I've said before, in lieu of any evidence to the contrary, we go back to the rape as being the catalyst. We find that George Shay tried to blackmail the rapist—"

"We *think* that," Gerald corrected.

"All right," Ransom said slowly, "we *think* it. But somehow the blackmail goes awry. Then when Harvey is released, Laura Shay seizes the opportunity to follow in her father's footsteps, and she's killed—cause and effect. So maybe—just maybe—Mrs. Shay decided to try the same thing."

"You're right," said Gerald, "that is a long shot. Especially since we don't have anything to prove that any of this took place, except for the fact that the Shays got a windfall to send their daughter away for a couple of semesters at U of C."

"Granted," said Ransom, blowing a stream of smoke toward the window. "But think back to when we last talked to Mrs. Shay. I said I was sure she knew the true identity of the rapist."

"Uh-huh."

Ransom raised an eyebrow. "You don't agree?"

Gerald smiled. "Well, as a matter of fact, I do. I just couldn't understand why, after you told her you thought the rape had something to do with the murder, she wouldn't tell us who it was if she knew." He stopped and Ransom spread his palms upward with a broad shrug. Gerald's face was blank for a moment. Then he grimaced and said, "Oh, Christ!"

"Exactly. If any of this is true it seems that Mrs. Shay was the last person we know of who knew the identity of the rapist."

"And she would know that she had him by the balls."

"That's a very apt way of putting it, Gerald." He paused and sighed. "Perhaps when they do an autopsy they'll find some sort of genetic deformity that would make an entire family tend toward blackmail."

They were silent for a few moments. Then Gerald said, "But do you really think all three of them would try to blackmail the same person, whoever it is?"

"If they were bitter enough—or foolish enough. Mrs. Shay seems to fit both categories. And Laura didn't have any reason to believe that she was risking her life by doing it, since nobody had been murdered yet, but her mother should have realized that there was danger in-

volved, if she was ever sober enough to realize anything.''
He stopped and thought for a minute, then said, ''More
and more I'm inclined to believe that Emily is right; it's
not so much that blackmail was paid initially that matters,
it's that the payments stopped. What on earth did the
Shays do that rendered them harmless to the rapist?''

''Did you tell any of this to MacNamara?''

Ransom leaned back in his chair again, took a drag
from the cigar, and expelled the smoke. ''Why would I
do that?''

''Jer...''

''It hasn't escaped my notice that you and I haven't
exactly been on the same page on this case. If you have
so much trouble believing my theory, how could I expect
someone else to?'' He curled his lips and added, ''And
it's not the least bit comforting that Newman was so re-
ceptive to it, but I think he'd go for any idea at this point
that at least gave the illusion of activity.''

There was a pause, then Gerald said, ''Look, it's not
that I don't agree, it's just...'' His voice trailed off as he
searched for the proper words. Finally, he smiled and said,
''It would be a lot more simple if Ben Harvey did it.''

IT WAS several hours before the report on Mrs. Shay's
phone calls was faxed from Area Two Headquarters, a
sign that MacNamara felt the request was a low priority.
Gerald was the one who brought it to Ransom, who was
immediately struck by the puzzled expression on his partner's face.

''Here it is,'' Gerald said as he handed the sheet to
Ransom, ''only one phone call, and you won't believe it.''

Ransom looked at the report, then glanced up at his
partner. ''But this is...''

Gerald nodded. ''Alice Peters.''

Ransom looked back down at the number, staring at it as if he half expected it to change into something that made more sense. "Didn't she say that she hadn't heard from Laura for several years?"

"That could still be true," Gerald replied. "We don't know why Mrs. Shay called her. We sure as hell don't know if Laura called her at all."

Ransom stared at the sheet a moment longer, then said, "You'd better call the wife and tell her we're going on overtime."

The drive out to the South Side was unbearably slow and frustrating in the late afternoon traffic: so much so that Ransom had smoked three of his cigars by the time they'd gotten off the expressway, much to Gerald's silent dismay. As they drove up the hill toward the Peterses' house Gerald gave a surreptitious sniff to the sleeve of his jacket and wrinkled his nose. He smelled as if he'd spent several hours in a bar. Fortunately, Ransom was too preoccupied to notice.

When Alice Peters opened the door in answer to their ring, her eyes widened with surprise.

"I didn't expect to see you again," she said, giving them a welcoming smile that was a bit more hesitant this time. It was clear she understood that their reappearance was not a good sign.

"There are a few more things we need to ask you," said Ransom.

"Of course. Come in."

They complied, and as she closed the door after them she offered them seats in the living room.

"Marc is just home from work. He's playing with the kids in the kitchen, so we can talk better out here."

They each took a chair in a small grouping away from the fireplace. Ransom got the feeling that Alice had

steered them away from her favorite spot for fear of taint-
ing it with whatever they'd come to talk about.

"Is something wrong?" she asked as she made a vain
attempt to tug the end of her skirt over her knees. "I really
don't think there's anything more I can tell you."

"Mrs. Peters," said Ransom, "I don't know if you've
heard about this, but there's been another murder."

"What?" Alice's face had the emptiness of someone
who truly can't believe what she's hearing.

"Laura's mother, Miranda Shay, was murdered last
night. Her body was found this morning."

"Oh, my God! Oh, my God!" she said, touching the
fingers of her right hand to her lips.

Ransom waited. He believed that if Mrs. Shay's call
had been innocent, it would be natural for Alice to vol-
unteer the information at this point. But she seemed to be
completely stunned. She stared straight ahead and continued to mutter softly.

"Mrs. Peters?" said Ransom. She looked at him and
the vagueness in her eyes dissipated. "So it's because of
this new murder that we need to ask you a few more
questions."

She didn't respond. She didn't appear to understand
what he was talking about.

"What is it, honey?"

Marc Peters was standing in the doorway from the hall
to the living room. He was fairly ordinary in appearance:
sandy hair in a business cut, blue eyes, and a round face
that signaled that if he wasn't very careful about his diet
he could easily run to fat. He was wearing the dark blue
pants of a business suit and a white shirt with the top two
buttons undone.

"Oh, honey, this is Detective Ransom and Detective
White."

They rose and nodded to Marc Peters as they were introduced, but nobody made a move to shake hands.

"Oh, yes," said Marc, "Alice mentioned that you guys talked to her yesterday." He looked from one detective to the other. "She thought you were done with her. Is something wrong?"

"Honey…" said Alice, moving to her husband and taking his hand, "Laura's mother was murdered last night."

Marc Peters' skin wasn't very dark, but it went noticeably pale at the news. "What? You're kidding!"

"No, it's true," said Ransom. He gestured to the chairs. "May we?"

Marc nodded and the four of them took their seats.

"I…that's terrible," Marc continued, obviously at pains to retain his composure. "But what does that have to do with us?"

"Well," said Ransom, "that's what we hope to find out." He turned to Alice. "Mrs. Peters, when we spoke with you, you said that you hadn't heard from Laura in years. Is that right?"

"Yes," Alice replied, the single syllable seeming to come forth from her without the benefit of breath.

"You haven't heard from any of the Shays?"

"No. Why would I?"

"Yes. As you said, after the rape, Laura really didn't have much to do with you, did she?"

"No. But she didn't have much to do with anybody, and she went away not long after, remember?" Alice replied.

Ransom stared at her for a moment, then said, "Mrs. Peters, Mrs. Shay's phone records show that she made one phone call just before she was murdered, and it was to this house."

Alice gazed back at him, her eyes so wide and blank

that she looked not only as if she'd been caught in headlights but as if she knew she was about to be struck down.

She shook her head slowly. "Mr. Ransom, I'm telling
you I didn't talk to Laura's mother. Why on earth would
she call here?"

"That's what we were hoping you could tell us."

"But I didn't talk to her. When was she supposed to
have called?"

"Last night, just before midnight."

Alice was silent for a moment. Then her face bright-
ened slightly. "Oh! You know, the phone *did* ring last
night, a long time after we went to bed. We're in bed at
ten, you know, with the kids and all. Marc has to get up
early." She turned to her husband and said, "You got up
and answered the phone, didn't you?"

Marc was looking at her without expression. There was
a beat before he said, "Yes. Yes, I did."

Ransom looked at the husband with new interest. "And
was it Mrs. Shay?"

"Yes, as a matter of fact, it was."

"Really?" Alice said with astonishment. "That's really
amazing! Why didn't you tell me?"

"I didn't…know you were awake. I didn't want to dis-
turb you."

"What did she want?" Ransom asked.

Marc took a deep breath. "To tell you the truth, I don't
know. She was drunk, and she was just rambling. I didn't
know what she was talking about."

"You know, if she was drunk—and she did drink, you
know, even back then—she probably just remembered me
and gave me a call," said Alice, obviously relieved that
it could be explained away so easily.

Ransom did not remove his eyes from the husband.
"Did she talk about money?"

"Well…as a matter of fact, she did say something about money. I didn't know what she was talking about, though."

"The Shays were always out of money," Alice offered. "She might've just thought we could loan her some, or give her some. But heck, we don't have any money to give anybody. We just get by ourselves." Her hand tightened around her husband's to reassure him that she didn't hold him responsible for that. Then she added, "Of course, she probably didn't know that."

Ransom glanced at Alice. "No, she wouldn't know that, would she?" He turned back to Marc and said, "But you did have money at one time, didn't you?"

"Well, my family does, yes."

"But your parents cut you off, didn't they?"

Marc glanced at his wife, then said, "I wouldn't exactly say they cut me off. My father just wanted me to make it on my own. He didn't want to just give me everything."

"I told you all that yesterday, Mr. Ransom," Alice said.

God, I've been a complete and total idiot, Ransom thought. His eyes narrowed and he said, "But you had money eight years ago, didn't you?"

"Like I said, my family did. It was never *mine.*"

"But certainly your father would help you out."

There was a long pause before Marc replied, "It depends on why I needed help."

"Hmm," Ransom said slowly. "Are you sure there wasn't another reason for your father withdrawing his support from you?"

"I told you," Marc exclaimed, his cheeks reddening, "he didn't cut me off. He just wanted me to make it on my own."

"So you said," Ransom replied. He crossed his legs

and began to drum the fingers of his right hand on his uppermost knee. He turned to Alice and said, "Mrs. Peters, what kind of girl was Laura Shay?"

"What?" Alice said, confused at the turn the conversation was taking.

"What kind of girl was she? Since we've been investigating her murder we've heard a lot about her character, most of it pretty bad, most of it having to do with sexual matters. But you were a friend of hers. What was she like?"

Alice hesitated. "I don't know what you mean."

Ransom sighed. "Did you consider her a good friend?"

"Well…yes. I did. She was loyal."

"Loyal?" Ransom said. "So she was trustworthy?"

"I guess."

"And you admitted that she was promiscuous, but was she trustworthy in that area, too?"

"I…I…really don't know what you mean."

Ransom recrossed his legs and explained. "She had another friend, Ruby Hawkins, who told us that she thought Laura was trustworthy when it came to men."

"Oh, yes," Alice said with something approaching a smile, "I remember Ruby…but…but I still don't know what you mean."

Ransom raised a single eyebrow. "You and your husband were going together in high school, is that right?"

"Yes," Alice said with a glance at Marc.

"Well, was Laura loyal? She was promiscuous, but was she the type of girl who would go after your boyfriend?"

"Oh," Alice said, a sigh showing that she was relieved again to at last understand. "No. No. She never would've done something like that. Not seriously."

"Not *seriously*." He turned to Marc and said, "Mr. Peters, did Laura ever flirt with you?"

"No."

"Oh, now, honey," said Alice, "you know she did. Laura flirted with all the guys." She turned to the detectives and added, "But she didn't mean anything by it. It wasn't serious. That's just the way she was."

Ransom continued to keep his eyes fixed on the husband.

"Did you know that she slept around?"

"Of course. Everybody knew."

"And she flirted with you." He let that statement hang in the air for a moment, then added, "Did you ever act on it?"

"No! Of course not," Marc said with indignation.

Ransom smiled. "That must've been difficult for you. I mean, if your friends were sexually active, to be hearing about things like that when you weren't."

"I had Alice. She was all I ever needed."

Ransom didn't miss the blush that quickly spread across Alice's face.

"Oh, I'm sorry. Then you and your wife were..."

"No, we weren't," said Alice, the redness deepening.

"Alice..." Marc said, his tone cautioning.

"I told you before I was a good girl."

Ransom turned back to Marc and said, "Oh, I really *did* misunderstand. You weren't sleeping together. So that must've been a very difficult time for you. It is for all teenage boys. And to be hearing about all your friends' exploits, and Laura being so available—"

"Mr. Ransom," Alice interceded, "you don't know what you're talking about. You didn't know Laura. She was my friend. She never, ever would have slept with Marc behind my back."

Ransom paused for just a second. "Not willingly."

Alice's face froze for a moment before her mouth

dropped open and her eyes widened. She looked as if the expected blow from the approaching headlights had finally been struck. She absently started to pull her hand away from her husband's, but he held it tight.

"Honey, he doesn't know what he's talking about. Don't listen to him." He looked Ransom in the eyes and said, "You're way off base, pal. And we've had enough of this! You get out of here! How the hell...how dare you come in here and make accusations like this! And you have no kind of proof at all! Get out!"

"Oh, not just yet, Mr. Peters. There are a few more questions to answer."

"No! No more questions!" He looked torn between his desire to get up and physically throw the detectives out of his house, and the fear that if he let go of his wife's hand he'd lose her forever.

Ransom flashed a malevolent smile. "I'm afraid I'm going to have to insist."

"I don't care if you insist or what! You have no right! You come in here making these wild insinuations, upsetting my wife for no reason, and you have no basis for them. I want you out of here!"

Alice continued to stare past them as if she were oblivious to what was being said and was watching her life crumble in the distance.

"Mr. Peters," Ransom said calmly, "there is proof of the identity of the rapist."

This brought Marc up short. His face went even whiter, and he almost lost his grip on Alice's hand. "What?"

"Are you aware that Ben Harvey was proven innocent of the rape?"

"Of course I am. Everybody is."

"And do you know how he was proven innocent?"

"Well..." he started to answer, then stopped himself. "No, I don't."

"Through a DNA test. It's something that wasn't widely used when Laura was raped, but it is now. The same test that freed Ben Harvey can prove who raped Laura Shay."

Marc's face was a complete blank for a number of seconds. He looked as if he were having trouble assimilating this new information. At last he said, "Well, you can't make me submit to any testing. Don't be crazy! That crime was a hundred years ago!"

Although Alice's expression didn't change, she suddenly snatched her hand away from her husband's. Tears began to run down her face.

"Perhaps not for that crime," said Ransom, leaning in toward the man, "but two people have been murdered. I guarantee you that in a double homicide, we can force the issue of the test."

Marc's breathing had quickened, and his eyes shifted back and forth. He seemed to be rooted in place and searching for a way out at the same time. When Ransom felt he'd let this go on long enough he said, "Maybe we should continue this at Area Headquarters."

"No," Marc said quickly. He paused for a moment, holding his breath, then heaved a sigh and said quietly, "I want her to leave the room."

"No!" Alice said loudly, her expression unchanging.

"It might be better, Mrs. Peters," Ransom said gently.

"No!"

There was a long, tense silence during which Ransom and Gerald kept their eyes on Marc Peters. Alice continued to stare straight ahead, tears rolling down her face, but she didn't make a sound. Her face had taken on a deadly pallor and seemed to have grown thinner, as if she were physically turning in on herself.

Marc said, "I don't want this to...I don't want the publicity. You don't know what that would do to me...to us. Any hope I had of...it would all be over."

"Two people are *dead*, Mr. Peters," Ransom said evenly.

Marc stared at the floor, his expression a mixture of hopelessness and anger.

"She was a tramp," he said without looking up. "She was just a goddamn tramp."

"What happened, Mr. Peters?"

"I didn't rape her. I didn't rape that . . . Laura."

There was a slight pause before Ransom said, "I have already told you about the evidence, now—"

Peters cut him off. "You don't know what it was like to be the only one who...who hadn't...in our senior year in high school. I was still a virgin, and everybody else... except Alice, of course." There was a touch of bitterness when he mentioned his wife's name, as if she could somehow be held at least partially accountable for his present predicament. She flushed but said nothing. "And Alice didn't want to sleep with me until we got married. But, you know how it is...and Laura was...there."

He stopped, and Ransom allowed a pause before he said again, "What happened, Mr. Peters?"

"I don't remember where Alice was—"

"The night Laura was raped," Alice cut in suddenly, "I was at a bridal shower for Dotty, my sister. I remember where I was."

Peters looked at her for a moment, then lowered his eyes back to the floor. "I was just out driving around. I don't remember what I was doing earlier. And then I saw

Laura. She was on her way home or something. I offered her a lift. And she was just like she always was. Tight dress, tight blouse, everything...just...she was...I'll never know why Alice had anything to do with her." If he was hoping for some explanation at that point, he received none. Alice's face had hardened to the point that she looked as if she might implode.

"But she wanted it. She wanted it. So I pulled into an alley, and we...we did it. But you've got to understand, she screwed everybody. She wanted it."

There was a long pause, then Ransom said soberly, "She was beaten, Mr. Peters."

"I..." He started to mount a defense, but apparently already knew that it would be useless.

"So you raped Laura Shay, and then what?"

Peters looked up. "What?"

Ransom sighed. "We already knew she was raped. I have some ideas about what happened after that, but why don't you just tell us?"

"After we did it, she...she got out of the car and ran away."

"Did she threaten to go to the police?"

"No. We didn't know anything about that until later. Mr. Shay called and threatened my father. He said they were going to tell the police I'd...what I'd done...unless my father paid up." He looked up at Ransom, his eyes open and pleading. "But I told my dad nobody would believe it, because Laura was nothing more than a slut, so there was no way they could prove anything. Nobody would believe someone like me would've had anything to do with her."

"*Prove* anything," Ransom said slowly. "But did you tell your father that what the Shays were saying was the truth?"

Peters's face fell and he looked back down at the floor. "I told him that I didn't rape her, just like I told you."

"But your father did pay the Shays off."

"That was because he knew that it didn't matter whether I was innocent or not. The newspapers—it would have been on the news and I would have been ruined before I even started. I was just a teenager. I had my whole life ahead of me."

"So did Ben Harvey," said Ransom sharply.

Peters was stumped for a moment, then said, "But I was going to Northwestern."

"Oh," Ransom said wryly, "and Ben was only going to a junior college. I see."

Peters couldn't meet the detective's eyes. "My dad knew I would never do anything like that. He knew me."

"I would say he knew you very well, seeing as how when all the dust had settled, he cut you off. It looks as if he was willing to break the law to save the 'family name,' but he wouldn't go on supporting you."

There was a silence before Peters continued, trying to ignore Ransom's remark. "The Shays said they wanted the money to send Laura to college. I suppose they could say they had a good reason for trying to get the money. If you could believe anything they said. Most likely they would've ended up drinking it all away."

Ransom was finding it harder and harder to control himself. It was apparent that despite what he had done and all that had transpired subsequently, Peters still didn't see himself as a rapist, or in fact guilty of anything. He tried to believe instead that the Shays had taken unfair advantage of his indiscretion.

"They did send their daughter to college," Ransom said, "but somehow they ran out of money. How did that happen?"

Peters looked at Ransom, then at Gerald, then back again. He seemed completely bewildered. "Well, after Ben was in jail there was no reason to keep paying them."

He said it so matter-of-factly that it was all Ransom could do to keep from reaching over and striking him. Gerald paused in his note taking and sat staring at Peters as if he were an ugly but fascinating insect.

"That wasn't all there was to it, though, was it?" Ransom asked.

"What do you mean?"

"Laura Shay became pregnant by that rape. She had an abortion."

Alice turned her horrified face to him and cried out, "No!"

Peters's face clouded over. "That could've been anybody's baby."

"Your wife told us that Laura was very careful to use protection with everyone. Except, of course, the rapist."

Peters shot his wife a glance that showed he believed she'd betrayed him. Then he said, "They were going to try to get more money out of us with that baby. But my dad wouldn't let them get away with it. He told Laura's father that if she had the baby, everybody would know that she lied to the police, and that she lied in court under oath, and no matter what happened to me, she'd go to jail."

Ransom shook his head slowly. "Everyone was left to think that Laura didn't keep the baby because it was the product of a rape. But she couldn't keep the baby, because it was yours. It wouldn't have been black. Everyone would have known the truth." He allowed a lengthy interval to elapse before he took a deep breath and said, "So Ben Harvey was released from jail and Laura decided to remount the Shays' little blackmail scheme. Is that what happened?''

Peters didn't respond. Ransom turned to Alice and said, ''Mrs. Peters, two nights ago did someone else call this house?''

''I don't...I wasn't here in the evening,'' Alice said vacantly. ''I was at my sewing class. I didn't get home till almost eleven. So I don't know...''

Ransom turned back to the husband and said, ''Did Laura Shay call you? We already know that her mother did.''

Peters still didn't respond.

''Mr. Peters, I'm afraid you don't understand the seriousness of your situation. Two people you admit were involved in blackmailing you at one time have been murdered. We know that one of them called you shortly before being murdered. We can trace the cause of the blackmail back to the rape, and that would mean that the fact that Ben Harvey was proven innocent would be a personal danger to you. Now, if you're unwilling to tell me whether or not Laura Shay called you, then let me ask you this: when Mrs. Shay called you last night, she asked you for money, didn't she?''

''Yes.'' The answer was barely audible.

Alice curled her fingers into fists and began tapping them on her knees with such determination she looked as if she thought it might keep her from blowing apart.

''Well, we know that you didn't have any money to give her, which makes your position worse because it means you didn't have anything to keep her from airing your dirty linen. Anything other than murder.''

''I didn't kill her,'' Peters said loudly.

''So when she demanded money, what did you tell her?''

Peters's head snapped up, his eyes flashing with anger. "I told her the same thing I told Laura! I told her to go to hell! I told her that thanks to her I was poor, too, so she wasn't getting another goddamn red cent out of me!"

"And what did you do after you got off the phone with Mrs. Shay?"

Peters looked confused. "What do you mean?"

Ransom spread his palms. "What did you do when you got off the phone? It's a simple question. Did you go out for a walk to cool down after getting so angry?"

"No I did not!" Peters exclaimed hotly. "I went back to bed! I never left the house. Not last night or any other night! I stayed home. I didn't sleep very well, but I never went out!"

Ransom took a long pause, then turned to Alice, who was still steadily tapping her fists on her knees.

"Mrs. Peters?"

"He stayed home," she said, her voice so low the detectives could barely hear her.

"I'm sorry, what did you say?"

She looked up and proclaimed loudly, "He never left the house!" She then turned on her husband so suddenly that neither Ransom nor Gerald could have stopped her even if they had wanted to. She pummeled her husband's face with her fists. After the initial shock, Peters raised his hands to fend off the attack, but he was no match for his wife's fury at the news of her ruined life. She kept up the barrage of strikes to his face and head as Gerald tried to pull her back. All the time she continued to yell, "He never left the house...he never left the house!"

TWELVE

"So, I REALLY AM sorry that I didn't make it here last night, but I had to have someone at Area Two track down MacNamara, and then of course it took forever to explain the whole thing to him. Oddly enough, he grasped it all fairly quickly and took Peters in for questioning." Ransom slowly turned the cup of tea around in its saucer with the tips of his fingers. "By the way, where's Lynn?"

Emily sat across the kitchen table from him, her usually incisive features having smoothed out into mild astonishment as he related the events of the previous day to her. She was concentrating so deeply on the story he'd just told her that his question took her by surprise.

"What?"

"Where's Lynn?"

"Oh," Emily said with a brisk shake of her head to bring her back to the moment, "she's gone to the store. She's making a roast for dinner and wanted to have some fresh potatoes."

"Ah," Ransom replied absently.

They were silent for several seconds, then Emily asked, "Why did you bring the matter to Detective MacNamara?"

"The only evidence we have against Peters concerning the murders at the moment is Mrs. Shay's phone call to him just before she was killed. Of course, there's the evidence of his raping Laura, but nothing other than that to connect him to the murders. But the rape evidence certainly gives him a good motive."

"Ah. I see." She thought for a moment, then sighed. "Well, of course, the news of Mr. Peters being brought in for questioning was in the paper this morning, and on the news, but from what you're telling me they didn't quite relate the *whole* sordid story." She sounded a bit disappointed. "I'd like to think that at my age I've pretty much gone beyond being shocked by anything, but I must say that what Marc Peters did, with the help of his father...well, really!" She stopped and took a sip of tea. She looked so cross as she considered this that Ransom would have laughed had he not been lost in his own thoughts. After a moment, Emily's features relaxed and she set the blue china cup down. "What I don't understand is, if the Shays intended blackmail, and the Peterses were willing to pay, why did they involve Ben Harvey at all? Why report the rape?"

"Partly because the idea of blackmail didn't occur to George Shay until after they went to the hospital, and partly because in order to have the Peterses over a barrel, they had to go through the normal process that one would go through after being raped. It was the only way they would have any evidence. They were just 'fortunate' in that Laura scratched Ben when he tried to help her, so they had a ready-made 'attacker.'"

"But why name anyone at all? Why not just say she didn't know who did it?"

Ransom gave a limp shrug. "I suppose it was because it was just easier. If she hadn't named someone, she would've been hounded by the police for a description, and the case would've remained open. I think it was less trouble all the way around to blame it on Ben and have the case closed and the whole thing over and done with." He paused, then added through thinned lips, "And everyone was more than willing to believe it. At least, every white person who heard about it was willing to believe it. Almost eager.''

Emily puckered her brow. "Not exactly a credit to one's race, is it?"

Ransom shook his head. "If it's any consolation, according to Ruby Hawkins, the blacks at the school were exactly the opposite. They were unwilling to believe Ben could've done it, no matter what evidence there was.''

Emily sighed heavily. "So the whole matter does no one credit. I'd like to think at my ripe old age that things would have changed by now.''

Ransom gave her a concerned glance. Ever since her heart attack and surgery, it worried him whenever Emily sounded forlorn, fearing that it might signal a relapse into postsurgical depression. But he needn't have bothered worrying. Emily readjusted herself in her seat and picked up their original thread. "Yes...yes, I see. So Ben ended up just being a pawn in their game of blackmail.''

"A game that failed," Ransom said, finally lifting his cup to his lips. He tilted the cup to take a drink, but at the last minute changed his mind and replaced the cup in its saucer. "Of course, we'll never know most of this for sure. The only people who could tell us are dead." He paused for a moment, then added, "At least Laura herself ended up being little more than a pawn.''

Emily folded her hands on the table and gently clucked her tongue. "It really is quite dreadful, what was done with the lives of those young people. Of course, the one I really feel sorry for is Alice Peters.''

"Why?"

Emily smiled. "Because her mother was right, as mothers have a way of being. She was the one who recognized the danger of befriending someone like Laura Shay. She was the one who thought Laura would end up ruining anyone with whom she came into contact. And all these years later, she's been proven right.''

"Laura wasn't the one who committed the rape,'' Ransom said pointedly.

"Oh, Jeremy, you know I didn't mean that. But she managed to ruin Ben Harvey's life quite literally with just one touch. Who's to say how any of these people would've ended up if they'd never come in contact with Laura?''

"I don't know,'' Ransom said reluctantly.

Emily smiled benignantly. "Perhaps I'm a little hard on my own sex. When I was young, it was commonly believed that if a woman behaved the way Laura Shay did, and something happened to her…well…that was what happened. These are more enlightened times, and now we understand that there's never an acceptable reason for attacking anyone.'' She paused and took another sip of tea, then gently put her blue china cup down. "But I still think it's dangerous to play with fire.''

Ransom went back to turning his cup around. "It still comes a little too close to blaming the victim. And I heard enough of that from Marc Peters. I really don't think he'll ever believe he did anything wrong.''

Emily examined her friend for a moment, then said, "Before you start thinking too much of Laura Shay as a pawn, remember that she didn't have to lie.''

He looked up. "What?''

"She didn't have to go along with her father. She didn't have to lie, but she did so in order to extort money. And it was her lies that sent an innocent man to prison.''

"That's true,'' he conceded, looking back down into his cup.

"Not only that, but she aborted her baby.''

Ransom raised an eyebrow. "I didn't know you were against abortion."

Emily drew back her head slightly and said, "It has nothing to do with whether one is for or against it. It has everything to do with *why* she did it. She had an abortion purely for self-preservation, to protect her lies. Any way you look at it, it was a despicable thing to do."

"Yes," said Ransom thoughtfully. His attention seemed to be wavering as he again become preoccupied.

"Well," Emily said brightly, trying to lighten the mood, "it must at least be pleasant to find that you were correct."

"About what?"

Emily elevated her eyebrows. "About Ben Harvey's innocence, of course."

There was a beat, then Ransom said, "Yes."

The corners of Emily's mouth turned down slightly with concern. "Jeremy, what's the matter?"

He was silent for a moment, then he looked up at her. "I know that Marc Peters raped that girl."

"Yes?"

There was a very long pause during which Ransom stared straight ahead, looking as if he were gathering the strength to go on. Finally, he said, "But I don't know that he committed the murders."

"What?" Emily exclaimed, her eyes wide with astonishment. It was the first time in their acquaintance that Ransom could remember seeing such utter surprise on her face.

"Emily, Peters more or less admitted to attacking Laura and to being the victim of blackmail, which alone would make him the prime suspect in the murder. But he said he told both mother and daughter to go to hell, because

he didn't have any money to give them, which we know
to be true.''

"Couldn't he have gotten the money from his father?''
Emily offered.

Ransom shook his head. "I don't think so. Not under
the circumstances. Apparently Peters's father pretty much
disowned him after settling the matter the first time. Besides, why tell *us* that he told his blackmailers to go to
hell? It only paints him in the worst possible light.''

Emily looked at him for a moment, then nodded in
understanding. "Oh, yes. Not having the money to pay
them off gives him an even stronger motive for murder.''

"Yes,'' Ransom agreed. "And he swears that he didn't
leave the house the nights they were killed, so he couldn't
have done it.''

"Isn't it natural for a murderer to profess his innocence?''

"Certainly. It wasn't what he said I'm having a problem with. It's what his wife said.''

"Yes?''

"She insisted that he stayed home. I hardly think it's
natural for a wife to give her husband an alibi right after
learning that he raped one of her best friends.''

Emily nodded. "Yes. I would say that was very odd.''

"And is it natural for her to go on giving him an alibi
as she's beating him over the head—which I'm ashamed
to add was quite gratifying, all things considered.''

Emily pursed her lips and pondered this for several seconds. "You're right. I can't be *that* hard on my sex. I
don't believe that she would continue to stand by him
knowing that he'd destroyed their family. But since
you've ferreted out all this information which points to
Marc Peters as the prime suspect, I don't see who else it
could be. After all, both Laura and her mother were killed,

and you said yourself that the rapist was the only other one who knew who was involved in railroading Ben Harvey into prison.''

Ransom suddenly stopped turning his cup. His head snapped up and he faced Emily. ''What did you say?''

Emily gave him a quizzical look as she replied, ''I said the rapist was the only other one who knew who was involved in railroading Ben Harvey into prison.''

There was a slight pause before Ransom said, ''Oh, my God!''

''What is it?'' She was alarmed by his tone and the distressed look on his face.

''Oh, my God, Emily, you were right all along!''

''What are you saying?''

His features sharpened as he leaned in toward her. ''When Ben Harvey was released from jail there were three people alive who knew who was responsible for sending him to prison: Laura Shay, her mother, and Marc Peters.''

''Yes…'' Emily said slowly, trying to discern what he was driving at. ''And Laura and her mother are dead, which leaves Marc Peters.''

''It also leaves Ben Harvey. I can't believe I've been so stupid!''

''Jeremy, I don't understand what you're saying,'' Emily said with the stern propriety of a schoolteacher trying to bring an unruly student under control. ''Ben Harvey couldn't be the murderer. He didn't know that Laura's parents were involved in the cover-up.''

''Oh course he knew!'' Ransom said, trying to control his mounting anger. ''He knew because *I told him!*''

Emily's face went blank for a matter of seconds. Then her eyes widened and she put her right hand to her mouth. ''Oh, dear God! You're right! That means…''

"That means that as of this morning's news, Harvey also knows who the third person is!"

THE EARLY EVENING crawl out to the South Side on the Dan Ryan did nothing to alleviate Ransom's sense of impending danger. He felt as if he were in a nightmare in which he was filled with a sense of mounting dread, but only able to flee the unseen pursuer in slow motion. He wove in and out of traffic, as did most of the other drivers, jockeying for a position that would allow him to move faster. It only seemed to succeed in slowing him down further.

Before leaving Emily, Ransom had called Area Two Headquarters and found that MacNamara had already left for the day. He spoke with Detective Roberts, who confirmed his worst fear: with no physical evidence yet against Marc Peters, they had released him late in the afternoon with the proviso that he not leave town.

"Mac questioned him till he was blue in the face," Roberts had said, using his affectionate nickname for their fellow detective. "Mac, I mean, not Peters. But his story stayed the same. Never changed. But we'll find something on him."

If you have the chance, Ransom thought.

He hadn't bothered trying to explain to Roberts that he thought Peters's life might be in danger, or that even though his suppositions about the rape and blackmail had been proven true, he now thought he was seriously wrong about the identity of the murderer. He knew it would take too long, and Roberts seemed so satisfied that Peters was the killer that it would have required too much effort to convince him otherwise at that point. And time was of the essence.

It took almost an hour to reach the 111th Street exit,

and traffic was no better on the street than it had been on the expressway. He drove slowly up the hill and down the street to Western Avenue, where he turned right, then made another right when he got to 107th Street.

Dusk was turning into darkness as he neared the house. Unlike on his two previous visits to the Peterses' home, this time the street was lined with cars on both sides, although there were still enough open spaces that parking wasn't difficult. He backed into a space in front of a house three doors up from the Peterses', turned off the ignition, and sat back. He'd spent the past hour more concerned with actually getting there than with what he would do once he arrived. And now that he was there, he really wasn't sure how to proceed.

He was still lost in contemplation when a light tap at the passenger window almost sent him out of his skin. He looked over and saw Gerald White's moon face peering in at him. He reached over and opened the door.

After Gerald climbed in, Ransom said, "A testament to how truly off the mark I've become. Not only did I not see you coming, you almost scared the hell out of me. What are you doing here?"

"Miss Emily called me," he replied with a shrug. "She was worried about you. She said you were in such a hurry to get out here that you might forget to call me." He eyed Ransom significantly.

Ransom sighed and gave a slight laugh. "She was being kind."

"And she thought you might need this." He tapped his holstered gun.

"Heavens," said Ransom with a smile. "I feel undressed. I didn't have time to go home before coming here."

"Did you at least call MacNamara?"

"Yes."

"Why isn't he here?"

"He'd gone home, and I didn't tell the detective I spoke with what I suspected."

"What?" Gerald exclaimed, his mouth dropping open.

"He was perfectly satisfied with Peters as the murderer. Who was I to burst his bubble?"

"Jer…"

"All right, I thought it would take too long to explain, and I didn't relish the idea of giving him a new hare-brained theory after the last one."

"The last one was right. You were right about everything—the blackmail, the rape, everything."

Ransom was slowly shaking his head even before Gerald reached the end of his sentence. "Everything except the identity of the murderer."

"You don't know that. Look, I thought you were off in left field on this case before, but you were right. And now we know that Laura Shay and her mother each called Peters just before being killed. Just because his wife vouches for him…"

"No," Ransom said firmly. He turned and faced his partner. "Gerald, you're the one who was right, painful as that might be for me to admit." He gave Gerald a slight smile. "It's easiest if Ben is the killer. You believed all along he was the one."

"So why do *you* believe it now?"

"Because of the murder of Mrs. Shay."

"But she was killed right after calling Peters."

"*That* is where coincidence comes into play. We were the catalyst for that. Or I was, I should say. If you think about what we did the day before Mrs. Shay was killed."

Gerald's face formed a puzzled frown. "What?"

"In trying to get Mrs. Shay to tell us who the rapist

was, I told her that we suspected him of being the murderer. That's what prompted her to try her own hand at blackmail.''

"But if she called Peters—''

"But we did something else," Ransom said, raising a hand to stop him. "After talking to Shay we talked to Ben, and I told him that Mrs. Shay knew about the rape. That was stupid and inexcusable. And it cost Mrs. Shay her life."

"No, lying and committing blackmail and helping to send an innocent man to prison cost her her life. You can't seriously believe it was your fault."

Ransom shook his head with disgust. "Harvey played me for a fool. And I was all too willing to go along."

Gerald didn't respond. He didn't think there was any point in trying to change Ransom's mind at that moment. Instead, he said, "So why the rush to get out here? Do you actually think he'll try something tonight? Wouldn't that be too obvious?"

"He killed Mrs. Shay right after finding out about her. I would think he would try the same here." He paused, then said, "When did you get here?"

"Just a few minutes before you."

"Have you seen anything?"

"If you mean did I see Harvey skulking around the house and breaking in, then no. The lights are on. What do we do now? Sit here and wait? We could be here forever."

Ransom stared at the house for a few moments. Marc Peters's part in all this—including the fact that he'd been brought in for questioning—had made the news that morning. He'd been released late in the afternoon, which meant that that had probably made it onto the evening news.

"But there's no evidence..." Ransom said absently.

"Huh?"

"There's no evidence in either of the murders. If we caught Harvey in the act of trying to kill Peters, we'd at least have something on him. Dammit." He hit his fist on the steering wheel, frustrated with his newly acquired indecision.

"So you want to wait here and watch for a while?"

"No," Ransom said with a sigh. "We'd better go and tell Mr. Peters that if he's not a murderer, his life may be in danger."

"He's not likely to be too happy to see us," Gerald said as they climbed out of the car.

"He's hurt so many people that I'm not terribly concerned about his feelings. And if he's in danger, he might be happier to see us than you think."

They walked down the street to the Peterses' house and up the front walk. As Gerald had reported, the lights were on, but there was no sign of movement within. Gerald pressed the doorbell.

"Maybe he didn't come back here," Gerald proposed after the wait became lengthy.

Ransom glanced at him and said, "Where else would he go?" They waited for a few more seconds. "Perhaps he just thinks we're reporters."

Gerald stepped up to the door, knocked, and called out, "Mr. Peters, it's the police."

There was no response. Finally Ransom tried the door, but it was locked.

"Let's go around to the back."

The narrow walk continued between the closely sandwiched houses to the back of the house. They turned the corner of the building and found the back door. Ransom examined the keyhole and found minute scratches, which he pointed out to Gerald. He then reached for the knob, but Gerald grabbed his wrist lightly and shook his head as he pulled his gun from its holster. Ransom gave a single nod, and stepped aside.

Gerald turned the knob and pushed open the door as quietly as he could. It slid open with only a slight creak, which sounded as loud as a gunshot in the stillness of the moment. The detectives slipped through the door and into the kitchen.

It seemed that all the lights were on in the house. The fluorescent light on the ceiling in the kitchen cast its harsh glare down on the speckled tiles, and although the two wall sconces in the hallway burned with a more muted glow, they still made the detectives feel uncomfortably exposed.

They made their way down the hallway, keeping close to the far wall out of habit, though they could hardly have missed being seen by anyone who happened to look in their direction. Gerald stopped at the archway to the living room, glancing to the left to make sure it was clear before entering. Then they both went into the room.

The first thing they saw was Marc Peters. He was sprawled in a heap in front of the fireplace, partly obscured by a high-backed wing chair. His face was frozen in a contorted grimace and an ugly red line was around his neck. Gerald stayed back while Ransom went to Peters, knelt beside him, and tried to find a pulse.

"He's dead."

The voice had come from behind Ransom, and he leaped to his feet and wheeled around to find Ben Harvey seated in the wing chair. His hands were folded in his lap and there was a length of wire coiled around his fingers. He stared down at the body with dull, half-closed eyes. He looked as if he was having trouble staying awake.

"He's dead," Ben repeated. For a few moments he continued to look down at the man who'd helped ruin his life. Then he slowly raised his eyes to Ransom and said, "At least this time I done it."

THIRTEEN

"LOOK WHAT I found," said Lynn, holding a single strand of her hair out for Emily's inspection. "Gray. My first one. I never noticed it before Maggie...before Maggie died. I suppose what they say is true. Tragedy really does make you turn gray."

Emily laughed. "Life makes you turn gray, my dear. Tragedy is just a part of it."

"Well," Lynn said with a glance at Ransom, who sat silently brooding over a cup of coffee, "I'm going to go finish packing."

Lynn left the room, and Emily gently smoothed the skirt of her dress, shifted in her chair, and folded her hands on the table. She gazed intently at Ransom, her forehead creased with concern. He was normally effusive once a case was over, and enjoyed sitting with her and performing a postmortem on the whys and wherefores of the problem solved. But this time was different. His mood bordered on sullen, and Emily found this to be a cause for concern.

"Well, I wish you'd explain it all to me," she said brightly, interrupting his reverie. "There's quite a bit I don't understand."

He looked up at her, an ironic smile playing about his lips. "I sincerely doubt that. You had the whole thing pegged from the beginning. So did Gerald, and Mac-Namara, and Mrs. Shay, for that matter. You always believed Ben was the murderer."

Emily shook her head. "Only because I thought his

reserve to be unnatural under the circumstances. But there could've been many causes for that.''

''But there weren't. He was waiting. And planning. You were right.''

Emily shifted again and tried another tack. ''But there *are* things I don't understand. He performed the first two murders so effectively, without being caught and without leaving clues. Why on earth did he stay at the Peterses' house after killing Marc?''

Ransom sat back in his chair. ''He said he got there just before we did, and after we'd rung the bell he figured he was caught. But I don't know...I don't know that he would have run away anyway. He'd done what he set out to do. He'd killed the people who sent him to jail. I don't think he really cared anymore.''

''But he didn't break into Laura Shay's apartment.''

''Only because she didn't have a back door. He knocked and when she answered . . .''

Emily shuddered. ''It's such a waste,'' she said with a cluck of her tongue. ''He was such an innocent boy when he went to jail.''

''And you were right about that, too,'' Ransom replied with a sigh. '' 'The villainy you teach me,' as you said. They taught him well in prison. He learned how to pick a lock and the quickest and most efficient way to kill someone. He slipped a wire around their necks and twisted it. One easy motion. They were dead almost before they knew anything was happening to them.''

They were silent for a while. Ransom went back to staring at the tabletop, and Emily eyed him with concern. ''There's something else I don't understand,'' she said, continuing her attempt to draw him out. ''Why was everyone so sure that Laura was enamored of Tony Thornton?

It seems clear now that he really didn't ever have anything to do with her.''

Ransom rolled his eyes. "The name game."

Emily elevated her eyebrows. "I beg your pardon?"

"The name game. Laura was a talker. She liked to talk about what she was doing. And according to Betty, her coworker at the drug store, she would use a fictitious name to talk about a man if circumstances prevented her from using his name. So at work, when she wanted to tell Betty about her dates with Bill Gibson, she would refer to him as 'Earl,' and Gibson never caught on."

"Oh, I see," Emily said slowly. "So when she wanted to talk about how enamored she was of Marc Peters, she referred to him as 'Tony' so she could talk about him in front of Alice." She smacked her lips with distaste.

Ransom nodded. "And everyone else, for that matter. She didn't want anyone to know she really was attracted to Marc Peters, because by most accounts she had *some* standards back then. She wouldn't have hit on her best friend's fiancé."

Emily pursed her lips. "But she thought nothing of *discussing* him with her, no matter how circuitously."

They fell silent again. Ransom sat slowly tapping the side of his cup with his index finger.

Emily said, "Jeremy, tell me, what's troubling you?"

He didn't look up. "Just that that's another area where I was wrong. Thinking that Tony Thornton had something to do with this business." He heaved an exasperated sigh. "I led us very far off the track."

"Oh, I don't know. It seems to me you were following up every possible clue."

"And missing the big one," Ransom replied, unwilling to cut himself any slack. "It's not just that I believed so strongly that Harvey was innocent. If I hadn't been so pigheaded I would have realized that Thornton wasn't the only one who was 'top of the hill,' as Alice Peters put it. Marc was, too, when he was growing up. I should have realized that the real reason Marc's father had cut him off was because he was involved in the rape. Or at least realized that his being cut adrift so soon after the rape was suspicious.''

''I don't see why you would have thought that,'' Emily said sincerely. ''After all, you had no reason to believe he had anything to do with anything. He was only mentioned to you in passing very early in your investigation.''

He finally looked up at her. ''I bungled it badly, Emily. If I hadn't been so intent on chasing smoke, I might've been able to save two people's lives.''

Lynn had just come back down the hallway and was about to enter the kitchen when she heard him say this. She paused in the doorway, thinking it might be better not to interrupt at that moment.

Emily straightened up in her chair and put her sternest expression on her face. ''Now, Jeremy, that's just nonsense! Ben Harvey was a clever young man, who I'm sure could have figured out for himself that Laura's parents helped her frame him, without your assistance.''

''I was wrong, Emily.''

''You were human. You wanted to believe something that turned out not to be true. But you wanted to believe it for a good reason.''

''That kind of humanity has no place in my job.''

Emily smiled at him fondly. ''That kind of humanity is inescapable, even for you.'' She paused, then leaned toward him and said pointedly, ''Jeremy, Ben Harvey chose his path. He killed those people, not you. It should be obvious to you now that he left prison with every intention of killing the people responsible for his incarceration. To believe that you were some sort of determining factor in his plans is as much as to imply that he is not responsible for what he did. That's all there is to it." She leaned back in her chair with a stately grace and thumped the tabletop once with her index finger. On her face was an expression that said that she had had the last word on the subject and would accept no further foolishness on his part. Ransom returned a sheepish grin.

Pleased with the effect, Emily relaxed and sighed. "I can't help thinking that Mr. Harvey could've avoided all this if only he'd read *The Merchant of Venice.*"

"Hmm?"

"Well, then he would have known that you can't exact your pound of flesh if you spill a drop of blood."

Ransom didn't respond. After a few moments his smile melted into a frown. "But if I hadn't—"

"Well," Lynn interrupted, finally coming into the room, "I'm all packed and ready to go."

"Oh," said Ransom, disconcerted by her sudden appearance. "Do you want me to drive you?"

"No, I've got my car."

"Are you sure you want to leave so soon?" said Emily, taking the young woman's hand. "You're welcome to stay as long as you like, you know."

"I know, and you're a dear." Lynn leaned over and kissed Emily lightly on the forehead. "You've helped me more than you can know. But I have to deal with it on my own sometime. You were right. You don't have to forget, you just have to accept what's happened and decide to go on with your life." She shot a glance at Ransom, then added to Emily, "I know it's going to be hard, but I'm going to try."

"Good for you," said Emily with a broad smile.

"I'll be back to clean next Tuesday, and I'd appreciate

it if you don't lift a finger until then," she said, tossing her tawny hair back off her shoulder. She then turned to Ransom and added, "And I'll see you whenever, Mr. Detective."

She gave him a wide grin and left the kitchen. A few seconds later they heard the front door open and close.

Ransom smiled at Emily. "Did you rehearse that?"

Emily returned a look of puzzled innocence. "Whatever do you mean?"

FATAL FLAW

FRANK SMITH

AN INSPECTOR PAGET MYSTERY

What drove seventeen-year-old Monica Shaw to take her life
with an overdose of insulin? The pain of being alone and
unwanted for the holidays at Thornton Hill Girls' School—
or something else? It's a Christmas murder for
Detective Chief Inspector Neil Paget.

Neither the village of Shropshire nor Thornton Hill School
can fully mask the secrets making the winter landscape
icy and treacherous for Paget as he navigates the fear,
desperation and dark deeds that hide the twisted motives
of the innocent…to find the fatal flaw of a killer.

Available December 1999 at your favorite retail outlet.

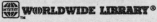

DEADLY VINTAGE

— A JACK DONNE MYSTERY —

WILLIAM RELLING JR.

In California's wine country, a heady
bouquet of money, rivalry and murder
gives ex-Treasury agent-turned-vintner
Jack Donne a case that turns deadly.

Neighboring vintner and universally
loathed Ozzie Cole makes an outstanding
product. So when Ozzie comes to Donne,
claiming somebody is counterfeiting his
best pinot noir, Donne reluctantly agrees
to look into it.

But Donne soon learns blood is thicker
than wine and there's a lot of it being
spilled—in his direction.

Available December 1999 at your favorite retail outlet.

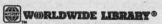

WILDCRAFTERS

A VENUS DIAMOND MYSTERY

SKYE KATHLEEN MOODY

A Hawaiian honeymoon and a new husband must wait while Seattle Fish and Wildlife agent Venus Diamond heads a massive search into the disappearance of a baby in the Bogachiel wildlife preserve. Natives believe the baby was snatched by "the Unknown," a half-man, half-elk creature of Native American lore. Venus suspects the incident may involve recent elk poachings in the area, and carcasses found with sawed-off hooves.

But what she discovers is a fanatical quest for eternal youth that drives human desires to hideous proportions where no one is safe...not even the most innocent.

**Available December 1999 at
your favorite retail outlet.**

NEXT WEEK WILL BE BETTER

— WILL BE —

BETTER

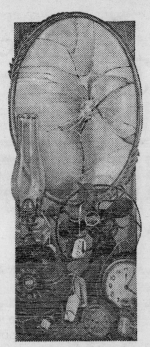

A CAT WILDE MYSTERY

JEAN RURYK

Spending the weekends rubbing shoulders in the summer heat with flea market hagglers isn't furniture restorer Cat Wilde's idea of fun. But she couldn't refuse her friend Rena, who needed someone to run her table at the flea market while she recuperated from surgery.

Luckily she has the space next to Old Sam, a true flea market diehard. But when Sam is murdered, Cat starts digging into the discordant world of flea market shopping, and discovers people will do anything for a bargain. Even kill.

Available December 1999 at your favorite retail outlet.

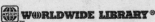 **WORLDWIDE LIBRARY®**

Visit us at www.worldwidemystery.com   WJR333

Denise Dietz

**AN ELLIE BERNSTEIN/
LIEUTENANT
PETER MILLER
MYSTERY**

Throw Darts at a Cheesecake

Fat Free Murder

At the weekly meeting of Weight Winners, losing
is everything. Group leader Ellie Bernstein herself
has shed fifty-five pounds, along with a cheating
husband and an unfulfilling life. But she quickly
discovers losing weight is not only murder,
it's downright lethal.

One by one, the group's Big Losers are being
murdered. Is some jealous member of the Friday
meeting a secret killer? Motive aside, Ellie's got
to watch her back as well as her calories before
she finds herself on the most permanent
diet of all...death.

Available December 1999 at your favorite retail outlet.

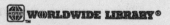

WORLDWIDE LIBRARY®

Visit us at www.worldwidemystery.com   WDD334